No One Cancels Christmas

Born in Staffordshire, Zara Stoneley wanted to be a female James Herriot, a spy, or an author when she grew up. After many (many) years, and many different jobs, her dream of writing a bestseller came true. Zara now lives in a cosy cottage in Cheshire, UK with her family, a lively cockapoo called Harry, and a very bossy (and slightly evil) cat called Saffron.

Her books include the popular Tippermere series (*Stable Mates*, *Country Affairs* and *Country Rivals*), and several standalone novels, including the bestselling *The Wedding Date*.

@ZaraStoneley
http://www.facebook.com/ZaraStoneley
www.zarastoneley.com
www.instagram.com/ZaraStoneley

Also by Zara Stoneley

Stable Mates
Country Affairs
Country Rivals
A Very Country Christmas
The Holiday Swap
Summer with the Country Village Vet
Blackberry Picking at Jasmine Cottage
The Wedding Date

ZARA STONELEY

No One Cancels Christmas

A division of HarperCollins*Publishers*
www.harpercollins.co.uk

HarperImpulse an imprint of
HarperCollinsPublishers
The News Building
1 London Bridge Street
London SE1 9GF

www.harpercollins.co.uk

This paperback edition 2018

First published in Great Britain in ebook format by
HarperCollinsPublishers 2018

A catalogue record for this book
is available from the British Library

ISBN: 9780008301057

Set in Birka by Palimpsest Book Production Limited,
Falkirk, Stirlingshire

Printed and bound in Great Britain by
CPI Group (UK) Ltd, Croydon CR0 4YY

MIX
Paper from
responsible sources
FSC
www.fsc.org FSC C007454

For my lovely sister Lynn, who is every bit as generous and kind as her namesake in the story.

PART 1
TANTRUMS AND TINSEL

Chapter 1

Dear Ms Hall,

I am not normally the type to complain, but (anybody who says this usually *is* the type to complain, and the *but* confirms it) *on this occasion I feel compelled.*

Over the years we have booked many holidays through your travel agency, and your aunt has always made sure we have had the very best. We have even swapped Christmas cards!

'*A*nd whilst I do not wish to place the blame at your door* . . . Ouch! Bloody hell, talk about passive aggressive.' The voice in my ear makes me jump.

'Don't read it out, Sam! It's bad enough just reading it in my head. Anyway, I thought you were busy booking that cruise for the Nifty Fifty's Gin Drinkers Association?'

'I was, but you've just ripped that drink coaster into shreds, so I reckoned something was up.'

'It's that bloody Will Armstrong again, at the Shooting Star Mountain Resort – I want to strangle him!' We don't

often get customer complaints, but this particular destina-
tion, and its grumpy owner, have been attracting a fair few
lately. And this particular complaint hurts more than most
because it suggests I'm the one at fault, and I'm not. 'He's
not happy just sabotaging his own bloody business, he
wants to drag us down with him.'

'Oh, come on, it can't be that bad. This guy can't actually
damage Making Memories, can he?'

I stab at the screen but can't trust myself to speak.

'. . . *we find ourselves at a loss at to why you should
recommend The Shooting Star Mountain Resort, as it is very
clearly overpriced and understaffed. Lynn has always ensured
we have value for money, and a fantastic holiday to boot.*

'To boot?' Sam interrupts her reading. 'Who says to boot?'

'Somebody who isn't happy at all. Keep reading.'

She does. Out loud, in an 'irate of the Home Counties'
kind of way.

'You sound a bit like your mum.'

She ignores me.

'*Quite frankly, our room was disgusting. The sheets whilst
clean were unironed.*' Sam pauses again, mid outrage.
'Unironed? What's the man talking about? I can't see how
that makes it disgusting, can you? I never iron the sheets;
it's like socks or knickers, who has time to iron things that
nobody else ever sees? Do you iron sheets?'

'Doesn't Jake see your sheets? And the other bits as well?'

'Well, yes, but I mean, the wrinkles stretch out, don't
they?'

'I iron everything. I always find crisp, flat knickers with a seam down the centre hold a certain sexy appeal.'

She stares at me, her mouth open.

I burst out laughing. 'God, Sam, do you honestly think I iron *anything?* I was kidding. Carry on.'

She gives me a funny look, then clears her throat. 'You don't really iron knickers, do you?'

'No, I really don't. Come on, before somebody comes in.'

The food was of variable quality and lukewarm. The final straw was speaking to the manager, who was abrupt and surly to the point of rudeness and suggested we vacate our cabin if we were not enjoying our stay. How could we possibly enjoy our stay when one of his vicious huskies had attacked our daughter, Ruby? I am sure she will suffer long-term consequences as a result, and now screams whenever a dog (including our own little Pippin, who wouldn't hurt a fly) approaches her. Little Pippin bit my wife as a result of Ruby's scream, and is now having to undergo veterinary visits as she is now nervous and snappy, and Ruby is booked in for counselling. My wife, meanwhile, has a bandaged hand which makes playing the piano extremely tortuous – and she is a music teacher!

'I have always trusted your recommendations, but am wondering if your lack of experience—'

I squeak as she reads out this sentence, I can't help myself. Sam and I stare at each other. 'Lack of experience! I don't know who I hate more, him or Will Armstrong.'

'. . . is becoming evident.

'As we were unable to book an early flight back, and the

5

nearby hotels were all fully booked, we had to endure the rest of our holiday under a heavy cloud and an even heavier blanket as the heating was woefully inadequate.

'Well, at least he gave them blankets!'

Sam always picks up on the positives. I roll my eyes, and gesture at the screen.

'*I am sure that ABTA and* Watchdog *would be more than happy to investigate my complaints. However, in a spirit of goodwill, I would like to give you the opportunity to offer us a full refund and compensation for the stress this has caused. Please find, itemised below, additional expenses incurred.*

'*I look forward to hearing from you by return post. If I receive no response within 7 working days I will instruct my solicitor.*

'*Yours faithfully,*

'*Stephen Latterby*'

'Blah, blah, blah.' Sam's dropped the 'outraged of Basildon' voice. 'Shit, look at that Sarah!' I look and wish I hadn't. 'Is that how much a dog psychologist charges? Wow, I think I need to retrain.'

'Sam! Just look at that total he's asking for!' I feel slightly sick, and faint. 'We can't pay that, we'll be bankrupt. Lynn will kill me!'

'But it isn't your fault. I'm going to pop across to Costa and get us a drink and chocolate brownie, this calls for a caffeine and sugar boost. Don't do anything until I get back.' She raises an eyebrow at me. 'I mean it. Promise.'

'Anything?'

'Well you can breathe and stuff, but please don't reply to that email. You need to think about this carefully.' She knows how impulsive I can be. 'And talk to Lynn. I mean, what if this guy does actually sue us? I'll never hear the last of this from Mum if we end up on Watchdog.'

We do the staring at each other thing again. She's probably thinking about dog psychology. I'm thinking about how much damage you can inflict on somebody without being arrested.

'I won't reply.' Which leaves things nicely open. It doesn't stop me firing both barrels at Mr Will Armstrong.

This is getting way more serious than advising him to stick some holly up and light the fires (which I have done several times – and been ignored).

I roll up my sleeves. Whatever this guy's game is, he is not going to drag us down with him. If there's any suing to be done it will be us, not Mr Latterby, or any of our other disgruntled customers.

We need to be seen to be acting. I glance at the photograph of Aunt Lynn on the wall. She looks happy, she looks inspiring, she looks like we all want to feel after a good holiday. We need to show we care.

Dear Mr Armstrong,

Please find attached a letter we have received from a valued customer.

What do I do now? I google the Dangerous Dogs Act.

I would like to draw your attention to the paragraph concerning your dog. I would be grateful if you could forward your risk assessment regarding the use of these animals. My understanding is that any dangerous dog should be muzzled, and that any contact should be supervised. It would appear, in this case, that neither applied, and this is of great concern as we (as do you) have a duty of care to our clients, and we would not expect dangerous animals to be roaming loose and unattended.

Secondly, our client has expressed concerns about the state of their cabin, and the quality of food served. I would like to refer you to the description in your brochure (and accompanying photographs) which promises 'cosy and comfortable accommodation, roaring fires and a restaurant offering food and drink that will round off the perfect day'.

Finally, I am concerned about the attitude of staff at the resort. They have, in the past, always been warm and welcoming, but our client complains of rudeness. Your service reflects on ours and I feel that our business relationship is now reaching the stage of being untenable.

This is a very an extremely serious situation, and I would be grateful if you could respond as soon as possible, before I am forced to take legal advice.

Kind regards,
Sarah Hall
Making Memories, Travel Agents

I hit 'send' and stare out of the window. Now what? Will Armstrong never replies to my emails, not even the jokey 'let's sort this together' ones. So why should he respond to a complaint like this? Maybe Sam is right, maybe I need to call Aunt Lynn. But I don't want to, not this time. I need to handle this.

There is a ping, incoming email. My God, it's from Shooting Star! Hell, if he's replied that means this really is serious, that he agrees we need to take action. Oh bugger, we're going to be ruined. Aunt Lynn will never forgive me.

Dear Ms Hall,

I do feel you are overreacting slightly. The Latterby family have no grounds for taking you to court or demanding a full refund for themselves or their dog (who quite frankly probably does need psychological support if this is what he has to put up with on a daily basis). At the risk of sounding unprofessional, I would classify Mr Latterby as a habitual complainer with over-inflated expectations.

Our husky, Rosie, was in her run at the time of the incident you mention. The Latterby's child had insisted on going down and feeding the dogs table scraps (of the variable-quality, lukewarm variety) despite clear signage forbidding this, and further signage requesting that no visitors enter the area where the dogs are kennelled without a member of staff.

Rosie, who has recently had puppies, reacted to the intrusion by jumping at the fence and the Latterby child slipped, falling on her well-padded posterior and screaming the place down. No blood was spilled, although I was very tempted to rectify that, as the welfare of our animals is important to me.

As far as rudeness goes, it is hard to remain civil when in the company of clients whose expectations stretch to spa facilities and fine-dining when our brochures and website illustrate very clearly that this is not what is on offer. Further, if they come to Canada in the winter, are icy conditions not to be expected? Much as I would like to play God, I am unfortunately not in a position to alter the weather conditions.

I suggest you use your tact, diplomacy and people skills to suggest they head 'Down Under' next year. I am not prepared to offer any compensation or discount but can give you the name of a good solicitor if you so require.

Is that serious enough for you?

Regards,

Will Armstrong

'Oh my God, what is he *like?*'

I hadn't heard Sam sneak back in.

I'm not quite sure how to answer, as I really can't decide *what* he's like. 'He doesn't seem to get it at all.'

'Well, he does seem to care about the dogs.'

'I know.' This bit makes me unhappy, not because he cares (who doesn't like a man who loves and protects his pets?), but because he doesn't seem to have a clue about where he's going wrong. 'But he's not got the first idea about customer service, has he? I mean, I know clients can be a pain in the arse—'

'You're telling me.' Sam rolls her eyes.

'But he's working in the service industry. Even if this complaint is a load of tosh,' which I suspect it might be, 'and this guy is pushing his luck, he still does have at least some grounds for complaints doesn't he? I mean look at the reviews . . .'

'It's not me you have to convince, Sare.'

'I know.' I groan. 'Maybe I should just send some of them his way, but I think he'll bin them before he even reads them, let alone do anything constructive.' Will is doing my head in, in a way he shouldn't. He obviously does care about some things, and he does have a point. 'Maybe he does get pissed off when people arrive expecting spa pampering treatments and ten different variety of gin, but why can't he see it's the little things that can make a difference? And,' I wipe a hand over my eyes, suddenly feeling weary, 'he doesn't see what he's doing to us. Does he? He could wipe our business out! And,' I stare at the email, 'he could at least be civil.'

'Well, he does sound pissed off, but it's not exactly rude, is it? More frustrated? Or just assertive. Maybe he's not used to getting it wrong.' Sam squeezes my shoulder, and hands me a coffee and a massive blueberry muffin. 'I wouldn't want to mess with him, would you?'

'I've got a horrible feeling I've got no choice.' Maybe, when you've got a pissed-off man, who thinks he's always in the right, then the only way to tackle him is head on and show him the error of his ways.

Chapter 2

Dear Mr Armstrong,

It is with regret that I am emailing to inform you that you really are the proverbial pain in the arse. Burying your head in the sand isn't big and it isn't clever. If you really are the Anti-Christmas then go ahead and ruin your own Christmas, but grow a pair and think about other people for once. Ditch the attitude, mate. You're happy to take our clients' money, so forget your 'bah humbug' – deck your flaming halls with jolly holly and answer my frigging emails!

Love and festive kisses, Sarah xxx

Making Memories, Travel Agents

I hit the final 'x' with a flourish and sit back. My hand makes contact with something soft and squishy that shouldn't be there, and there's a yelp.

'Ouch!' Sam has her hand over her nose, and a pained expression on her face.

'What on earth are you doing, peering over my shoulder?' She ignores the question and starts to rub her nose,

13

which makes her words come out all funny. 'You can't send that, Sarah!'

'Why not? I'm starting to hate the man.' Following hot on the heels of the threat of legal action yesterday, I have arrived at work to a second disaster. Will Armstrong might not have been prepared to take me seriously yesterday, but I want to make sure he will today. Even if my approach is not quite as professional as it should be.

'But you still can't—'

'You think I should have put ass instead of arse? Is arse too British? I was a bit worried about that bit.'

'Bloody hell, Sarah. You can't say arse *or* ass. What would Lynn say? Delete it! All of it! Now!' She's gone a bit squeaky.

'Stop pulling my wheelie chair.' I hang on to the edge of the desk by my fingertips. If I let go now I might whizz across the office and end up in the potted plant. It's happened before. 'Do you think it's too much?'

'Far too much.' She's given up on trying to move me away from my desk and is nodding her head vigorously and rubbing her nose at the same time.

'Are you okay?'

'Sure.' It comes out as 'dure'. 'I was fine until you threw your arms out in a finale and hit me in the face with your elbow.'

'Did I?'

'You always fling your arms about when you're pleased with yourself.'

'Do I?' I'm pretty sure I don't, but as I've just squashed

my best mate's nose it doesn't seem the right time to argue about it. 'But you were snooping. You get more like your mum every day!' I love Sam's mum, and she knows I do. But we both know that Ruth is a total expert when it comes to creeping up like a ninja, so she can listen in on private stuff.

'No, I do not! She listens to stuff that's none of her business. This *is* my business. This is work, and you can't send that. What the hell has happened now?'

She's right. This is work. She's also probably got a good point as far as the email goes.

'You're right. And there are too many kisses, I hardly know the man.' I delete one and am careful not to throw my arms in the air. 'Not through want of trying, mind you. We'd have a flourishing relationship by now if he replied to my calls; instead I can't even get past first base. Idiot.'

Sam giggles and backs off to her own desk so there's a safe arm's-length distance between us. 'Very funny, but you know I didn't mean that!'

Even though she's known me a few years now, Sam, my best friend and lovely workmate, takes me far too seriously. She's gullible. Or wise. It could be that she's actually very, very wise and knows that my twitchy fingertips are actually dying to hit 'send' on this email, even though it might look like I'm just messing around.

What she doesn't know is *why* he's upset me so much. I'm trying to be cool about this, to laugh it off, but inside it hurts. Inside it feels like a little bit of me is being destroyed, and last night in bed I decided I wasn't going to let him, a complete stranger, do this to me. To us.

Sam pushes a packet of Hobnobs in my direction. 'He's probably scared of you.'

I realise I'm clenching my teeth. It's what I do when I'm upset. My shrink said it's important not to do that when I talk, or it will make me sound angry. She also said it's better to express how I feel. So how does that work? I feel angry, I'm expressing it through clenched teeth. I'm beginning to think most of what she said was bollocks.

I take a deep breath and unclench everything, then take my frustration out on a crunchy biscuit. 'I am not scary. *Real* men appreciate the direct approach.' I try and blow the crumbs out of the keyboard. The letter 'T' is already a bit dodgy; if this ruins W and A I'll have lost one of my favourite words.

'He might actually be quite nice. I'm going to look on their website. What's he called again?' Sam pokes me in the ribs when I don't immediately answer.

'Armstrong.'

'Armstrong, what?'

'William.' I sigh, I can't help myself.

Sam swings round on her chair so she's facing her own computer again and does some rapid key-tapping.

It stops, and I'm pretty sure I know what's coming next.

'Oh wow. He's . . .' She pauses, her head tilted as she stares at the screen. Then rests her chin on her hand. There's a long silence.

'I can tell you're struggling.'

'No, I'm not.' She flashes me her best headmistressy stare. 'Have you *seen* him? I mean look! If I didn't already have Jake I would be straight over there myself, to hell with crap reviews about his place. Look!'

'I've seen.' I try and act bored, but the truth is I've looked at William Armstrong's photograph more than once. The man confuses me, because when I first rang him (after seeing that photo on the resort website) I thought he'd be nice, charming. But he wasn't. He was curt, rude, and muttered something that sounded like 'I'm going to string him up by his baubles for this' before putting the phone down on me.

'But he does look quite sexy, admit it.'

'Are you for real?' I'm not going to admit it, even though he does have a certain something about him. 'Not my type I'm afraid.'

'Aw, come on, he's not that different to that guy you went out with before Callum.'

I roll my eyes. 'Exactly. He looks a lightweight.' I stare at the image. 'And smug, like he thinks a lot of himself.' *That guy* before Callum spent a hell of a lot of time staring at himself in the mirror and it's kind of put me off the well-groomed look. I mean, have you ever known a man to be checking himself out while you're having sex?

I thought he was reciting the alphabet backwards in his head or something, to try and delay the inevitable; turned out he was checking out if his hair gel was holding up. That was it for me. End of.

'He's good-looking, so cute!'

'And he knows it.'

'Rubbish, how can you tell that from a photo? He reminds me of that guy in *The Mentalist*.' She's staring at her screen and has moved in closer, as though she's going to start licking it any moment.

'Mental's the right word. Who are you talking about now?'

'You know, I know you do. What's he called?' She does some more googling. 'There you go, Simon Baker. All twinkly-eyed and cute, but a bit naughty.' We both stare at the images.

'Pfft.'

'He's cute.' I think she's back to our Mr Armstrong now, but who knows? 'Look at those dimples. I bet he's fun.' I don't know which set of dimples she's going on about, but it doesn't matter.

'I am not interested in his dimples, or his cuteness. He is duplicitous.'

'That's a very long word.' I can tell by Sam's twitching fingers that the online dictionary is about to get interrogated, so I pull her and her wheelie chair away from the desk. Very handy these chairs, a good investment.

'Well, he is.' I can't believe that somebody could portray themselves as so – well, fun and carefree, when in fact they're rude and curt. 'His face contravenes the Trade Descriptions Act.'

'His face?'

'His face. He is definitely not nice, however cute he looks in that picture. In fact, I bet that's not even him, or it was taken years ago, and he's gone all mean and bitter in his old age.'

'Maybe he's having a mid-life crisis and realises that his life is meaningless.' Sam sighs, rests her chin on one hand again and reaches for another biscuit with the other. I roll my eyes. Not at the biscuit, but her fantasy.

'Running a business is not meaningless.'

'It is if you always wanted to swim with dolphins, or ride a camel, or drive to Monte Carlo in a Ferrari.'

'Sam, that's your bucket list, not his. Do you honestly think he looks like he wants to swim with dolphins?'

'Maybe not, but you don't know, do you?'

'And I don't care, to be honest. Look, he is taking our clients' money, giving them a shit Christmas in return, and refuses to talk to me about it properly.' I don't know what annoys me most, the fact that he's totally, single-handedly, ruined what used to be our most popular festive location, or the fact that he is refusing to take my calls, to discuss it. 'Whatever happened to *the customer is always right*? He's just plain rude.'

We're on the build-up to the festive season, and it's not just the nasty email that came yesterday: bookings at the Shooting Star Mountain Resort are spinning into reverse. Which is so not how it should be. I mean, it should be the perfect place to spend Christmas. Crackling log fires, massive mug of hot chocolate, sled rides with a pack of huskies and some ho ho ho from Santa as you shove carrots at his real-life reindeer. Not to mention all that après-ski to warm you up after a day rolling about in the snow (I can't ski, all I can do is roll and face-plant).

'It should be fan-bloody-tastic. The brochure and website make it look like total magic.'

'Maybe they're a bit out of date?' Sam is looking worried. And I was beginning to think the same. 'But you don't need to send him an email like that.'

'I flaming do! It's not just that Latterby guy threatening to sue, it's worse. You know the Wilsons who came in the other day?'

'Oh yeah, they were lovely. They were so excited about going even though it's nowhere near Christmas yet, and they were SO loved up.' Sam has got that dreamy look on her face. She's pretty loved up herself, with the lovely Jake, and I think she's subconsciously started to plan the wedding of the decade. 'Getting married in a winter wonderland, can you imagine?'

I can imagine. 'Wedding in a Winter Wonderland' was already on a mental poster I was going to stick in the window after they'd sent me some of the photos. They'd be swathed in rugs, surrounded by presents on the prettiest reindeer-pulled-sledge imaginable. Kissing. All the best bits of Christmas and weddings rolled into one.

They'd be curled up together in front of a roaring log fire, sipping a shared hot chocolate as the snow fell softly outside, and the whole scene would be bathed in candlelight that bounced off the bauble and tinsel-laden Christmas tree.

And they'd be surrounded by friends and family, swapping presents, then gathered round a food-laden table as they tucked into a mammoth Christmas dinner that had absolutely everything. Even the bits you don't like.

'Well.' I blink, and the image disappears. 'They're not.'

'What do you mean, not? They were so perfect together, he was—'

'Oh, the wedding is still on, just not at Shooting Star. They cancelled first thing and have already rebooked at another resort online.'

'What?'

'This.' I switch screens on the computer and open the video link they sent me. 'Matt Wilson was looking at reviews and found this online on *The Worst Christmas Ever* blog. It's from last Christmas.'

It's quite a professional video, actually, with captions and music, specifically 'Do they know it's Christmas?', which says it all.

I have already watched it several times; it's like one of those horror films that you know is going to scare you to death, but you can't help yourself. You have to see it, even though you keep half turning away and squinting. Then you have to watch the worst bits on a loop.

Sam and I watch in silence. The family are wearing party hats, which is a handy clue, or you really wouldn't know it was Christmas at all. They are also wearing coats. And scarves. With tinsel over the top.

One solitary marshmallow floats on the top of what might or might not be a mug of hot chocolate, and a vat of mulled wine is poked about in vigorously until a single clove studded orange bobs to the surface.

A child drops a sprout, which bounces across the table like a frog on steroids, and is pounced on by a cat.

The fire looks like it stopped 'crackling' two days earlier, and the turkey looks like it's been on a diet.

And the tree. I don't want to talk about the tree. Christmas trees should be glorious. They should be the biggest tree you can carry home, and they should have every single decoration on that you can find (I need to stress that you can never have too many). This one is like the orphan of Christmas. It is the tree Christmas forgot.

It has been starved of attention, it is practically naked apart from a strand of scraggy tinsel and a job lot of candy canes.

'Wow, have you seen all those candy canes.' Sam points, unnecessarily. 'Have you ever seen so many?'

'Nope. And I never, ever want to see that many again.'

The video pans to the window where the snow is falling, and there's an unmissable sign taped to the glass: *Boxing Day Party Cancelled*.

I close the video down and we both stare at my email. 'This is *so* bad. The only people who are actually going to book are the ones that don't know how to use Google. I don't want to give up on the Shooting Star Mountain Resort, and strike it off our list, but honestly Sam, what the hell are we supposed to do? We can't let them book a holiday that we know is going to be shit.' How could the man be so good-looking, but so totally bah-humbug? What a waste.

'I know, but, maybe it's got better since last Christmas?' I love Sam for her optimism. 'He might have bought some new decorations?'

I position the cursor over the 'send' button and hold my finger up high over the mouse theatrically. Just to see the look of horror on Sam's face.

'You wouldn't dare!'

'Sam, the man hates Christmas, he is Scrooge with knobs on!'

Sam is not like me; she is a bit dippy, but she is also kind, logical and sensible. I am not often accused of any of those things. And I am mad, as in very cross. Mr Armstrong is driving me nuts, which is quite an achievement seeing as I've never even met the man.

He is upsetting our clients but, more importantly, he is upsetting Auntie Lynn. She was so agitated yesterday when she heard about the latest complaint (I had to tell her, no way can I lie or hide things from Aunt Lynn, though I avoided mentioning a lawsuit), that she cleaned the oven. This is unheard of. That is why Mr Armstrong needs sorting. He's also upsetting me, but we don't need to go into that. 'Do you really dare me?'

'No, no, I take that back. I didn't mean it, no dare, just don't!' Sam knows that I will rise to any dare, that saying the word 'dare' to me is like saying the words 'hot chocolate fudge cake' to her. Irresistible.

'That man needs a kick up the butt. Has he any idea how much commission we're losing on this? It's all me, me, me with some people.'

She giggles and waves a biscuit in front of my face. 'Ha ha, instead of you, you, you? You're just taking this all too seriously, it's not personal. Have a Hobnob, they're chocolate ones.'

I do take it seriously. This travel agency on the high street is my Aunt Lynn's business, and knowing exactly where our clients are going is our USP. We have gone for small, friendly, and special. Boutique. Auntie Lynn was a bit of a hippy (from what I can gather) when she was younger. As in what I call her pre-me era. The time before she took me in and took the place of my mother.

She loved to travel, to explore the world. Live life in a way that most people only manage through reading books.

She thinks the rest of the world is special.

She thinks holidays are special.

We are, she says, selling dreams, so we have a responsibility to stop them turning into nightmares. Our edge is that we care about our customers; we know that we're selling a holiday that will suit somebody to a tee.

Except it's all gone wrong with Will Armstrong.

I used to love hearing about how much people enjoyed their holiday in this place, how much it meant to them. It made me feel all warm and fuzzy inside, as though I was somehow responsible. Aunt Lynn and I would share a secret smile as we read the reviews together. And now Mr Armstrong has buggered it up, and it's pissing me off.

'It *is* personal.' I narrow my eyes and stare at the screen. 'This place is one of the first that Auntie Lynn visited and fell in love with. He's screwing up her happy memories as well as our reputation.'

When my aunt set this business up, it was to promote the places she'd been to. Places she loved and wanted to share. Then, as it grew, she made a point of visiting every location. Experiencing for herself what they had to offer, and more often than not she had taken me along with her. She said we were the two musketeers, though I did sometimes wonder if it would have been better for her if she'd been able to add a third.

Anyway, back to Mr Pain-in-the-arse Armstrong. To give in to temptation and hit send on this email, would be to admit that he has got to me. That he has made me forget my professionalism. It would be easier to just find another, much better resort to recommend.

Except it isn't that simple.

The lovely log cabins with roaring fires, lashings of hot chocolate and deep white snow outside had sent our customers flocking to the Canadian Rockies for a cosy Christmas. Once upon a time, this place had created memories that could never be replaced. And sometimes we all need memories to hold onto the good times.

'It's bloody annoying,' I know I sound a bit like a spoiled

child, but I'm peeved, 'that place was perfect, not commercialised, and everyone who had stayed there thought the same. They all came back starry-eyed, saying how it had been the best ever Christmas. Until Mr Festivity-bypass got his hands on it.'

Last Christmas had been a bit sparse on the old festive spirit, and even the holidaymakers who'd gone for the ski-ing and snowboarding had written terrible reviews about the equipment and facilities. As an outdoor resort it was pretty bad: as a festive resort it was the pits.

'To be fair,' Sam always tries to be fair, 'it has definitely been slipping the last couple of years; last winter somebody said the huskies kept stopping for a pee instead of pulling the sled, and the mistletoe was plastic.' She does have a point; the sparkle has been wearing off for a while now. 'Faded plastic.'

Plastic mistletoe has to be the pits, but faded old plastic mistletoe? I ask you, who's going to pucker up under that?

She shrugs. 'We can suggest people go to Lapland instead, or to see the Northern Lights, they're popular. I wouldn't mind going there myself. Do you want this last biscuit, or not?'

'Yes, seeing as you've had the rest.' I reach out. 'Shit.' I had wanted the last biscuit, but now I don't, I really don't. 'Holy crap. How did that happen?' Oh God, why did I position the cursor there? Why was my stupid bloody mouse right where I could catch it with my elbow? Why do biscuits even exist?

'What?'

'Shit. Bugger. I am sooooooo dead. I hit send!' I cover my eyes with my hands, and peep through. Sent. Gone for ever. Even if I delete it from my sent box, I will know I did it. Aunt Lynn will kill me. 'It's fine, fine.' Take a deep breath, Sarah. 'He won't read it anyway. He usually never reads my emails.' Only he did yesterday. I nibble on the biscuit frantically, like a demented hamster.

'You idiot.' A packet of Oreo's appears on her desk as if by magic. 'Emergency supplies, to treat shock.'

'Oh nooooooo!'

'I thought you liked . . .'

Her voice tails off, probably because I'm pointing at my screen. This can't be happening, I need gin, not Oreos. 'I've got a reply!'

'It will be auto generated, out of office, or something. Nobody types that quick.'

It isn't.

Apparently, some people can type quickly.

Chapter 3

Dear Sarah,

Thank you for your recent correspondence. How nice to hear from you again! (I suspect this is sarcasm.) Unfortunately, in this part of the world there is no sand to bury one's head in, therefore one has to use snow, which rather freezes the brain and leaves one temporarily incapacitated and thus incapable of carrying out simple tasks such as responding to phone calls.

I am currently reviewing our 'flaming halls' and other client requirements, though as far as I am aware 'growing a pair' has never featured on any feedback form.

Many thanks for your interest in our resort, and we look forward to welcoming you here in the future.

Regards. Will Armstrong (The Anti-Christmas).

Shooting Star Mountain Resort

'Well at least he's got a sense of humour.'
'Hilarious.' Dry I think they call it. I'm busy typing as I speak. What a cheek! Welcoming, huh, he doesn't know the meaning of the word.

Dear ~~Will~~ Mr Armstrong,

Many thanks for your prompt response. If you are not currently suffering from brain freeze it would be very helpful if you could spare the time to pick up the phone so we can discuss our requirements.

Our clients have reported a far-from-warm welcome – in fact, it has been coined 'frosty' in one instance – and there has been little in the way of flaming recently, in fireplaces or halls. The only feature in your brochure that you seem to provide, is snow. Maybe a new, more specific, feedback form would be in order?

'You can't send that!' Sam is back peering over my shoulder, dropping crumbs down my cleavage.

'You said that before.' I drum my fingers on the desk, well away from the danger zone of the mouse, and wriggle the crumbs out of my bra. 'You know what I'm seriously tempted to do, though?'

Sam raises on eyebrow, and surreptitiously nudges the mouse out of my reach. 'I don't like the sound it, whatever it is.'

'Go.'

'What do you mean, go?'

'Go there. To the resort. He said he'd look forward to welcoming me in the future, so maybe that's the answer. I mean, he can't ignore me if I'm standing in front of him, can he?' I minimise the email screen and log on to the booking system. 'I could see for myself just how welcoming

Mr Brain-freeze is and whether there's any hope of salvaging some magic. And if there's not, I'll cancel all the bookings our clients have made and move them.'

'No! You can't just go, we're busy, *you're* busy!' Sam is staring at me. 'Anyhow, all the good resorts are booked up now, so you can't move people if it really is that crap. It's too late.'

'Well, I'll think of something.'

'You have got to be kidding!' Sam frowns, then bites the side of her thumb. 'Have you totally lost your marbles this time?'

She might have a point. But not one I intend to concede to. 'I could be the undercover hotel inspector, poking about in his dark corners and uncovering the truth. I've always fancied myself as a bit of a sleuth.'

'You said you wanted to stand in front of him, so he can't ignore you.'

The girl has a point. 'Stop being picky. Anyway, that's after I've poked about and written a witty and scathing piece about the state of his ski-lifts and skirting boards.'

'Skirting boards?'

'That's where the dust gathers, apparently.' Not that I'd know; I'm not a big-on-dusting kind of girl.

'Do log cabins have skirting boards?'

'Sam!'

'Sorry, just trying to help.'

'Anyway, I'd get a staff discount.' Always look on the bright side, as my Aunt Lynn likes to say, and the one very bright side to working in her travel agency is that I get to travel on the cheap.

'They should be paying you to go there.' Sam taps a few buttons on her computer, then draws a deep breath. 'Listen.' I don't really need to listen, I know the crap reviews off by heart, but she's going to read them out to me anyway. '*The worst Christmas we have ever had. The only good bit was the hot chocolate—*'

'*– until they ran out of marshmallows.*' I finish the review for her. 'But I could always take some with me.' She ignores me. 'I mean, who runs out of marshmallows? It's like . . . like . . .'

'Running out of wine?'

'Like a margarita without the salt round the rim.'

'Serious stuff, then.'

'Well, you'd feel cheated, wouldn't you? And how about this one? *Cosy this place is not – unless you're related to a polar bear, it was warmer out than in.*' Sam glances up to check I'm still listening. '*The website promises husky-drawn sleds, and the nearest we got was being allowed to take the dog a walk.* Aw, I quite like the idea of that. Jake's thinking about teaching Harry to pull a sled, but there's never any snow here, is there?' I refrain from commenting. Cute as her boyfriend's dog Harry is, I'm pretty sure sled dogs are usually twice his size. 'And this one's from last Christmas, *Guide refused to take us ski-ing because it was snowing! Cheese fondue was ace, let down by untidy dining room and rude waitress. Amazing place, just a shame the new owners have let standards slip. A magical Christmas this was not.'*

'So, I should go, shouldn't I? Look, that place used to be the best on our books; it was magical, fabulous, festive – you know, all those F words.' I've run out, but she knows what I mean.

'And now it's a flop, Sarah, but it's not our job to put places right, is it? We just recommend somewhere else. You don't have to actually *go* there.'

'Aunt Lynn used to.' I think I might be sounding a bit sulky.

'To check places out, see if they were holidays she wanted to sell. Not put them right. Oh Sarah, why not just drop it, find somewhere better?'

'Because . . .' Well, partly because I'm stubborn and don't like to admit defeat. 'It's not just Auntie Lynn that loved it.' I take a deep breath as the prickly heat of tears in my eyes takes me completely by surprise. I mess around with the paperclips on my desk so that I don't have to look at her. 'It was where she and I spent our first Christmas together.' There's a lump in my throat that shouldn't be there, and I'm blinking faster than the lights on a faulty pelican crossing. I swallow, hard. 'I want to thump Will Armstrong.'

'Oh hell. Why didn't you say? Not the thump bit, the Christmas bit, I mean.' Sam squeezes my hand and I pull away slightly, because sympathy always does me in. I don't want to end up in tears, not here, not at work. Well, not anywhere, really. Crying is something I learned not to do a long time ago. It's pointless.

Zara Stoneley

Our first Christmas at the Shooting Star resort had been magical. Which I suppose is what Auntie Lynn intended.

She'd never been that close to her sister, my mum, they'd been too different. Camembert and brie, as Lynn liked to say, and the subtle differences had run deep. Mum had married young, had me, taken me off on magical mystery tours in a camper van. Lynn was single, resolutely childless and loved to spend time in unexplored corners of the world. They both had wanderlust, but their lust and their wandering had taken them in very different directions.

Up until then, I'd hardly known Aunt Lynn; our paths had never really crossed until that Christmas.

The Christmas when she'd been there to try and save my little family, and instead had been left with me when my parents had left. Without me. For a 'spot of adult time' as Mum had laughingly put it, and I'd never seen them again. That jokey comment and her tinkling laugh are the last I remember of her.

She didn't wear perfume, so there was no lingering smell of lavender or Chanel N°5 to give me a part of her back. She didn't even leave a discarded jumper, or treasured trinket. Life isn't like always like they tell it in the movies. There was nothing; no part of her for me to hold on to, except for the sound of her laughter and a hazy memory of her big, green eyes.

It had been my last Christmas with Mum and Dad, my first with Auntie Lynn.

We'd spent another week there. Just the two of us. I'd

been bewildered, feeling lost, waiting for my parents to appear at the door and for everything to go back to normal. They didn't.

Mum would never be able to go back anywhere now, she was sleeping with the stars. And Dad? Well, as far as I was concerned, my dad no longer existed.

That Christmas we'd spent our days building snowmen, walking in the snow, patting the huskies and feeding the reindeer. And in the evenings we'd curl up together in the log cabin, staring into the flames and making wishes. The same wishes I'd carried on making for years afterwards. Until I realised wishes never come true anyway.

I blink away the past and ignore the one tiny tear that manages to squeeze its way past my defences.

'It doesn't matter. That's not the point, is it?'

Sam is frowning at me and doesn't look convinced, so I ignore her and tap away on my keyboard, which means I can brush away the dampness on my cheek without her noticing.

'But what about Lynn? You always spend Christmas together.'

Sam is right again. Ever since that one in the Shooting Star Mountain Resort, Aunt Lynn and I have spent every Christmas together. She's my family, my whole family, the only one I've got, and she's amazing.

I love Auntie Lynn. Totally. If it hadn't been for her my life would have worked out totally differently. I would be an insecure, unloved mess and I would also be totally boring and bored. Auntie Lynn has brought me up with cuddles and creativity, and she has taught me that being the only guardian at parents' evening with striped hair and questions about what I thought rather than what the teacher thought is something to be celebrated, not be ashamed of.

'But I'm not going for actual Christmas.' No way do I want to spend Christmas there ever again. Even if the place had still been perfect (which it certainly isn't), I don't think I could face that. 'I'll go just before, or after. Actually, now might be a good time.' No time like the present. 'I could try and get some of it sorted before he has chance to ruin Christmas for another load of people. One more bad Christmas could finish the place off for good. I am not going to let him screw up like this: no one cancels Christmas!'

'But you can't just up and leave me!'

'I'm not leaving you on your own. I'll have to clear it with Aunt Lynn, but she did say a while ago that she thought maybe we should start to visit places again. She's thinking of taking a temp on to cover here, so that we can get out more. You'd get to go to places too.' I give her a sideways glance. 'She knows you want to travel.'

Sam goes bright red. She thinks she's hidden the way she feels, but she is one of those people who just can't hide their feelings – they're written all over her face. She's changed in a good way, lately, especially after she got over her tosspot two-timing ex, and met her dishy boyfriend Jake. It's been obvious that she's come out stronger. She's still the funny girl I love, but she's now much more determined to live the life *she* wants. And she wants more than just sitting in a goldfish bowl in the high street.

'Lynn doesn't want to lose you, Sam. I don't either.' I can't imagine life without Sam. We're totally different, but we just get on. She's giving me a look, like she might hug me, and I can't cope with hugs right now. 'Hang on, this will timeout if I don't complete the booking.'

'Leave it.' She tugs at my chair again so that I can't reach the keyboard. 'Come on, they aren't exactly going to get booked up if you leave it a few minutes, are they? And don't you need to check dates first?'

'I can provisionally book.' Not that there is much need – there is availability on every date I look at. 'Then I can call Aunt Lynn.' Sam doesn't like the impulsive side of my character, it makes her uncomfortable. She likes to know where she stands, whereas I – with my wobbly past – tend to view each day as a new challenge. And right now, locking horns with Mr Armstrong in the Canadian Rockies sounds like a good diversion.

'Why don't you call her now?'

'Okay, okay, I'll talk to her first if it makes you happy.' Sam does have a point, but it's a quiet time and I'm sure my aunt will be more than happy to cover for me for a few days; she likes to 'keep her finger on the pulse', as she puts it.

'It does make me happy.'

So I dial out on the office phone and put it on speakerphone so that Sam will be in no doubt at all to Lynn's response – even though I know she will like this idea. She says travel broadens the mind and shrinks the butt. She will definitely like this idea.

'Aunt Lynn?'

'Oh, I'm glad you rang, dear.' She says this as though we never talk, whereas we talk at least once a day. 'I wanted a little chat.'

Sam raises an eyebrow, and I half wish I hadn't put Lynn on speakerphone.

'I'm a bit 'tied up at the moment,' she does sound distracted, 'but come for a spot of coffee and cake.' I stare at the phone, then glance at Sam, who is doing an 'I haven't a clue' gesture.

'Er, fine. It's just I wanted to—'

'Will it keep until Wednesday, dear?'

She sounds as if she's not really listening anyway, so I nod, even though she can't see me. 'Sure.' What difference will a couple of days make? 'Or tomorrow?'

'Oh no dear, I've got Hedgehog Rescue tomorrow, had you forgotten?'

There's the tiniest note of reproach in her voice. How could I forget Hedgehog Rescue? Not to mention Purrfect Cat Rescue, Sanitary Towels for the Homeless, and Baby in a Box. That last one did worry me a bit, until I researched and found out it was a care pack for newborns. The image in my head hasn't changed, though: the perfect next day delivery service for the childless.

Aunt Lynn believes in paying it forward, and because

she is so nice people shower her with little acts of kindness. There is, therefore, a lot of paying forward to be done.

'It's the big weigh in, followed by a hog roast.'

'That sounds vaguely inappropriate.'

She laughs, a hearty belly laugh. 'Oh, get you! We can have a good catch up, and I'll tell you all about my plans.'

'Plans?' That sounds ominous.

'Shall we say three o'clock, then?'

She is obviously not going to enlighten me. Although with Aunt Lynn there is never a need to rush, and she is the least inquisitive person I know. If somebody says they've got something to tell me, I will mull it over, dissect the tone of their voice, list all the possible reasons, worry. Lynn will forget about it. 'Sure, if you can't—'

'Rushed off my feet, darling! Oh dear, oh dear, I really have to go.'

'Shall I bring cake?'

'No, no.'

'It's no bother, I can grab some from the café across the road?'

'Just bring yourself, dear. Take the afternoon off, I'm sure Sammy can cope. Now, I really am going to have to rush, Lionel is dangling from the chandelier, he's so adventurous!'

Sam splutters biscuit crumbs in all directions, and I shout 'bye' and slam a finger hard on the end call button, as though it will disconnect it quicker.

'Clean that dirty mind of yours.' I stare at Sam disapprovingly. 'Lionel is her neighbour's cat.'

'Ah.' She's grinning, and I can't help it, I have to grin back. We know we're both thinking the same thing (as she does know my Aunt Lynn quite well), and Lionel could quite easily have been a man she'd picked up. Qualifying for a bus pass hasn't slowed her down at all.

We sit in silence for a moment, savouring the image that has sprung into our minds. It's Sam who shakes the thought out of her head first. 'Do you think it's okay? The cat?'

'Oh yeah, he's done it before. He waits until she's halfway up the stepladder then lets go and stalks off.'

'Oh. That's good.' The look of relief turns to a little frown. 'That was a bit weird, the cake and coffee thing. She never asks you round for cake and coffee.'

It is weird (even weirder than the Lionel thing) and worrying on many counts.

'I know.' Lynn doesn't really do 'coffee', I might pop in for a chat, or she sometimes calls by my place and stops for a drink, or even a meal. But we don't invite each other round for coffee. And definitely not for cake and coffee. The whole conversation is out of character. Something is off kilter. This feels like bad news and has made me feel all uneasy and icky inside.

What does she need to talk about that means I won't be up to work afterwards? Is she selling up? Is she ill? My God, is she getting married?

I feel more than uneasy now. I feel sick.

I take a deep breath. It can't be that urgent if it can wait until Wednesday and be lower priority than Hedgehog Rescue. Surely?

But even though Wednesdays are quiet, she knows that leaving Sam running the place single-handedly could be an issue.

Sam is ace at selling holidays to people who aren't sure they want them, but she tends to get distracted. And press the wrong buttons on the computer (unlike me of course, ha ha). So why would Lynn suggest I take time off, unless she has something major to tell me, something that can't be discussed on the phone?

And secondly, Auntie Lynn definitely doesn't bake cakes. Her occasional spontaneous baking sessions in the past have resulted in deconstructed scones and melt-in-the-middle Madeira cake. Yes, she knows there is no such thing, but that is what usually happens. And you know those recipes that are impossible to mess up? Well, I've got news for you, Mr Super-chef.

When I was little I thought they were the most amazing creations ever – nobody else had smashed banana and crisp sandwiches with a side of pancake pieces in their lunch box. I was special.

The fact that we are meeting at her home and not in a café, where cake is provided and guaranteed to pass health and safety requirements, is even more worrying.

'You don't think it upset her, talking about booking to go to that place?'

I shake my head. 'I didn't even get that far, did I? It wasn't *my* plans she was interested in, it was *hers*. She said she'd tell me all about her plans.' This is the third, and most unsettling part of it all. What plans? Lynn doesn't plan things, she does things. And she doesn't save things up to tell me about later, we fill each other in as we go along.

Sam and I both frown together. 'I'm sure it's nothing. She just wants a chat with you, that's all.' Sam doesn't sound convinced, and nor am I.

What hasn't Lynn been telling me?

Chapter 4

Auntie Lynn's house is warm and welcoming, and smells of fresh baking. I lived with her until I was twenty, at which point we both agreed that it might be better if I moved out. Lynn is more free-love than I am, and it was getting awkward and, to be honest, a bit embarrassing to bump into her lovers wandering about in the nude. Especially as some of them seemed a damned sight sexier than the men I brought back. And more interesting. And even, on one memorable occasion, younger.

'Now dear.' She pushes the plate of tarts in front of me; they're a bit of a strange colour, with weird stripes that look like petrified goldfish immobilised in a sea of strangely translucent custard. 'Lemon curd and marmalade – I ran out of lemon, but oranges and lemons go together perfectly, don't they?'

I take a tentative bite. A sour sweetness explodes in my mouth, along with a chewy bit that could be orange rind, and my tongue goes kind of numb. I think my eyes are wide and watering, and I seem to have developed lockjaw.

'I've got a bit of news.' She is smiling, but watching my face closely, slightly nervous – as if she's expecting me to keel over any second. 'It's all been a bit last minute, but I wanted to have a chat about it and explain.' This obviously isn't about her cooking. This is about 'her plans'. The reason I'm here.

There is a long pause. I don't like pauses, they come before bad news. I'm also not keen on the word 'explain'. I put the rest of the tart down.

'I'm going away for Christmas.'

My locked jaw is suddenly slack and I understand her nervousness now. This isn't about her culinary skills. 'But we never go away for Christmas, we always have it here.' We have the biggest tree we can find, too much glitter, and pretend cotton-wool snow if the real stuff doesn't appear. We make mulled wine and weird-shaped mince pies, we go to midnight mass in our wellies and swap a special present just before we go to bed. We help feed the homeless and then walk the dogs in the shelter, and then we watch the Queen's speech and play Monopoly.

'I know, love. But this year,' she sighs, 'I'm afraid I have to go and see Ralph.' She stresses the 'I', which I realise I'd missed before. I as in her, not us. Not *me*. There's a hollow pang of emptiness inside me, and my heart is racing away as though it knows I need to run and hide. It's that feeling I remember from school, when I knew I wasn't going to get picked by anybody to be on their team.

'You're spending Christmas without me?'

She leans forward and squeezes my hand, and I realise I sound like a five-year-old child, not the independent woman I insist to the rest of the world that I am. Except Aunt Lynn isn't the rest of the world. 'You're leaving me on my own?'

'Only for a few days.'

'And who's Ralph?' Is Ralph a dog? Why have I never heard of Ralph before?

'He's in Australia.'

'*Australia?*' I do realise I'm just repeating everything, but she's saying all the wrong things.

'I need to do this on my own, darling.' Lynn sits back, and I watch mesmerised, as she stirs her mug of tea and the words swirl round inside me. 'He's an old friend,' the way she says 'friend' makes me look up, into her eyes, 'and he's dying. This will be his last Christmas, and I'd really like to spend it with him. You knew I was in Australia just before you came to live with me?'

I nod. I have some vague recollection of being told, but I was little more than a toddler back then, and all I remember is the strangeness. Aunt Lynn was strangely brown and wore odd, flamboyant clothes, all bright and swirly. Big skirts that swished as she walked, big beads that jingled together, that I played with as I sat on her knee.

Her house smelled different to my old one, all scented and smoky. *She* smelled different, all warm and inviting. She'd hug me to her chest and sing to me, and even her hugs were different to all the ones I'd had before. Only

Aunt Lynn hugged me that way, as though she'd never let me go.

A silly lump is lodged in my throat, and I sit and blink like an owl at her.

Christmas has always been about the two of us being together. How does Christmas work without her?

Oh God, I can't spend Christmas all alone, I haven't even got a cat for company!

I know, I'll take Callum up on his offer. He texted this morning asking if I wanted to spend the day at his parents' house with him, and I'd been horrified. I'd nearly rushed round there and then to say no, to explain I had to be with Aunt Lynn. That's we always spend the day together. But something had stopped me. I blink some more. I don't want to be with Callum. If I say yes now, it will be for all the wrong reasons. I'll be using him.

'I came back for you, Sarah, and I left Ralph behind. But now it's time to go and see him. One last time.' She squeezes my hand again and her voice is gentle as she studies my face with eyes that used to be piercing blue but are now softened with age, and the sadness of life. 'I am so sorry, love. I know what Christmas together means to you, it's important to me as well. But you can come with me if you like? Ralph won't mind at all. I just didn't think you'd want to share Christmas in a strange place with a man you don't know who's dying, and I know it won't be the same as Christmas here, but . . .'

'It's all right. Honest.' I'd rather have Christmas anywhere if it meant being with her, than being at home without her, but I can see that this is something that really can't be shared. Ralph needs her. And I've got a feeling she needs him.

'He's only got a few weeks left; he might not be here to see the new year in, so it's all been a bit rushed, you see. It was the earliest flight I could get – the silly idiot had put off telling me until now.' There's real anguish, mixed with tears in her strangled voice. 'I just hope I'm not too late.'

I've never thought of her as old, or sad before, but now the mist of my own selfishness is breaking up and I realise she's more than just my Auntie Lynn. She's a woman with a past of her own.

Aunt Lynn has never said much about her other life. Her pre-me life. Before my parents disappeared. But as I grew up, and studied the photographs, the discarded rucksack shoved to the back of her wardrobe, and the small mementoes of different places and people that adorned every shelf, nook and cranny in her house, I pieced together her real life as best as I could. And I saw a carefree, happy, hippy lifestyle that she'd willingly abandoned, and that she made sure I never felt guilty about.

How can I not be happy for her if she has a chance now to go back to that life? I am all grown up, and she can be free again. I swallow down my desire to shout 'don't leave me', ashamed that I'm struggling. 'Tell me about Ralph.'

So she does. And all the time she speaks about him she has a wistful smile on her face, her voice soft and sing-song, her mind miles away from the life she and I have been sharing.

'You shouldn't have left him.'

'I had you, love, and besides, the time was right. Are those a bit tart? I was worried the orange rind would go chewy, but I only had the thick-cut marmalade. Would you like a bit of flapjack? It's a bit crunchy – I didn't know whether to smash it up and call it granola.'

I can't think about granola now. I'm thinking about Aunt Lynn being sad and putting a brave face on things. And spending Christmas on my own.

Lynn smiles, a bit uncertainly.

'Actually, I've got plans myself.' What am I saying? 'I'm going away.' I'm what? How could I say that?

'You are?'

'I am.' I nod. Confidently. And feel slightly sick, but now I've started this, I can't stop, can I? 'I'm going to Canada!' That's it! That will show her! I'm all grown up now, I can do Christmas on my own. Spending Christmas with Callum would definitely be wrong. In my heart I've known for a long time that things aren't quite perfect between us, that we've been running out of time. Oh no, I'm not going to spend Christmas with him. I'm going to see this as an opportunity and fix Will Armstrong once and for all.

'Canada?' She's got a puzzled frown on her face, which isn't surprising. Inside I'm a bit confused too.

'I'm going to sort out the mess at the Shooting Star Mountain Resort. That's what I wanted to talk to you about,

I've already made a provisional booking; all I need to do is confirm.'

'The Shooting Star resort? The one where . . .'

I nod, less confidently now, feeling even more queasy.

'Well, that is a surprise. Good for you, darling. Going back and—'

'I'm only going back because of all the crap reviews, and the fact the jerk that's running it seems to be determined to totally wreck the place and get us sued in the process.'

'Sued?'

I think I might have got carried away and said things I shouldn't. I'm not sure flapping my arms in the air in what I thought was a nonchalant gesture is removing the frown from her face, but it's worth a try. 'Oh, it's nothing to worry about, just empty threats.' She doesn't look convinced. 'But that's why I'm going.'

'*The* Shooting Star resort?'

I nod.

'And you'll be all right on your own?' She's looking even more worried now, and I don't think it's anything to do with being sued.

'Definitely. I'm a big girl, now.' But feel like a tiny, abandoned toddler inside. Man up, Sarah, you can do this.

'I'd come with you, but I need to do this for Ralph – and for me, if I'm honest. He needs me, Sarah.' That is Aunt Lynn all over: she is there if people need her, like she's always been there for me. 'Why not wait until the new year and we can go together?'

'Honestly, I'll be fine.' And why spend Christmas on my own, when I can be with Mr ruin-it-all Armstrong? 'It needs sorting now.' I think I might be trying to reassure myself here, convince myself I've made the right decision.

What am I thinking? It's not only Mr Scrooge himself that I'll be tackling. I'll be back *there*. The place where it all went wrong, when I found out just how little I meant to the two people who'd meant everything to me. My world.

Aunt Lynn is right. I won't be all right on my own. I want her there, holding my hand. I don't want to pull warm mittens on all alone, to look at the spot where we built the biggest snowman ever without her at my side.

I don't want to curl up on a rug, looking at the flickering flames, and see my parents wave goodbye in my mind.

I can't go back alone to the place that broke my heart. In fact, I swore I'd never go back. I'd closed that door forever.

I can feel the hurt bubbling up in my throat. Threatening to break out in a babble of words, saying I can't do it, that it won't work, that I'll never ever be able to go back there again.

But it doesn't.

I can't expect Aunt Lynn to be there, watching my back, forever. This is my battle now, not hers.

And anyway, this isn't about the past, about me. I'm going because of the business, and I'm going because I need to prove to Lynn and myself that I'm all grown up now.

I blink hard, shut out the image of a husky dog licking

my fingers, tickling my face with its fur until I giggle, until Mum laughs and swings me up in the air.

'I want to go.' Swallowing hard clears my throat and digging my nails into the palms of my hands helps the lie. 'If I don't go now, it'll be too late.'

'Okay.' It's long and drawn out. 'Well, if that's the case, I'm going to shut the agency over the holiday period, so that you don't have to worry and can have some fun.' She stands up abruptly, as though she's made a sudden decision, and walks over to the dresser. 'And I've got a little surprise for you too. Consider it an early Christmas present!'

Chapter 5

A unt Lynn and I have one thing in common with the royal family. I'm pretty sure it will only be the one thing, but who knows? Anyway, we decided many years ago to go for inexpensive gifts that will make us laugh. We have a strict spending limit and it's all about trying to get something that will make the other person chuckle, but something that they'll love and cherish because it's so 'them'.

Aunt Lynn has always collected knick-knacks from her travels, but says that each item, however seemingly worthless, has a memory attached and means something to her. And that, she says, is the important thing. What's the point in spending lots of money on something that is emotionally worthless?

It took me quite a while to get my head round this (and she did bend the rules rather a lot when I was little), but as I got older, the gifts she gave me started to mean more, which meant I treasured them. I don't keep much; I'm not a 'stuff' type of person, but each gift she has given me has captured a memory, a place or a feeling, and I've kept them all. My emotional me is spelled out on my dressing table, if anybody ever takes the time to study the weird assortment of items and work it out.

These days we laugh as we rip the wrapping paper off, but behind the laughter there is a shared 'knowing'. An anticipation. Our flippant gifts prove how much we know about each other, how closely our lives are meshed.

Today, though, this feels wrong, and is making my heart twinge with dread. It is not Christmas morning, and the envelope she has just fished out of the drawer does not look funny, or cheap. It looks ominous. It feels like something terrible is about to happen, that the one tradition we've stuck to, the one certainty in my life, is about to explode and shatter into little pieces.

'I'll keep it until—' I'm not usually a wimp, or melodramatic, but I don't like this at all. The reality that we're not spending Christmas Day together is still sinking in. I don't want any more shocks. Changes.

'Open it now, love.' She doesn't let go of her end, as though she knows I'll stuff it in my bag if she does. There's a little tussle between us, until my gaze meets hers dead on and she knows I'll do what she's asked. 'It's not a proper present really, more like a promise.'

'A promise?' The envelope is burning the tips of my fingers.

I don't want to open it now, but I know she isn't going to give me a choice. For all the hippy-chick free love-living and happiness vibe she gives out, on the inside Lynn is tough. And determined. Appearances can be deceptive.

The envelope isn't even sealed, the flap is just tucked in, but it seems to take an age for my clumsy fingers to find a way inside it.

To drag out the slip of paper.

'Oh.' It isn't at all what I expect. Not that I know *what* I'd expected. You can't cram Christmas with all the festive trimmings into an envelope, can you?

'But . . .' It doesn't make any sense at all. This isn't like our normal presents, this isn't about making new memories. This is terrible.

My world wobbles. Coffee and cake at Lynn's had seemed weird, but this is starting to feel like it should be happening to somebody else. 'Why?' The single syllable rocks me. She *hasn't* tried to cram Christmas into an envelope: she's tried to cram responsibility in, commitment. The future. She's not just leaving me for Christmas, she's leaving me for ever.

Oh shit. 'You're,' the words are choking me, 'you're staying there? In Australia? Or you're ill?'

'Oh Sarah, don't be ridiculous! I might be getting a bit old in the tooth, but I'm not going anywhere, and I'm not about to pop my clogs any day soon.'

'But you're getting rid of—'

'I'm not getting rid of anything. In fact, this is all about giving me some time to let my hair down before it all falls out. I didn't have time to sort out all the legalities, but I'll do it before I go and then we're straight for when I get back. A new year, a new us, eh?'

'But, I can't—'

She shifts the sheet of paper so that it's between us on the table, then puts an arm round my shoulders. 'This isn't about me leaving you, Sarah. This is about sharing, about the future.'

I stare at the sheet of paper. Flatten it out with fingers that seem to have an agenda of their own. A wobbly one.

I am now – well, soon will be, joint owner of Making Memories Travel Agents. My initial 50 per cent share will rise gradually over the next five years until I take full control.

My bottom lip is now as wobbly as my fingers and I feel very stupid. 'I thought it meant . . . Oh God, I'm sorry Auntie Lynn.' I throw my arms round her, trying not to rub my runny nose on her shoulder. 'This is so nice of you, so . . .' I wipe the back of my hand across my face, and resist wiping it down my jeans like a child. There's this massive blockage in my throat that physically hurts, but my brain can't work out what to say next.

My eyes sting with the burning tears that are trying to explode from my eyes. But I don't want to be all emo and pathetic, and blubbering. Though to be honest, I'm not sure what I want to be. This is massive. Giving me a job was one thing, but an actual share in the company? It's generous, it's kind, it's trusting, it's . . . madness.

I've never been responsible for so much as a potted plant before, let alone a business. Well actually, I'm lying. Somebody gave me a poinsettia one year and it didn't go well. Let's just say that by Christmas lunch it was looking even more worse for wear than I was. And that's saying something. I think I'm more of a cactus person. Minimum nurturing and commitment. This is forever! This is bigger than a five-year plan. Callum would think it was hilarious.

Oh God, how am I going to do this? A business! Aunt Lynn's business. Letting her down would be the worst possible thing in the world. I can't say no or scream for help.

So, I smile. Hope it comes across as confident and not manic. I'll work out how to handle this later, when I'm alone and can talk to myself in private.

She puts a finger under my chin, and looks me straight in the eye, like she used to do when I'd come home after a shit day at school. 'Who else could I trust with our little business, Sarah? We set this up together, and I've always expected you to take over one day.' She suddenly smiles and looks lighter than she has since I arrived. 'Actually, you going to the Shooting Star is a fabulous idea, Sarah. I was going to suggest you started to visit some of our resorts and searched out some new ones as well. We need to shake things up a bit! Going back there is a splendid idea.'

'It is?' I'm glad at least one of us thinks so.

'Oh yes. And now is the perfect time to make your peace with the past, isn't it? Before you sail into the future.' She waves a hand.

'Is it?' Making my peace with the past isn't on my agenda. That would involve accepting things, facing up to my dad, forgiving them both for what they did. I'm not sure I will ever be ready for that.

Her voice is soft and seems to come from a long way away, 'I think it's the perfect time, don't you? I think it's something you need to do, isn't it? Go back?'

'I'm going to sort all the problems out, make it perfect again.' Even I can hear the defensive note in my voice.

'Oh Sarah, this isn't really about the problems with the place, is it love?' Her voice is so gentle it brings silly prickly sensations to my eyes. 'This is about you. The past.'

'I don't do the past, I do the future.' Looking back has never helped me. Just hurt me.

'Sometimes, love, you can't find a future until you've found peace with the past.'

I've never really got what that means. Peace with the past? I mean, how can you stop those feelings of anger? There's no on-off switch for something like this.

How can you say, yeah, fine, it was a great idea to dump your kid and do a runner, to not come back. To cause fucking havoc in her life and mess with her head. To make her feel useless and cast aside like some coat you didn't want any more.

Talk about a dog being for life and not just for Christmas! Just thinking about it is stirring up all the anger and resentment in my chest, all the emotion I try and keep squashed down. I don't feel self-pity any more, I just try and block it out. And when I can't do that, I seethe. Maybe that's what 'peace' means for me.

'I *have* found peace.' I say it anyway, to reassure her, 'I've got you, work, everything.' My life works. I like it. I'm busy and the people that surround me are there because they want to be. And if I ever suspect they don't want to be, then I move on.

I don't let my parents mess with my head any more. They're old news. I'm done with them and all that.

Going to the Shooting Star is about the future, not the past.

Aunt Lynn smiles and pats my hand. 'Good, well that's fine then. You know what you're doing and this can be your first trip representing the agency!'

Oh God, now I've got added pressure. I'm not just going to shout at Will Armstrong and inspect his dusty crevices, this is my future well and truly at stake. I need to be even more professional than I was going to be.

'And while I'm out of your hair seems like the perfect time for an adventure. I'm being a bit selfish as well: that place means a lot to me and I don't want us to strike it off our list and walk away on a sour note.' Her voice has regained its normal briskness.

I stare at the sheet of paper again. There is no choice now. I need to go the Shooting Star resort, this is *my* business at risk.

All I need now is a booking for one, all inclusive. I will experience all the horrors our clients have told us about, a frosty Will Armstrong and a draughty cabin. I will make an objective, professional judgement about whether our clients deserve somewhere better.

The moment I get back to the office that provisional booking is being confirmed.

I'd said to Sam that I'd go, sort out all the issues, confront Will Armstrong, but I hadn't meant for Christmas. No way. I had never intended to go back for the festive season, to stir up the memories of a time that broke my heart and changed my world. Those bits of me needed to be left untouched, so that I could pick out the nice bits in my head, remember just the happiness and plaster over the hurt.

I'm not sure how this is going to work, how I'm going to feel if I relive that Christmas again. Except I know it will be different. I've got to prove to Lynn that I can cope with anything, and I suppose I've got to prove that to myself, too. And I've got to sort Will Armstrong out once and for all. Whatever Sam said before, this *is* personal now. Nobody is going to mess up my business. (I quite like the sound of that, *my* business.)

'You can do it, love. I know you can.' Lynn squeezes my hand. 'Do you remember what it was like? That little log cabin? It was lovely, wasn't it?' Her wistful smile is reflected in her voice. 'And that very nice couple who ran it then, you won't remember them.'

'I do. They were like Mother and Father Christmas.' Warm, cuddly, ever smiling. I'd felt like I'd been wrapped in a blanket of love and protection, and even back then, so young and confused, I'd clung to their kindness.

'They were sweethearts, but getting on a bit even then.

They sold the place a few years ago, to two brothers. It seemed to be much the same for a long time – the younger boy, Ed he was called, was running it. I had some lovely chats with him, but then something happened and his brother took charge.'

'Will.' I'm not really listening to her, all I can think about is the last day I was there, at the resort. When I hadn't wanted to walk away, because how would Mum and Dad know where to find me if I left with Auntie Lynn?

It wasn't until later that I realised one of them would never be able to look for me, and the other didn't care.

'Will, that's right. Well, he's a totally different kettle of fish to Ed.'

'Cold fish rather than kettle I'd say,' I mutter, but I'm pretty sure she's heard because she's giving me her 'look'. 'And he's ruined the place.'

'Well, we don't know all the facts, do we, love? And from the brief emails we've swapped I'd say there's more to him than meets the eye.'

Oh God. Emails! Has he said anything to Aunt Lynn about those? Oh shit. What exactly did I say to him? What's Auntie Lynn said to him?

'Sarah, are you all right, love? You don't usually gobble up my cakes like that.'

I swallow hard, and I mean hard – this pastry is quite a challenge. I hadn't realised I'd been shoving food in my mouth as a stress-reliever. 'There's something I need to tell you.'

How do I put this, without making her snatch my early Christmas present away before it's made legal?

'After you saw all those horrible reviews, that made you clean the oven, I emailed the resort.'

'Oh, I wasn't cleaning the oven because of the reviews, love. I did it for some thinking time, to work out what to do about Christmas.'

'Oh. But I thought . . . Well, it is important to you?'

'Of course, it is. I'll never forget that first Christmas, Sarah, but it's all,' she taps her forehead, 'up here. I have the trinkets we brought back, and I have you.' She smiles. 'The biggest trinket of all. But places change, and we can't expect a stranger to preserve our memories for us, can we?'

I shake my head.

'But it was a lovely place, and very popular with clients, so I'm sure if you can chat to this Will and sort it out, it will be wonderful. Otherwise we'll have to start sending people to see the Northern Lights, won't we?' She stands up. 'Now, I don't want to be rude, love, but I promised to bake some cakes for the homeless, so I'll talk to you tomorrow, shall I?' She's already handing me my bag. 'Lots to do before I go away. And I'm so pleased you're keen to go back to the Shooting Star, Sarah. I think it means you're ready to move on, don't you?'

In my heart I know what she wants me to do. The thing she's gently hinted at over the years, the thing the shrink less gently hinted at. She wants me to talk about what happened to Mum, to ask all the questions, to forgive her last actions. And she wants me to talk about Dad. To talk *to* Dad. To stop harbouring the hate, the mistrust; the feeling in my heart that it's always my fault, that I can never be quite good enough. That it's always better to move on before people find out that I'm not the person they were hoping I was and leave me.

She wants me to stop picking boyfriends that I know from the start aren't within a million miles of being 'the one' and to think about *the future*. Live in the moment has always been my motto. I'm not sure how I'm going to deal with all this responsibility and dealing with the past shit.

If anybody else was asking, I'd be out of here. But this is Lynn. And Aunt Lynn wants me to do some adulting stuff, so I guess it's time to try.

It's as she pushes the door firmly shut behind me that I realise that I never got to explain to her what I actually said in my emails to Will. And she has no idea how rude and impossible Will Armstrong is, and that he thinks I'm the most unprofessional travel agent ever. She is clueless about the fact that I'm heading towards the worst Christmas ever.

And that, before I go, I have to burn another of my bridges.

Chapter 6

'It's blue.' Callum is propped up on one elbow staring at me. Well, when I say me, I mean my hair. He seems to be mentally circling me, like a sheepdog.

'Callum, are you listening?' It's taken me ages to work out the best way to break the news, and now he's not even listening.

'It's blue!'

'Yes, I know. I—'

'It was blonde, shoulder-length and had pink bits last time I saw you.' He's frowning now and looking a bit miffed. 'And that was only two days ago.'

'Pink hair is so old hat.'

His text yesterday morning had made me uneasy, and then my chat with Auntie Lynn had decided it for me, even though in my heart I'd known for a while that we were running out of time.

After I'd left Lynn I'd called my friend Liz, who also happens to be my hairdresser. It was time for a change and I always find it easier to deal with moving on if I've done something different. It's an outward sign of the inner feeling. Or at least, that's what the shrink said after the teenage me had screamed 'you're not my mother' once too often, and Aunt Lynn had declared we needed professional help.

'But it's black and blue, and . . .' Callum leans around to see better, 'short.'

'Don't you like it?' To be honest, it doesn't really make much difference if he does or not, because the deed has been done now and there is no going back. And I like it. But it would still be nice if he did, too.

'Is that a green streak?' He's now pulling at it as though we're monkeys having a grooming session.

'It might be. So, you don't like it?' He's obviously not going to listen to what I really need to say to him until we're got the hair thing over with.

'I didn't say that. It's er, just a shock. Hang on. I need to check if the carpet matches the drapes, don't I?'

I put a hand out to stop him, because there is a sensible discussion we need to have, but he's already lifting the sheet with a grin on his face, shaking his head.

Callum is my toyboy, the cocktail shaker I picked up in a bar, the guy who I love to shock and who likes to be shocked.

I grin back as he dives under the covers and wait for the yell – or shocked silence. I never quite know how he'll react. Which is half the fun.

In a way, we're perfect for each other. Or we were. Until that text.

Until he asked me over to his parent's house for Christmas Day.

This means he has mentally crossed a line that I never intended going anywhere near – he's strayed into 'meet the family' territory.

Meet the family is scary shit. They will see the things he's hasn't: that I will never be the perfect girlfriend, that I am a million miles from daughter-in-law material. I have blue hair (which was pink) and wear unsuitable clothes. I carelessly lost my parents and haven't a clue where they went. I get over-excited. I am older than he is. I do not have a five-year (or even a five-minute) plan.

See? It's not going to go well, is it?

Callum and I are a good fit now because he's young and a post-grad student with a sparkling career ahead in astrophysics. One day, when he's a bit more grown up, he will want the family I can't give him. He will realise this and then dump me.

And if he doesn't realise, his parents will. And they'll tell him to dump me.

It is much better to realise that we are approaching the end of the road before we get there. While it's still fun.

I've been practising in my head what to say to him, and I'm still struggling. No bloody wonder, really, when I hadn't planned on doing this in bed. How was I to know that he'd greet me at the door stark-bollock naked with a battered gladiolus clenched between his buttocks (he said it had been a healthy specimen at the start but had been harder to hold than he'd thought and had taken several tries)?

Anyway, that was then, and this is post-then.

It's not you, it's me.

No, no, no. I can't say that. Totally not. It's so wrong on so many levels. I mean it *is* me, but just as it takes two to make a relationship, it takes two to break it, doesn't it? The other person might not realise it at the time, they might not realise they're not the perfectly fitting jigsaw piece. But when they're told, they'll feel like the damaged bit, the piece that the dog chewed. And Callum is not damaged, he's just not the fit I thought he was.

Which brings me back to *me*.

It always starts out so well, so full of promise, and then I find I can't live with it. Whatever *it* is.

Although *it*, in this case, is definitely linked to commit-ment. I mean, Christmas Day? That's the start of the end. The start of getting serious, which always wrecks things.

We really hardly know each other. We share fun, pizza, movies, our bodies. We don't do 'meet the family', and Christmas. Even *thinking* about it now is making me hyper-ventilate.

Christmas is for sharing with loved ones. And my loved one is Aunt Lynn, not some cute guy who makes me laugh and orgasm.

I could just say I have to spend the day with Aunt Lynn and leave it at that. But that wouldn't be fair. And it would be a lie. He asked a question that is far more complicated and loaded than it appears, and now there is no un-asking.

Getting serious spoils things, doesn't it? Everything becomes about settling down. If you're not serious, then you can't be horrifically dumped. I'm not ready for serious; in fact, I'm not sure I ever will be.

'Holy Moley!' Don't ask where he gets language like that from, but I like it. I have a rather weird turn of phrase myself, apparently. He resurfaces, and his eyes are wide. 'That looks more like a no entry sign than a landing strip.'

Freud would have a field day with me. And so would a masseur – I didn't half get a crick in my neck (and a bit bog-eyed) giving 'down there' a makeover. 'Callum, we need to talk.'

Callum sighs, drops the bed sheet and edges back up so that his head is at pillow level. His gaze drifts to my hair, then back to my eyes. 'Is the whole hair change thing symbolic, then?'

Callum isn't daft; he is a star astrophysics student. I will be insulting both our intelligences if I do the glib get-out.

I can at least try and keep it light and jokey though.

He picks the bedsheet up again, for another look, and gives a low whistle, which helps. 'Is this because I asked you over for Christmas? You're moving on, aren't you?' He doesn't look me in the eye, he's studying our naked bodies under the sheets, but not in a lustful way.

'I'm going to Canada.' I blurt it out.

'You're moving to Canada? Wow, that's a bit extreme, even for you.'

'Not moving. Just going for Christmas.'

'Oh.'

'And . . .' I shake my head. Callum is sweet, and we've had loads of fun. He's been up for anything, and he's always seemed to get me – until now. 'Well, to be totally honest,' I need to be, 'if Auntie Lynn had been at home, then I'd want to spend Christmas Day with her. Look Callum, you're brilliant, but I can't do the whole settling down, meet the parents, thing.'

'Cool.' He shrugs. 'No problem, there's plenty of time. There's always next year.' The grin is a bit lopsided, but totally sweet, totally Callum. 'Or I could come to Canada? They won't mind.'

I hate myself.

'No, I need to go on my own, it's work, and,' I take a deep breath, put my hand over his and do my best to look him in the eye. 'Who knows what I'll be doing next year? I don't know if I'll ever be ready, Callum.' I go back to studying his neat finger nails. 'You need a nice, sweet girl you can marry, have kids with, and I'm not that person.'

He opens his mouth to object, and I put my fingers to his lips.

'Not now, maybe, but one day. You're wasting your time with me.' I shrug. 'Settling down isn't my thing.'

I hate doing this to him. To us. I hate to chase the happiness away. But I can't help it.

When I look up, he's shaking his head in denial, but I can see it in his eyes. He does know. He knows me well enough. 'You've already decided, haven't you? The hair, everything. You're not going to change your mind.'

'I have.'

'Sah, I don't want you to take this the wrong way.' From the look on his face, I think I probably will. 'Don't get me wrong, I do love you, and you're fab, and a total laugh, and daring but . . .'

'But?' It's my turn to wait for the 'but'.

He squeezes my hand. 'You do need to get your shit together you know, you can't keep running away from people.'

'I don't run away.' I can hear the indignation in my voice – and the hurt – as I pull my hand away from his.

'Forget I said it, I'm sorry, I shouldn't – let's drink to Canada, shall we?' He's already out of bed, and dragging his jeans on over his naked, toned butt, and pouring vodka shots out before I've even got my T-shirt over my head.

We perch on the edge of the bed and drink in silence, punctuated by awkward attempts at conversation. The link is gone. Broken. We aren't the same any more. We aren't a couple.

'Hey, I do like the hair. Blue is good.' He kisses me on the nose as we stand at his front door, both knowing our lives are about to head off in different directions. 'But don't forget your pink side, will you?' His voice has a wistful edge that makes me feel like a naughty child.

'I just needed a change.' I run my fingers through my cropped hair.

'One day a lucky guy will come along who you don't mind being pink for, and,' there's a long pause, 'who you want to spend Christmas with. I'll miss you, you mad mare.'

'I'll miss you too, Callum.'

And then he winks and opens the door wide for me, shoves his hands in his pockets, and that is that.

Chapter 7

'Sugar.' Sam is pounding the keyboard of her computer frantically when I get in to work. Luckily there are no clients (or Aunt Lynn) around to witness the abuse. Although it does occur to me that the keyboard will soon be my property. My responsibility. Shit, all this responsibility could be totally weird. The nearest I've come to commitment before has been to book a flight more than four weeks in advance. Now I've got a boulder-sized slab of obligation hanging over me and I'm not quite sure how I feel. They say love and hate are close buddies, don't they? Well, so are petrified and proud. Right now, it's anybody's guess which one will win the day. I'm either going to end up crushed or feeling like I've done Aunt Lynn proud and shown her what I'm made of.

I'm not Spiderman, though, I haven't got great power, just responsibility. I wish I was Spiderman, actually, I'm sure he could sort this out in a jiffy. He could whizz over and truss up Mr Armstrong in a super-strong web, and he wouldn't care a fig that the one person he loves isn't going to spend Christmas with him.

'You're frowning.' Sam has stopped pounding.

'No, I'm not.' I force my face into what I hope is a chilled expression. But is probably just looking down my nose pop-eyed. 'What's up?'

'I just accidentally booked my mum on a non-refundable last-minute deal to Kenya.'

'And she doesn't want it?' Sam's mum is funny. She's one of those mothers who is so well-meaning it gets embarrassing, if you know what I mean. But she is lovely, and totally means well. Like mother, like daughter.

'Does she buggery.' Which figures. She is more big-hat hunter than big-game hunter. 'She wants to go to Lapland, not bloody Kenya.' Sam goes back to abusing my assets.

'You can't actually undo what you've done just by typing fast you know.' I sit down and push her wheelie chair, and her, to one side. You see? This is what I meant when I thought it was weird Aunt Lynn leaving Sam on her own. At least this is a family booking cock-up, and not a customer. 'Pressing delete doesn't work when it isn't on the screen any more.'

'I know that.' She suddenly smiles. 'Actually, maybe that's the best idea I've ever had, and my brain just hasn't realised. Sending Mum off on her own would solve all kinds of problems.' The frantic typing stops. 'Christmas can be such hard work if we're all together. A few days with just me and Jake on our own would be ace.'

She's got a dreamy look in her eyes, and for a moment I feel a pang of jealousy. Sam has got a lovely boyfriend, a wonderful family and she's all set for the perfect Christmas. Unlike me. I'm just about to book a ticket to hell. This was not a good idea at all. Me and my big mouth. Why can't I think before I speak? Just once would be nice. I think they call it 'filtered', whereas I'm more another f word.

And I *so* like Christmas. What have I done?

Sam frowns. 'Unless she gets eaten by a giraffe or something.'

'What?'

'Mum, in Kenya!'

'Aren't they vegetarian? They eat leaves and stuff.'

'Well, a lion. Or what if a rhino tramples them? I mean, you know how she likes to be centre stage, she'll be throwing her arms around and projecting!' Sam's mum is into amateur dramatics and sees herself as the next Dame Judi Dench. 'How good is the health and safety at these places? They must do risk assessments, yeah?'

'Yeah, of course they do! They have to, and you don't often hear of tourists getting chewed up or trampled to death, do you?'

'Well no, not often but there was that alligator—'

'That was in the swamps, and that drunken twat decided to use it as a paddleboard. I don't think your mum will be trying anything like that, will she?'

'I suppose not.'

'They'll be far more careful than Will Armstrong,

anyway; he probably wouldn't know a risk assessment if he fell over one.' Oh God, I can't get that stupid man out of my head. All roads lead to Will. Literally. Sam looks alarmed – even though she doesn't know the chaos that's going around in my head at the moment. Honestly, I'd rather be in Kenya being trampled by wildebeest, right now.

My face must have done something it wasn't supposed to, because her attention zooms in on me.

'Anyway, what are you doing here? I thought you had the day off?'

'I just thought I'd check you were okay.' Maybe popping into work, on the pretence of checking everything was okay, was a mistake. But the truth of the matter is I couldn't face being at home on my own today. I now have no Callum, and no Christmas. 'And I need to stalk Will Armstrong.'

'You've already googled him.' Sam grins. 'You just want to stare at that photo don't you? Go on, admit it, you think he's cute.'

'It doesn't matter how cute he is—'

'Ha! I knew you did!'

'This is business, I need to google him better. The Wi-Fi is better here than at home, and,' I pull out my chair and do a quick spin on it, cracking my knuckles as I go to show I mean business, 'I also need to book my Christmas break.'

'Christmas break?' Sam is frowning and has stopped her attempts to unbook her mother's wildlife trip. 'Where are you going?'

'Canada.' I watch while it sinks in. 'To see Will Armstrong.'

'But I thought . . .'

'There's been a change of plan.'

'Christmas! Wow, you're going for actual Christmas with Lynn? Is that what she suggested when you told her about what's been going on? Gosh, the pair of you together will soon sort him out.' Sam claps her hands, looking so happy it seems a shame to put a downer on things.

'Not the pair of us, just me.' I stop my googling and look at Sam. I think it might be time to mention the cakes, and Ralph. And the business. Which is the really awkward one. I mean, we're mates, we work together and in the new year it could all turn a bit weird if I've kind of become her boss, and don't do this properly.

'And Callum?'

'No, not Callum. Callum and his buttock-clenching glad-ioli have gone.'

'Buttock clenching?'

'Later. But it was a good job he hadn't decided to say it with roses.' Thorns do not bear thinking about.

'So why are you going to Canada for Christmas, then? I don't get it.'

Nor do I.

'Tell.'

'Pass the Hobnobs first, my stomach needs reminding what food should taste like. Lynn's cakes were a bit . . .' I pull a face and rub my stomach, and Sam laughs. 'Lemon curd and marmalade.'

'They sound okay; my mum does lemon curd tarts, sometimes.'

'Lemon curd and marmalade together.'

'I think you need a Jaffa cake.'

Sam plunders the supplies, then she watches intently as I nibble the chocolate off, then remove the sponge, and finally savour the orange bit.

'Wow, I needed that.' This could be the closest I get to orgasm for a while. I take another. Sam can't bear the suspense and snatches the box away.

'So, what was so urgent? She's okay is she? Not ill or . . .'

'She's fine. More than fine.'

'Oh God, she didn't find out about that nasty email you sent to Shooting Star?' She clasps her hand to her mouth.

I shake my head. 'Not quite.'

'What do you mean, not quite? Tell me, woman!'

I haven't quite worked out how I feel about this yet, which is why I suppose I've been reluctant to say it. Because once it's out there, then there's no going back. 'Aunt Lynn has sprung a surprise. She's got to go to Australia to see her old mate Ralph.'

'But . . .'

'He's dying. Might not last until the new year.'

'Oh.'

We both take a moment, and another Jaffa cake.

'So why aren't *you* going to Australia? I mean, Australia's nice. You could have Christmas on the beach!'

'I don't want to be a gooseberry, or kiwi, and she needs to be on her own with him. So, I said I was going to see Mr Brain-freeze Will Armstrong. I kind of jumped in without thinking about it, so she wouldn't feel bad.'

'Aw, that's so nice.'

'Look out world, Saint Sarah is coming.'

'Well,' there's a heavy undertone of doubt, 'you did want to go, I suppose. But, not on your own, not at Christmas.'

'It's fine.'

'I know! I can come!'

'You've got Jake and your family. And I'll be fine, Sam.'

'But, on your own?'

'I'll meet people, you know I'm good at that. And I am working, remember?'

She stares at me. 'But for actual Christmas?' I nod. 'And you deffo can't take Callum?'

'Nope, I dumped him last night.'

'Ah, so that's why your hair's blue.' She knows me well.

'It might have a bearing.'

She raises an eyebrow and ploughs on. 'But you can't spend Christmas all on your own.'

'Well, I won't be completely alone. Mr Armstrong hasn't frightened off all his guests – yet.'

'You know what I mean. You're not going with Lynn, or anybody?'

I shake my head, not wanting to voice the fact that there isn't an 'anybody', and instead grab another Jaffa cake. I need sugar.

'Well that explains why she rang and told me she was shutting up shop for two weeks over Christmas, then.' She gets up and puts the kettle on. 'Paid leave!' She smiles. 'How generous is that?'

So, Sam gets paid leave and I get a fully inclusive break in a snowbound, rundown holiday resort with the Anti-Christmas.

And he's already decided I'm an idiot.

'There's more.'

'More?'

I hand her the slip of paper and watch the emotions flicker across her open features. If it was me, there'd be a hell of a lot of conflict going on there. Fear, doubt, envy, disbelief. Sam just grins.

'Bloody hell, Sare, this means you've got a five-year plan! That is so—'

'Not me?' Sam know what I'm like. She knows I always like an escape route. That I can't even commit to a hair colour, let alone a man or a job.

'So amazing! It's brilliant.'

'It is? Sorry, I mean it is.' I try and sound positive.

'You love working here, and you'll be able to look at new places, and redecorate.' I raise an eyebrow; she's getting carried away. 'And tell Will Armstrong where to get off. It's ace!'

'I've never thought about even a five-day plan before. Five years is a bit . . . well, a bit somebody else, not me.'

'You don't have to think of it like that, though, do you?

I mean, you were never going to just up and bugger off and leave Lynn and me in the lurch, were you?'

She has a point. 'Well, no, but—'

'This is just kind of giving you more power!'

I stop my self-indulgent worrying and give her a big hug. 'Oh Sam, where would I be without you?'

'Buggered, which means you can't sack me!'

'I'd never sack you.'

Her eyes are twinkling. 'But you *are* going to sort Will Armstrong out?'

I take a deep breath, disentangle myself and turn back to my computer. 'Yep, my first priority as,' I pause; it seems a bit out-there to say it, 'a company director.'

I click a button on the keyboard, my fingers crossed under the desk.

Booking confirmed.

'All done, an all-inclusive break at the Shooting Star Mountain Resort. Watch out, Will, here I come.'

Bugger, what have I done?

Chapter 8

Do not believe any magazine article or blog that tells you packing for a week in the Canadian Rockies is easy. That is bollocks. They have never done it. Or they have servants who do it for them.

I am totally exhausted. Winter holidays in minus thirty degrees are not the same as summer *scorchio* ones in Spain. If they tell you that all you have to do is roll your clothes up and they will fit miraculously into one small bag (which works on my normal trips), it is a lie. It is as much of a lie as somebody telling you that if you go back and face your past it will help you make a better future.

I am a travel-light-with-a-rucksack type of girl; I do not have *stuff*. Well, I didn't until now. The sheer volume of stuff (and totally scary amount of money I have spent) is enough to give a person like me a panic attack. The only way I have managed to cope with this has been by repeatedly telling myself that it is an investment; in the business, in my future.

My normal backpack has room for flip-flops, shorts,

skinny vests and bikinis, but I am now officially a lug-the-massive-suitcase type of traveller. Even on a good day, seeing my bed strewn with the type of clothes I would never normally be seen dead in, apart from the gorgeous leopard-skin base layer, would be a nightmare.

And today is not a good day.

I stare at the enormous pile of colourful clothes, and my stomach feels all hollow and empty.

Sam told me, with the authority of a girl who went on school ski-ing trips, that I needed 'Jeans, base layers, ear warmers, hat, gloves, mittens, snow-boots, socks, neck warmer, sunscreen, chapstick and moisturiser,' she'd taken a deep breath, 'minimum.' So that is what we bought. The minimum. Which is rather a lot.

My main find had been what looked like leopard skin print pyjamas (but turned out to be a base layer), although they nearly didn't make the grade. I had gone shopping, fully intending to project a businesslike image that would show Will Armstrong just who he was dealing with. Then I remembered the real 'me'. I am not the type of person who dresses to impress a jerk who is out to ruin my business. Sod convention. I am not padded-ski-slope-princess, I am blue-haired leopard! And I think my inner big cat needs to be unleashed if I am to survive.

Sam had rolled her eyes. 'I suppose it is one way of getting Will Armstrong onside.' Which was worrying. I do not want him to think I am even more unprofessional than he already does. He will think rude flippant emails, and seductive base layers are all I have to offer. He will think I am no threat whatsoever. He will destroy our business as well as his own.

Leopard-skin sexiness was what Callum would have loved. But I'm not going with Callum for a cosy Christmas, I'm going on my own. I'm on a mission. Then it hit me, all I needed was a serious top layer. He will not be peeling away my layers, so it's only the top bits that count, surely?

Unless I have a crashing fall on the slopes, and have to be unpeeled by medics, while Mr Armstrong stands on the sidelines, tutting and saying, 'Why should I listen to a girl like that? She knows nothing'. Oh to hell with businesslike; I need to do this my way. I need to make sure Will bloody Armstrong meets the real deal, I'm not going to pretend I'm something I'm not, just to impress him.

But I do need him to take me seriously.

There's a little shimmy deep in my stomach, a bit like when you're poised at the top of the big dipper and know there's no turning back. I'm not scared of him. Okay, maybe I am a bit; well, not scared of *him*, more scared of what's going to happen. I don't want him to ruin the resort. I don't want to get there and find he's trampled over my memories with his big snow-boots. It's important I get this right, but it's also important I do it my way. Something tells me that if I don't he'll just head me off, like he's deflected all the emails and crap reviews.

I shove a pair of massive pink knickers (that Sam insisted

on) into a corner of the bag. By the time anybody gets all these bloody layers off, sex will be the last thing they'll have on their mind. How does anybody get a quickie out there?

Then it suddenly dawns on me that I may have found the key to Mr Armstrong's lack of cooperation. Maybe the poor man just needs unwrapping, and beneath the layers I will find a soft centre.

Or maybe not.

***

Today I am wearing biker boots, thick black tights, denim shorts and a T-shirt I found in the charity shop. 'Life's a Mountain, Not a beach' is emblazoned across the front and it seemed strangely appropriate when I saw it. A bargain buy at two quid, as opposed to the several hundred quid price tags which I've just spotted on some of this clobber.

I feel a bit queasy. My bank balance is not fit for 'designer' it is more 'buy one, get one free'. But I do want to look the part. And I am determined to show Aunt Lynn that I am up for this. One, because the business will one day be mine, and two because she's leaving me at Christmas and I am not, repeat NOT going to let it get to me.

But today is not a good day. I have Will Armstrong waiting for me, along with limping huskies, lumpy custard and leaky cold cabins. Although I always try not to pre-judge people, in my heart of hearts I know I have already put him firmly in the 'spoilt, upper-class preppie idiot who doesn't give a damn about anybody else' category. I can picture him cuddling up to his chalet girls and having a good time while his visitors freeze.

I think this mean judgemental streak also has a lot to do with Bear Cabin. The name is imprinted in my memory, and from the moment I committed to going back to Shooting Star Resort, it was there in my head. Which is weird. How come I remember that so clearly, when I was only a little girl?

Granted, I've only got hazy little-girl memories of Bear Cabin, but in my mind it's the perfect log cabin in the middle of snow-covered mountains. Maybe it wasn't really like that, maybe time has distorted it. Or it was half imagination and half real. But it was all my fairy-tale dreams come true. Even now I can remember the softness of the fur throws beneath my fingertips. I'd never felt anything so soft, so warm, it was like being buried in a real bear hug. Without the danger of claws and teeth. I remember the smell of wood, the crackle of burning logs in the evening, the glow as the flames reflected off every surface. And there was a tree. A small but perfect tree in the corner of the cabin. It was the first real Christmas tree I'd ever seen and I used to stand in front of it and stare as the tinsel shimmied and the baubles reflected my face and seemed to dance. And I stole the tiny polar bear that hung from one of its branches and tucked it into my pocket.

Aunt Lynn found it, the day we left, and told me to give it back. And the lady on reception hugged me and told me to keep it.

Bear Cabin was perfect, but now I know it won't be. Will Armstrong has ruined it, I'm sure he has. Going back would be a mistake. It would dash away the only good memories I've got locked in my head. All I'll be left with is the bad bits. Do I really want to go back at all?

And yet, some part of me wants – no, needs to see it. Some tiny childlike part of me that hangs onto the hope I can step back in time and maybe turn back the clock and start over.

I realised last night, in bed, that in my heart I hadn't really meant it when I'd told Sam I'd go on a problem-solving trip and sort things out. It was just one of my big-mouth comments. I mean, why would I want to take a trip down such a muddy and horrible bit of memory lane? Scary.

I really don't want to go. Will anybody notice if I burrow under my duvet and spend the Christmas holiday at home, alone, instead? I can treat myself to Christmas dinner special sandwiches on a meal deal and eat mince pies by the box full. I can play Mario Kart and watch *The Holiday* for the thirty-fifth time as I eat a family-size box of Quality Street.

I don't like snow. I don't ski, I hate ice, I hate unfriendly, stroppy Will Armstrong. I don't want to go to Canada. I don't want to wear massive pink thermal knickers, bala-clavas and six pairs of socks.

I want to be here, with Aunt Lynn, laughing at stupid cracker jokes, eating the flaming pudding that one year set the curtain alight, beside a completely OTT Christmas tree that takes up half the living room and means you have to crawl to the door.

I don't want to be on my own. I can't do Christmas on my own.

The ginormous padded trousers that Sam and I had thought were hilarious when I tried them on are lying on the bed as empty and unloved as I am. I'm being pathetic, I need to grow up. Not going away is not an option.

'This is not all about you, girl.' I do talk to myself sometimes, I probably should get a cat, or a bird, or something so that I seem less mad. 'This is what Aunt Lynn wants you to do, and you owe her. So, you're going to bloody do it.'

I don't need to 'move on' but I do need to do my job and kick Will Armstrong's ass.

It is the perfect opportunity to see what is wrong through objective eyes, when I am not caught up in all the emotions of a family Christmas.

Once I've got going on the rolling and shoving in the bag routine though, it's not so bad, though I am breathing pretty hard by the time I cram the last pair of gloves (who thought gloves could be that big?) into the pocket and sit on the bag so I can pull the zip round.

I sit there, astride, panting, which could possibly leave any intruder who might come across me with a very uncomfortable image, and nightmares. Then I lean over and grab my tablet before I change my mind.

Dear Mr Armstrong,

Ref. SSMR/18/100342

Regarding the above booking, made in my name, I would be very grateful if you could reserve Bear Cabin for me.

Kind regards, Sarah

Making Memories, Travel Agents

Okay, I might be mad. I *am* mad. But I have decided upon the 'in for a penny in for a pound' approach that Aunt Lynn normally adopts. Otherwise known as full-on confrontation.

If I don't stay in Bear Cabin I will spend the whole holiday (if you can call it that, maybe 'break' is a better word, but to me that would be tempting fate) edging round it. Wondering if it's still the same. I might as well go the whole hog and stay in the damned thing. For a start, you can bet that Aunt Lynn will quiz me about it when I get back.

And although I haven't 'addressed' the past, this will work much better. I can be there, and prove exactly how over the whole parents-abandoning-me thing I am.

The past means nothing to me. Nada. I have moved on. I am so over all of that.

I'm sure I am. Well, I'm soon going to find out, aren't I?

But I mean, it's only a place to sleep, after all, isn't it? It's just a cabin, and it was a nice cabin. I'm all grown up now, it will be totally different from when I was a kid.

I hope.

It would just be nice if I could stop feeling as though my stomach wants to turn itself inside out.

Dear Sarah,
No kisses this time? Have we fallen out?
Will

Dear Mr Armstrong,
This isn't funny. I'm being serious.
Sarah

Dear Sarah,
Unfortunately, the original Bear Cabin was demolished several years ago and is now the site of the new dog kennels. I'm not sure you'd want to share with them. Rosie snores.
The cabins are all, however, furnished to the same high standard, with the same view, and one will be allocated to you on arrival.
Regards. Will Armstrong (The Anti-Christmas).
Shooting Star Mountain Resort
PS Please do call me Will

Demolished? Dog kennels? Dog kennels! A bunch of hairy dogs are peeing on my past? I hate him. Even more than I did before.

Bear Cabin might be where horrible things happened, but it was also amazing. And it's where life with Aunt Lynn started. Where really good things happened. And it was magical. I'll never, ever get to stand in front of that Christmas tree again, and see the reflections of me, Aunt Lynn, Mum and Dad, all happy and smiling. Laughing. I'll never get to peer up the chimney like I did with Mum and see if we could see the stars.

It's all gone, like they have. Forever.

And it's all Will Armstrong's fault.

Another email pings in, maybe he's going to make the dogs homeless, let me sleep there.

PPS You'd also have to sleep on straw. Scratchy.

I bounce on my bag with frustration and there's a funny sound which might, or might not, be tearing fabric. Bugger.

I ease myself up off the bag and put my head between my legs to check it's not my new, very expensive bag that has let me down. It isn't. There is however something fluorescent pink poking out of a hole that really shouldn't be there. In the shorts, not my bag.

Double bugger. How late can you order online and still get next day delivery? Why haven't we got those delivery drones that drop your goodies in the back garden within ten seconds of ordering stuff yet? Although knowing my luck they'd land on the roof, and I'd need a ladder to rescue them. And the last time I went on the roof, to try and sort the aerial, nosy Mrs Gerard from number 35 rang the fire brigade. Which would have been fine, except they had to send the oldest, baldest, most halitosis-ridden firefighter in the whole world up to 'rescue' me. I understand now why cats have claws and hang on for grim death sometimes. Except not even a cat gets thrown over somebody's shoulder (I don't think he needed to do that, he was showing off) and arrives back on terra firma, head first.

Why is life so complicated?

I'm beginning to hate 'call me Will'. I'm also beginning to wonder if he actually exists. I think some aliens have taken over the resort, and he is a computer-generated image based on random facts they have found on the internet.

Stalking Will Armstrong is like stalking the end of the rainbow. There is no gold, there is nothing to hold onto. Just as you think you've got there, he dissolves into thin air.

I wasted a whole three hours of my life trying to find out more about the man. Well, when I say 'more', I mean anything.

'Well, that's half a day of my life I'm not going to get back.' All I have for my troubles is a load of cobblers about random Will, Willy and William Armstrongs who live everywhere from Land's End to Timbuktu. Why does the man have to have such a popular name?'

And none of them are him. Which made elimination quicker. In fact, elimination couldn't have been any quicker or more complete if I'd had a vindaloo curry with a laxative chaser. I have nothing left. Just the one photograph. Which is bloody annoying.

What is it with the man? It's like he's hiding. Maybe he is *in* hiding and the resort is just a cover? Maybe that's why he's determined to put clients off? He could be an escaped convict who has to keep a low profile, so can't promote the business because it will attract attention. Or perhaps he's a bankrupt who has sold all the logs and blankets (and marshmallows) off to the highest bidder? Or a junkie. Yeah, maybe he's selling everything to feed his habit, or no, no, hang on, even better: he's being black-mailed. He's being blackmailed because he's killed off his lovely, well-liked brother Ed and buried the body in an avalanche, and needs to get out of there before the snow melts and all is revealed.

Or maybe he's just a weirdo who doesn't know how to run a business.

It's then it hits me. That I've been so caught up in worrying about the resort, about grumpy Mr Armstrong, about Aunt Lynn, about it being different to every Christmas I've had before, that I've missed the point. I normally like different, and ignoring the bad bits, the Shooting Star Mountain resort was the absolute best place in the world to spend Christmas. And however bad the reviews are, it can't have changed that much, can it?

'I'm going to Canada!' I say to myself, grinning. I think it might be a bit manic, but there's no one here to see me. I'm going to have a proper snowy Christmas with real, still-stuck-in-the-ground fir trees! And it's going to be fan-bloody-tastic. Snow, sleighs, log fires, toasted marsh-mallows! I'll take my own, just in case Scrooge has run out. It is Christmas, everything a girl could want at Christmas. I am going to show Will Armstrong the best time of his life.

PART 2
DESPERATELY SEEKING SANTA

Chapter 9

'Why are you on your own? Haven't you got any friends? I can be your friend if you like.'

I keep my eyes closed and thank the Lord and the airline company for providing me with an eye mask. Along with some heavy breathing for authenticity, I reckon I can get away with convincing a child that I am either asleep, or dead. Either way, she might leave me alone.

But the kid is not to be distracted. I get a sharp jab to the ribs from a bony elbow. How old are children when they evolve from cuddly round creatures into pointy ones?

'Leave the lady alone, Poppy, she's sleeping.'

'No, she's not, I saw her move.' Poppy kicks me in the calf with an accuracy that comes from a lot of practice. I bet she's one of those cherub-faced horrors who can do no harm in their parents' eyes, and who teachers hate.

'People move in their sleep, darling. Do you want some crayons?'

'I can't draw properly because the plane keeps bumping.'

The armrest is lifted and Poppy wriggles closer. 'It's okay if you want to pretend,' she whispers, rubbing a sticky cheek against mine. 'I'd want to hide too, if I didn't have anybody to come on holiday with.'

'Any refreshments, madam?' This is so not fair. If I progress to pretend snoring I will have a sticky face, bruised calf and no drink. I push the mask up with a resigned sigh and open one eye. A pair of bright blue eyes stare right back. She is so in my face, the drinks trolley is completely obscured.

'Yes, yes.' I flap a hand frantically and appear to have a handful of flight attendant trouser. He's stopped so abruptly his trolley has run off course and clanged into the seat on the other side of the very narrow aisle.

'Gin please, or prosecco, or vodka, or anything!'

A miniature gin is dangled just out of reach. I know it would be rude to throw Poppy out of the way, but I'm honestly considering it when she sinks back onto her own seat.

Now, I do not have a drink problem. I am the same as most other girls who are hanging on to their twenties desperately. And I don't often *need* a drink, I just like one. But today, I think I might need one. Today I would like something to distract me from what lies ahead, to soften the edges so that I do not give in to the temptation to leap on Will Armstrong and strangle him the second we meet. Which would definitely fall into the unprofessional category, and solve nothing. But give me great satisfaction.

'Ice?' Damien (he has a badge with his name on) smiles, folds down my table for me and puts the drink down. He must have seen a look of panic on my face because he deposits another miniature bottle next to the first and winks, his finger on his lips. 'You better not tell the others, they'll all want one.'

Poppy is still studying me. She actually isn't as pointy as I'd thought from her elbows, and is actually quite pretty, with blonde hair that has been dragged into a pigtail, and a very earnest, grown-up look on her face. She is frowning.

She has a pink streak down the side of her face, which I think explains the stickiness. I now suspect I might have a matching one on my own face.

'Poppy, leave the lady alone! I'm so, so sorry, she's not usually like this.' Poppy's mother smiles apologetically, and brushes hair away from her face. She looks one 100 per cent hassled. 'She's just so excited, and,' her voice drops, 'my husband was plying her with sweets in the airport lounge, I didn't realise until all the wrappers fell out of his pocket when I asked for a tissue.'

'It's okay, don't worry. She's fine.' What am I saying? I'm not a nanny. I haven't got a clue what you do with children.

'If you're sure?'

'Absolutely.' It's worth the total lie just to see the look of relief on her face before she sinks back into her seat.

'You could buy a baby.' Poppy is back in full flow.

What makes children come out with statements like that?

'So that you aren't on your own. It's boring being on your own.' Ah. 'The lady next door to us got one, I know she bought it cos she was never fat like Mummy was with Jack.' She nods earnestly. 'I'd rather have a puppy, though.'

'So would I.'

'Mummy says they pee everywhere.'

'So do babies.'

'But they have nappies.' She frowns. 'But puppies have proper legs, they don't fall over all the time.'

'True.'

'And you can leave them when you go out shopping.' She gives a heavy sigh. 'We have to take Jack *everywhere*, even to swimming practice. He smells, and he cries.'

I glance across at the chubby little baby that is sittiing on their mother's knee, chewing on what I hope is a teething ring. He beams back.

Poppy prods me to get my attention again. 'Why haven't you got any friends of your own?'

I'm no expert on children, but I hear they can do this. Keep on and on until they get an answer. Why seems to be a favourite word.

'I have got friends, but this is a business trip.'

'What's a business trip?'

'Work.'

'Why? It's Christmas. Mummy and Daddy don't work at Christmas, only Father Christmas does.' She pauses. 'You aren't his wife, are you?'

'No, Father Christmas is too old for me.'

'God works on Christmas Day as well, and Baby Jesus. I know you're not Jesus cos he's a boy. He's in all the school plays. We did a nativity play – do you want to hear my lines? I can still remember them.'

'I'd love to.' The gin fizzes over my ice in a very satisfactory way.

'I was a goat.'

I'm not sure where goats figure in the nativity scene, or what a goat would be saying, but it isn't going to stop Poppy.

***

Discussing talking goats at 30,000 feet in the air isn't quite how I imagined I'd start the trip to seeing Will Armstrong. But after a chat, and a snooze (my shoulder now had dribble on to coordinate with the sticky patch on my cheek) and a snack and another drink, a good portion of nine hours has gone by.

In fact, by the time I've had my third drink, I'm not bothered that the plane seems to be filled with kids on a sugar high, and am in such high spirits I join in with the Christmas carols. Well, when I say spirits, that could be the gin speaking.

But I am actually feeling much more relaxed than when I was waiting in the departure lounge at Heathrow reading the emails that Will Armstrong had sent.

Dear Will, wouldn't it be easier to text?
  Sarah.

Dear Sarah, not really. As you'll find out when you get here!
  Will

This one scares me. And makes me completely forget all the other questions I wanted to ask before I got there.

Dear Will, what do you mean?

My heart is thudding much harder than it probably should. I think I'm knocking days off my lifespan.

Dear Sarah, phone reception isn't great here, but who cares?

Who cares?! What do you mean, who cares? How am I going to do stuff?
  Panic has definitely set in.

Chill. You'll be fine. It's not another planet. And there are emails.

Chill? Chill! I hate him.
  The panic has died down a bit now though. After all this is a holiday as well as work. I can pretend I've been whisked back to the olden days when there were simple pleasures, and no apps.

And no running water or electricity.

I hope there is running water and electricity. Specially the electricity. Lucky I had my hair cut extra short so won't need a hairdryer.

You do have running water and electricity?

There was no answer to this last message. Which might mean they haven't. Or it could be because a bossy air stewardess told me it was time to go to 'flight mode'.

I have also hardly thought about not spending Christmas with Aunt Lynn. Well, I've thought about it a little bit, because it's impossible to imagine Christmas without her, but the constant interruptions have stopped me getting to the stage of wishing I could turn the plane round. And the excited chitter-chatter has been kind of infectious. I want to go to the resort: I just wish Aunt Lynn was going there with me. If there was a degree in distraction, though, this kid would be star pupil.

I almost feel like hugging perky little Poppy. Almost.

Instead, as I step off the plane I wave goodbye to her and her family and head off in search of my very big bag and super-expensive puffed-up clothes. I practically dance my way to the baggage collection.

'Watch out fugitive Will, I'm a-coming to get you!'

Chapter 10

'There's Sarah! There's Sarah!'

Something, or rather somebody, cannons into the back of my legs and nearly sends me flying. Straight into the smiley, slightly plump man who is holding a 'Shooting Star Mountain Resort' sign in one hand and a clipboard in the other.

'Oh, my goodness, come here, Poppy. Oh, I am so sorry. Poppy, stop bothering the lady.' Poppy's mother is juggling the baby, a duty-free bag, has a handbag dangling round her neck and what I imagine is a baby's changing bag threatening to strangle her. 'Oh, it's you! Sorry, so sorry. Are you off to Shooting Star as well?'

I nod.

'What a coincidence!'

Indeed, though I suppose given its supposedly 'family friendly' features there was a good chance at least one or two of the families on the plane would be heading that way. I look at Poppy, and all I can see is the non-family-friendly child-molesting husky called Rosie (who I really mustn't mention, and upset anybody), and feel guilty. I've actually got quite fond of her. She's tapped into the happy, non-adulting side of me that has been a bit squashed lately.

Poppy's mother smiles apologetically at the sign holder. 'Sorry we're late.' Her husband staggers in her wake, mega rucksack on his back and dragging two massive holdalls on wheels behind him. Poppy is bouncing about unfettered. If I ever wondered about the true effect children have on your life, here is the answer. They look totally knackered. The parents, that is. The children look fine. 'You've no idea how long it takes to wrap a baby up for this weather.'

'I could kill a drink.' Poppy's dad gives me a wry smile as he drops one of the bags. 'Craig Harris. Pleased to meet you.' He shoves a hand in my direction, which I duly shake as Poppy somehow manages to grab my free hand. 'And this is Tina, plus Jack – and you've met Poppy.'

'I am so sorry.' Tina, puffing and pink in the face, passes Jack over to her husband. Well, at least I guess it's Jack. Obviously wrapping a baby up suitably for sub-zero temperatures is an art form. She wipes one hand over her brow, while the other finds a place in the small of her back. 'Christ, my back is killing me. Do you know how long it's taken to wrap him up like that? And once we get on the bus I have to take all layers off, then put them back on again before we get there. It's like bloody pass-the-parcel. How we ever thought this was a good idea, I don't know.' She looks slightly accusingly at her husband, but there is affection there as well. 'He thought reliving our youth might spice up our sex life, but I ask you!' She gestures helplessly towards both her children. 'Really? Men can be such jerks, can't they?'

Craig laughs. 'You'll thank me on Christmas Day when you've had dinner cooked for you, this pair are in bed and we're sitting in front of a log fire.' He winks. 'Romance, they call it.' Then he rubs his hands together and spoils the effect. 'Rumpy-pumpy, I call it.'

We all laugh, and I feel a twinge of fear. I hope they didn't book through our company; I hope that things aren't as bad as the reviews suggest and they haven't run out of logs and blankets. I hope there actually *will* be a Christmas dinner, and I hope Rosie's puppies have all grown up now and she's no longer quite as hormonal.

'All present and correct, then? Ready for the Shooting Star Mountain Resort?' Our meeter and greeter, who definitely doesn't look anything like Will Armstrong, ushers us out into the cold and swings the door of the minibus open.

'I'm sitting with Sarah. She hasn't got any friends.' Before I can object, Poppy is onboard and patting the seat next to her. Tina smiles apologetically and, dumping all her bags at the feet of her husband, clambers up with the smiling Jack gurgling away in her arms.

I don't know whether it's because I'm sitting next to an excited little girl who is clutching my arm and oohing and ahhing at everything, or whether it's just the sheer beauty of the landscape we're passing through, but as the miles pass by I forget that I'm tired. I forget that I'm a little bit scared, and that I'm worried about what I'll find. I forget that it hurts that Aunt Lynn has chosen to head off on her own, and I start to remember what it was like last time I arrived here.

The glass has gone all misty, and my nose is cold, but I've gone all shivery for a totally different reason.

The memories are distant – I've been an expert at blocking them out. Straying back here, even in my mind, has always involved the risk of too much pain, so I've veered away. The odd time I've seen a picture, or smelled a smell, that reminded me of this place, it's felt like a physical blow, reminding me of the worst day of my life.

I can see, quite clearly now, that I've built a barrier between then and now. Between my early childhood and a couple of years into my life with Lynn. No shrink had ever been able to explain that, but now it's as clear as day.

Subconsciously I've found new associations for the smell of pine needles, the whiff of mulled wine, the warmth of a log fire. Associations that are all to do with Aunt Lynn and nothing to do with the Shooting Star resort where my parents abandoned me.

It surprised me, the other day, how the memories of Bear Cabin had rushed back into my being, filling a void I hadn't known was there, and now it's quite a shock how, just being here, has jolted me straight back to those days. It's as if it was only a short while ago, it's so vivid and so real.

I remember pressing my nose to the glass of the big coach, just like Poppy is doing now in this minibus, her flurry of words being replaced by gasps. I remember wiping away the mist of my warm breath, desperately searching for a glimpse of Santa Claus and his reindeer amidst the mountains and lakes, and it brings a lump to my throat.

Banff was a magical winter wonderland, everything a child could desire. It was like being whisked away on a magic carpet, or Santa's sleigh, like suddenly stepping out of the dreary, dank wardrobe and into Narnia.

It's startling, but also strangely exhilarating. Almost like I've been kick-started into a new adventure. The little fluttery feeling inside me isn't dread now, it's excitement. Butterflies of anticipation. I just know this is going to be good. Will isn't a problem, I can sort him, I can sort this place. I can spend Christmas wrapped up in a big fur blanket, slurping hot chocolate and watching the flames of a roaring fire.

'Here we go then, folks. Everybody out.'

Out? What does he mean out? I wipe the window just in case I'm missing something. There is nothing 'out' there, apart from snow.

'Reception is just up the path.' Our driver has already thrown the door open and is busy flinging our cases into a mini snowdrift, which has been created by somebody doing a half-arsed job of clearing the path. Path, huh!

We follow the suitcases.

Probably because he knows what to expect, the driver has left the engine running and is back in his seat and driving off before anybody can demand assistance, or (more likely) try and jump back in.

It's freezing (which I suppose you'd expect, with all this snow), and my arm is dead, because Poppy fell asleep on me and seems to have cut off the blood supply. But the place still takes my breath away. It's stunning. Nature certainly knows what it is doing, even if Mr Armstrong doesn't, and the cabin that serves as a reception looks lovely and rustic from the outside. I mentally tick off that box. Then we go inside.

'Holy crap.' I untick the box again. It is cold, and it is dark. I think the low lighting and candles are about saving electricity, not about creating ambience.

Squinting helps. Though 'helps' might not be the right word. I half expect to see one of those giant singing fish on the wall, or a smiling moose head. Something corny. But I don't. It is worse.

My breath has been stolen again, but for all the wrong reasons this time. I'm sure that last time I was here this place was all bright and twinkly. That I'd stared around in awe as my parents and Lynn signed us in. And that there was a plate of gingerbread men that smelled like gingerbread had never smelled before.

Today there is no trace of that memory. I could cry, but I won't. I have to be jolly for the rest of the guests. Then, when I get Mr Will Armstrong on his own, I'll let him know how I really feel.

'Whoever said the seventies were over?' I stare around slowly. Parquet floor, a mustard-coloured rug and a mish-mash of patterns was so not what I was expecting. This room definitely doesn't feature in any of my memories of the place. 'I think I've walked onto an *Abigail's Party* film set.' The mustard, orange, green and yellow colour scheme is making me think I just have to be hallucinating. Or having some weird out-of-body experience. Or I'm in that bit between life and death that you hear about.

Somebody was proud of this ill-advised makeover, but I reckon that was a long time ago. Or my off-the-wall idea that Will is in fact an alien in human form is actually correct.

All we need now is a lava lamp and a soda siphon and we're cooking.

'Who's Abigail? Is she your friend?' Poppy tugs on my hand.

'Er no, it's an old film made before you were born, before *I* was born.'

'That old? Did they have films then?'

'That old. My aunt made me watch it.'

I don't remember it looking like this last time I came, but I suppose at that age you just accept things, don't you? Or it was *totally* different.

'Can I sleep on that ginger chair with Sarah?' Poppy looks at her mum, her big eyes wide open.

'I'm hoping we get a cabin.' Tina pulls a face and gives a very strained laugh. 'It's freezing in here.'

It is indeed freezing. It is also worryingly free of a receptionist.

And of tinsel, holly, baubles or anything else remotely festive.

113

This is going to be the Christmas from hell.

Tina is looking around slightly anxiously as Jack starts to whimper. 'It didn't look like this in the pictures, Craig. There were cosy rugs and log fires, weren't there?' She does a full 360 degree turn, slowly. I think she's taking this even worse than I am. 'And really pretty fairy lights and candles. It looked so gorgeous.' I'm a bit worried she might start whimpering soon as well.

But I totally get it. She's just had the journey from hell with two small kids in tow and has promised them Christmas with bells on.

'They obviously don't want to waste money on the reception.' I try and be jolly, but as warm welcomes go, this is definitely not happening. I now understand the review that said something about a 'frosty welcome'.

I was expecting somebody to appear to help us bring the luggage in, but nobody has materialised.

'Hello!' We all spin round. A vision of loveliness glides towards us, in the way only five-inch heels on a parquet floor can do. I think I am hallucinating. She has swinging shiny blonde hair, a glass in her hand and a smile on her face. I want to hug her. This is more like it!

Her smile falters and she comes to a halt. 'Oh. I thought I heard Ed. You don't know where the advocaat is, do you?' She is posh. She says it like 'ard-vo-caaaar'. We all shake our heads, stunned into silence. I suspect she is not here to welcome us. She is a guest. 'Oh, what a pain, he promised me a snowball and that cutie who mixes the drinks has done a runner. Where's a sexy guy with a shaker when you need him, eh?' She grins. I am still speechless. 'You will point him in my direction if he turns up won't you, babe? Tell him Bianca will need emergency resuc soon, though knowing Ed he'll jump at the chance! Laters.' And she's gone before we can say another word. I'm tempted to run after her, help her find the advocaat, make us all snowball cocktails.

'Well, they're expecting us, they sent the bus, so somebody must be around.' It's then I spot it. A bell.

'Ring for attention' says the little (and I mean little) sign next to it. So I ring. In fact, I ring several times. And then Craig has a go.

'Can I have it, Daddy?'

I practically throw it at Poppy, who can't believe her luck. She dives off, ringing like billy-o and starts to hop and skip her way round the very scraggy excuse for a Christmas tree (undecorated). Jack is now fully awake and smells rather pongy. He has stopped smiling. I think any minute now he's going to scream. I don't blame him.

'I could just . . .' I start to edge round the table that seems to be serving as a desk and stare at the big book. I know this is totally out of order, but there is nobody in sight and I'm knackered. We're all knackered. Even Poppy has lost some of her 'pop'. I'm sure there'll be some kind of list in here, saying who gets which cabin.

'What on earth . . . ?!'

I drop the book guiltily. The man walking towards me is not Will Armstrong. It is a cross-looking man with a limp. He also has a pained expression on his face, which I think has less to do with whatever is wrong with his leg, and more to do with the fact that I have just dropped his booking system (well, I can't see a computer, so I guess this book is it).

'We booked a cabin.' Craig steps forward as though he guesses I might be on a short fuse. Killer huskies have nothing on me. 'The name's Harris.'

The man gives a sigh as though we're a massive inconvenience, then holds his hand out. 'Passports.'

We all stare, but Craig hands his over obediently.

There is total silence while he scowls at the passports, then fills in some paperwork. It is like being at a funeral. Our holiday spirit (including quite a lot of gin) has dispersed. 'Sorry I wasn't here when you arrived, there was an emergency.' He doesn't expand on that. 'Right.' He dangles a key just out of reach. There is a long pause. Even Poppy is standing to attention. Tina appears to be trying to juggle a wriggling and very slippery Jack without drawing attention to herself. All I can say is, if you ever have babies, don't wrap them in shiny snowsuits. Matte all the way. Preferably with a handle of some kind.

'No boots in the cabin, please.' He looks rather pointedly at the puddles that have formed around our feet. 'Wet clothes to be left in the drying room. There's a charge if you need extra logs and the meal times are posted in your cabin.' He doesn't even take a breath. He's practised this. 'Activities are posted in the entertainment room, you can hire skis and snowboards if necessary, and we'd ask you to consider other guests and keep the noise down at night. I think that covers it. Unless there's anything else?' We wouldn't dare. We're all staring at him, open-mouthed. Even Jack, who Tina has managed to jam down her jacket. Then he spoils it by suddenly passing wind. Loudly. I stare, half expecting her jacket to inflate, but it doesn't. She turns pink, Jack is bright red with the effort.

'We're short-staffed. So leave your cases and I'll bring them over once I'm finished here. Turn right out of reception, follow the path, third on the left.'

The man needs to go on a customer relationship course. Urgently.

Craig nods dumbly and is just talking hold of the key when there is a Poppy-sounding squeal. I'm still mid-turn, and can see a blur of green out of the corner of my eye, but Craig is already on the move. I guess it's parental hormones that are responsible for his turn of speed, but it's still quite impressive. 'Fu—' What's less impressive is that his feet seem to be going faster than the rest of him.

I'm rugby tackled at speed, and we're both going down, slipping in the melted ice we've left on the floor.

I look up from my spot on my bottom, still winded, and with Craig's hand locked painfully onto my forearm, to see our grumpy receptionist supporting the toppling tree with one hand and holding Poppy by the scruff of her neck (well, jacket) with his other.

She dangles limply like a kitten, who's not sure if its dinner.

How did the man move so fast (especially with a limp)? Does he have supernatural powers or something? Is he superman? Are all the staff here actually aliens (I'm warming to this theme – it's the only thing I'm warming to though, right now).

Poppy suddenly realises her feet are off the ground, and she is less impressed by our alien host. She bursts into tears, loud tears, as the man of the moment pushes the tree back into an upright position. Then he wordlessly extracts the bell she's still clutching from her little hand and sets her back on her feet. She doesn't even object, just makes a dash for the safety of her mother and hides behind her legs. I don't blame her.

'At least it didn't have decorations on.' It's the best redeeming feature of the incident I can muster, but grumpy-drawers seems to have taken it as a criticism. He's glowering at me. My God, if looks could kill. 'I could, er, help decorate if you've got some baubles?'

The scowl deepens.

'After you've fixed it back up a bit more firmly.'

Kill me now. Although I might be making it a bit too easy for him, lying splayed out on the floor like a sacrifice.

I kick my legs, it's all I can move.

Craig gets the hint. He struggles to his feet, yanking me up. 'Sorry, love.'

'No probs.' I rub my arm, trying to make it look casual.

'I was trying to get the pussycat.' Poppy, clinging on to her mother's inner thighs, seems to have recovered quicker than the rest of us. My bottom was not designed for parquet floors. I don't know which to rub first, my elbow or my rear, or the bit of arm that Craig nearly amputated. That man has a strong grip. 'The poor pussycat was stuck in the tree. I only went to help it.' Tears are bubbling up in her eyes again.

At least there was something, I suppose, though tinsel and baubles might have been better as far as health and safety goes.

'Cat?' Superman frowns. 'You saw the cat?' He's down on his hands and knees peering under the tree and looks vaguely nice-human for the first time. Well, the back of him does. 'She's been missing for two days. Chloe? Chloe!'

There is no sign of the cat, but who can resist warming to a man who has a cat called Chloe, who he clearly loves? Well, by warming, I just mean thawing slightly. I can't blame the cat for doing a disappearing act. Maybe aliens eat them.

'She went up there.' Poppy points towards the staircase in the corner of the room, and I swear for a moment superman is going to abandon us and go in search of his cat. Or maybe I'm kidding myself, maybe he has no redeeming feature – because he's resisted the urge and is glowering at us again.

'We'll, er . . .' Craig has brushed himself down and is looking awkward. 'Sorry about that.' He gestures at the tree.

'I'll get a mop.' Superman looks pointedly at the puddles. But, I mean, what kind of a surrounded-by-snow winter-wonderland resort has slippery parquet flooring and no proper doormat? It's asking for trouble, isn't it? And shouldn't trees be firmly affixed? And who'd have thought there'd be a cat up there?

I suddenly realise that the family have scooted off and it's strangely quiet. Just me in a puddle, and superman. Who is staring. Which is a bit unnerving. The Harris family were acting like a very nice protective blanket, and now I feel all exposed.

'And you are?'

Do I come clean, admit who I am? Or do I do an impression of an undercover hotel inspector. Incognito. Which might be a good idea, until I find out if Mr Armstrong is an alien, bank robber, bankrupt or druggie.

'Hall.' Phew, no sign of recognition.

'Passport?' He's staring at me.

'I need to talk to the manager.' I refuse to be intimidated. I had a list of issues in my head before I got here and it's already got a lot longer. If Poppy and her family are going to stand any chance of a happy holiday (and I really would like them to) then I think I need to act sooner rather than later.

'Why, what seems to be the problem?' He's raised one eyebrow now, and is looking at me quizzically, as though nothing could possibly be wrong.

I splutter. Problem? Where do I start? 'Cat, floor, tree . . . cold.' I am gesturing wildly, trying to cover just part of the problem, then I stop myself. This needs thinking through. And explaining to the right person. 'Life is too short.'

'Sorry?'

'It's silly going through everything twice.' I can tell, just by looking at him, that if he had a choice the only thing he'd fix would be the clients – he'd send them all home. He must be related to the boss. Although they do say that attitudes start at the top.

'No, I mean, sorry, what does cat, floor, tree, cold mean?'

He's leaning rather strong-looking forearms on the desk and studying me, so I study him back. I always like to look people in the eye, and this guy seems to have the same idea – which might not be that good an idea. Locking horns, or rather eyes, he might not give me an easy get out. We could be here some time, eye-to-eye combat.

His eyes are actually quite nice, though. Well, very nice, in an unusual-intensity slightly-unnerving kind of way. If he smiled he might actually be attractive, if you liked his type. As in the all-man, outdoorsy, not-happy type. Which isn't my type at all. No way can I imagine him with a gladiolus gripped between his naked buttocks, or giving himself the once-over during a sex session. I think I might be going a bit beetroot-y coloured. I need to concentrate. So I look away. Sometimes you've got to lose the battle to win the war.

His fingers are laced together; mid-length, strong-looking fingers. With short nails (no manicure here). Capable.

'Just, er, things that might need fixing. I'll write a list.' My brain is getting overloaded and the rest of me, for some unknown reason, is getting embarrassed, so making a note on my phone seems a good idea. A start. After all, the sooner I start, the more chance that the guests will have at least something resembling a holly-jolly Christmas.

'What list?' His hand is over mine, or rather the phone. It is indeed strong. And he doesn't sound happy. I snatch my precious mobile away (we're very attached to each other; it's outlived most relationships), before it gets confiscated. I wouldn't put anything past this guy.

'Can you tell me where to find Mr Armstrong.' He raises an eyebrow. 'Please.'

'If there's anything—'

'Or give me an extension number and I'll ring him in a bit.'

'There's no phone in your cabin.' The corner of his mouth quirks up briefly, then drops. If I hadn't been studying him closely, I'd have missed it. It appears he has a very well-hidden sense of humour. But even that doesn't lighten his face. In full-on twinkling mode I bet he could be devastating.

But as I'm never going to be treated to that sight, I'll add smart arse to the list of things I don't like about him. 'If you really can't, it's fine, I'll find him myself. And you are?'

'Mr Armstrong.'

'O-kay.' Didn't expect that. A lack of customer service must run deep in this family. 'I want to speak to *Will* Armstrong.' Surely Will has to be better than this one? He's probably off out enjoying some après-ski while his new arrivals have to deal with his less-helpful relative. He really needs to be told that this is not a good first impression. I'm tempted to add that to my list, but daren't take my mobile out of my pocket. I'm never going to remember all this.

'That's me.'

I could have sworn he said . . . 'Sorry, you're *who?*'

'I am Will Armstrong.'

'No, you are not.' I am quite sure of this. I have evidence.

'Really?'

He's giving me a slightly amused look now. Don't you hate a know-it-all? 'I think you'll find . . .' I dig out my phone (but keep a strong grip on it), '*this* is Will Armstrong.'

He gives it a cursory glance, then looks back at me. It's weird; in one way I want to take a step back, in another I want to stay right where I am. Maybe even move a little closer. Like I said, weird. 'No.' There's a long, unnerving silence which I'm tempted to fill with babble. 'That's Ed.'

'Ed?' I am confused. An alarm bell is ringing deep in my subconsciousness. Aunt Lynn had mentioned an Ed, posh advocaat-girl Bianca had been after Ed. I ignore it. 'No, it's not. It's Will. Ed was the owner and—'

'He's the co-owner.'

'But I've been emailing Will. You . . .' My voice tails off as I try and get this straight in my head. I've been emailing this man, while I've been thinking I'm talking to somebody who looks quite different. Ed. 'You're not just the receptionist?'

My voice might have lifted with hope. There might still be a chance this is a mistake.

'No, do I look like I am?'

'Well, not really.' He doesn't. 'Receptionists smile.'

He smiles, a full-on smile. It only lasts a second, but it makes my eyes open wider and my stomach dip. It's like no receptionist smile I've ever come across, and I've seen a few.

I have no clever comeback. So I swallow hard. Press on, Sarah, press on. 'I'm Sarah, from Making Memories.'

I look more closely at Will, now I know he's Will. I need to do some readjusting in my head.

'Ah.' There's something that looks suspiciously like a grin twitching at the corners of his mouth, the hint of a dimple. Which is annoying. 'That figures.' He crosses his arms. Smile, folded arms, we're getting mixed messages here. And I'm not sure I like the way he just said that.

'I am Will, Sarah,' his clipped tone has veered closer to a drawl, 'I'm Ed's brother. It's me you've been chatting to.' He's telling the truth, I can tell. It slowly sinks in and I can feel myself changing colour. Forget ice and snow; boy, is it hot in here. Gawd, this is embarrassing.

'But that photo?' It's come out as a squeak. I don't need to press on, I just have to say something. Any idiot can see there's a faint resemblance between him and the photo on the website. He's just lacking the friendly, cute part. 'And he was in the video!'

'What video? We haven't done a video.' There's a hint of alarm on his features.

'The one somebody posted on *The Worst Christmas Ever* website. The one with bouncy sprouts and no marshmallows.'

He's looking at me like I've grown an extra head.

'And a third-world turkey and rubbish . . .' I glance at the slightly bent and very lopsided tree, 'Christmas tree.'

'Oh.' He shrugs. How can the man shrug off stuff like that? 'Well, that was last Christmas; I wasn't here then. But Ed's the face of the resort, not me.'

This explains a lot. Ed might not have a duplicitous face after all. He just has a face, a nice face.

Ed, Aunt Lynn said, was nice, she also said that Will was a totally different kettle of fish.

He is. And he has an interesting, if grumpy face. And not a 'welcome to my resort you'll have fun here' kind of face.

'But, if you want to talk to Ed,' he shrugs, 'I'm sure he'll turn up at some point if he can be bothered.'

'Ed was in charge last year then, when that video was made? Worst Christmas ever?'

I think he might have flinched, it's hard to tell. His jaw has tightened, though. I now know why the term 'chiselled' is sometimes used. This one has been hewn from granite. 'He was.' He might even be doing my trick of talking through gritted teeth, or his jaw is just so tight it just looks that way.

I'm very tempted to reach out and trace a finger along his chin, but I don't. He might bite it off.

It's my turn to frown now, though. Lovely Ed, the one Aunt Lynn liked, had already started to ruin the place, before 'couldn't give a monkey's Will' had taken it on. Except it looks like he does give a monkey's (at least a baby one), or he wouldn't be looking at me like he is. Hmm.

Or he's just very cross with his brother, and the fact he's had to step in. On the lead up to Christmas, which at a guess he hates.

'*You* are in charge now.' Just to check. So I know what I'm up against.

The corner of his mouth quirks. 'I am in charge now.'

'It's you I've been talking to?'

'It's me you've been talking to.'

Oh shit. This is worse than I thought when I was back in the safety of Making Memories, blithely making promises to sort the place out. I've got to deal with a man who barks orders at his guests, hates his brother, hates Christmas and is looking like he's not very keen on me either.

'Where's Ed?' I want Ed, I desperately want Ed, I don't care what he's done. I'm sure he'll be much more amenable to fixing bullet-hard sprouts and wonky trees. Maybe he just needs direction.

'I've taken over on a temporary basis, but he's around.'

'Is he ill?' That could explain why things have gone wrong lately. Maybe poor Ed had a breakdown? Couldn't cope. Hence the disastrous Christmas last year and why it's all gone downhill from there.

He gives a short laugh. Not a funny one. 'That's one way of putting it. Now, what can I help with?' He pauses. 'A key for your cabin maybe?'

I settle for the key. I'll write that list and tackle the rest as soon as I've unpacked. 'Would you like me to take a photo of you, for the website?'

'No.'

It's not exactly an explosive no, but it sounds pretty definite. I wave my phone in the air anyway. 'No bother, this takes really good qua—' I need a photo.

'No photo. I'll show you your cabin, shall I?'

This is annoying, I'd really like to take a photo so I can send it to Sam and show her just what I'm up against. I also think one needs posting on the website. Forewarned is forearmed and all that. Not that guests should need to be armed.

'Fine.' I need to approach this in a new way. A sneaky one.

He picks my bag up effortlessly, then does a kind-of-smile that crinkles the corners of his eyes. They are steel blue. Bright and clear. I know, because he is staring straight at me and sending a don't-cause-trouble message straight to my brain. Like telepathy. I don't like being telepathized, or told what to do, but I seem to be just standing here, mouth gaping like a goldfish.

'It's not exactly festive, is it?' I try a bit of social chitchat out as we go out in the cold. He doesn't comment. 'A bit gloomy?' I've got to start somewhere and getting him to see the problem is the first step.

'What do you mean, gloomy?' This could be more difficult than I first thought. 'This place is fantastic, what the hell do people expect? If people spent more time at looking at what's around them—'

'I take it you mean outside, not that?' I wave back towards the reception area we have just left, he ignores me.

'And stop expecting to be spoon-fed entertainment.'

'Well, you should market the place as white stuff, lots of white stuff available.' I think I've grown an extra head, or he's trying to make me disappear. 'White stuff is, er, good.'

'Snow. For ski-ing, it's a winter resort.'

'Well, say that: lots of snow for ski-ing, don't say winter wonderland.'

'I never said winter wonderland. It's not the type of thing I'd say.'

'I can believe that.' I make a mental note to double check. I also want to scream out that this place used to be a winter wonderland, and he's ruined it. But I don't.

'Well, there you go.'

'So you definitely didn't say that, in the brochure or online anywhere?' He shakes his head. 'So that was just me, then?'

'I guess so.'

'I think we have a problem here with expectations; lots of those bad reviews are because you do advertise it as festive, and it isn't.'

'I also advertise it as an outdoor resort, which it is.'

'Fine. So you've got plenty of snow, for skiing. But what about inside? In there it's not wonderful, or fantastic. Where's the . . .' I wrack my brains, trying to come up with a list of all the things I thought were in (or suggested in) the brochure. 'Hot chocolate, log fires, cosy evenings?'

He stares. Does this man hate Christmas, me, or just guests? 'There's a tree.'

We both stare at the tree. 'They normally have decorations, a bit of tinsel, the odd twinkly light. And you could have a shiny star on the top . . .' My voice tails off. It isn't just because of the way he's looking at me. It's because now I'm here I can picture that tree from when I was a kid, like it was yesterday. It was the biggest, brightest, greenest, smelliest (in a good way) Christmas tree I'd ever seen. Dad lifted me up high in his arms, saying I could be the fairy on the top, his warm arms hugging me close. Safe.

My eyes are misting over, the rubbish scraggy tree blur-ring into a green and brown mass, and so I step closer, to be sure he can't see my face.

'I haven't had time to dress the tree yet.'

'But it's nearly Christmas!' Indignation always works when I'm upset.

'Really?'

I think he's being sarcastic, but it still makes me smile. Will is funny, and I'm not sure if I want to hit him or hug him. He's the most exasperating man I've ever met.

'In the brochure . . .' I try again. We need to be on the same wavelength here.

'Look, the brochure is out of date. That was last year, this year we've not got round to it yet. It will be done for Christmas Eve.'

I close my eyes, in an attempt to block out the crappy tree and picture this place as it was last time I came. It's hard, given how cold and bleak the reality is. Doubly hard when I know he's staring at me.

'There should be a roaring fire, and decorations, fir cones, candles, cinnamon sticks.' This is what *all* places should have at Christmas time – no past memories need dredging up for that.

'There are candles.'

'They're not festive, they're functional.' I've had the chance to study them while I was waiting. 'And they're the only lighting in the place. Has there been a power cut?'

'Sorry?'

'Well, it's a bit dark in here, isn't it?'

'Look, I've not got time to chat. Feel free to decorate the tree later if it'll make you happy.'

For the sake of my own sanity I'm going to have to convince myself that he is just wowed by my professionalism and very expensive ski jacket. And is not trying to brainwash me or planning on burying me in a snowdrift.

'It will make me happy. I'll do it. Now, tomorrow, soon. In fact, I'll write you a list.'

'Fine. Ready?'

I'm not ready to move yet. I fold my arms; mentally, I'm digging my heels in. 'Can you supply a bit of tinsel? Holly?'

He raises an eyebrow.

'Berries?'

'Don't push it!'

'But it's Christmas! And what about some mist-le-toe.' The word gets slower and slower as it comes out of my mouth and dies like an out-of-date sparkler on a damp night. The look says it all. I need to approach this with more tact, or just act first and ask later. I have exceeded the boundaries, strayed into no-man's land.

'So, that's a no, then.'

'Right.' He's moved on. Decisively. 'I'm afraid I didn't have time to get a fire going for you, but I can come and do it once I've stopped by the kitchen.'

'No, no problem. I'm sure I can work out how to do it. Dib, dib, dib and all that.'

'Dib dib dib?'

Oh God, what made me say that? I can feel myself getting hotter than a smoking barbecue. Dib, dib dib? He shouldn't raise his eyebrow, though, or do that lop-sided grin thing. He'll ruin his grumpy image. It's a good job I know I'm all hot and bothered because he's now bound to think I'm a complete weirdo.

'Boy Scouts. Be prepared and all —'

He shakes his head. 'Kill me now, but I can actually see you in the Boy Scouts, trampling all over those fragile male egos.'

I'm not quite sure if this is a compliment or an insult.

'I won't kill you yet – it would look bad in my report.'

He shakes his head again, and there is no trace of a smile now. 'Ed might not be happy if you hammer the final nail in our coffin, but you know what? You might be doing us all a favour.'

'What do you mean? Doing you a favour?' There's something not right here. Why has he stepped in, if he really hates the place so much?

He ignores me and carries on walking.

'Look, I'm not trying to finish the place off, I want it to

be like it used to be, better. I've got ideas.' I dodge round him and block the way. He needs to stop and listen. He doesn't and I just end up walking backwards, which is not a good idea. I also get another of his 'looks'. But I'm not stopping here, I need ideas, quick. Instead, I get to be on my bottom, quick. 'I'll decorate the tree, I'll go through your brochure and make sure it matches what you have when we've made it better, obviously.' I carry on talking, because I am effectively blocking the way and unless he steps over me he's got to listen.

'Obviously.' He doesn't look convinced. But he does hold a hand out and grabs mine. It's a big, warm capable hand. Very warm, and strong, and tanned. There's a scar over the knuckles, a white line that stands out starkly against the olive brown. I'm tempted to run a finger over it, but it's almost like he senses it, and snatches it out of reach. Slightly embarrassing. How can you take in so much of a hand in just a few seconds? I blink, avoid looking at him, until I get back in my stride.

'I'll help you redo your website. I know, I know, I've got it!' I'm on a roll here, Lynn would be proud. 'We'll do a new video, show people what to expect, the ski-ing snow, because it is wonderful snow – it's a gorgeous place, awesome.' He gives a half-smile, which is nice. Not exactly cute, but it warms up something inside me that it shouldn't. 'And the tree, when I've decorated it, of course, I'll film that, and the food, the cat.'

'The cat? No chance, you'd have to catch her first.'

'Well, other stuff, and . . .' I'm thinking on my feet, and it's just come to me! I grab his arm. 'We can live-stream! People love stuff like that! That's it, we can livestream an evening of fun – I'm sure Craig and his family would join in. We can do a carol service, or nativity thing, or some sing-song, and, and, and – you can be in it!'

'No!' If I thought the previous photo-taking no was a bit emphatic, this is explosive. And so is the way he stares at my hand. I disengage, feeling all hot and bothered.

'Sorry.'

'No livestreaming, no way, and if there's any videoing to be done, I'll do it. I am not appearing in anything, got it?'

He holds his hand up to stop me saying anything. So all I can do is bite my tongue and nod. 'Okay, okay I get it.'

'Here's your cabin.' The door is flung open, I'm bundled in, and my bag dropped at my feet. 'Any problems, you know where to find me. Welcome to the Shooting Star Mountain resort, we sincerely hope you enjoy your stay.'

That funny Will? No trace. Gone.

And I'm not sure about the sincere bit, but he has made me feel totally in the wrong. But it's not my fault he's ruining the place, is it? Final nail! He's being totally unfair, this is his problem, and I'm the one trying to help here. I'd tell him, but he's already backed out and closed the door very firmly behind him.

Chapter 11

'He is seriously fit.'

'He is *so* not fit.' I'm still seething inside from the totally unfair talk about coffins and nails and being totally barred from livestreaming. That idea was brilliant! What is wrong with the man? Is he determined to stop me doing anything that might help, apart from decorate the flaming tree?

Also, the Wi-Fi here seems to have come from the same decade as the furnishings in the reception hall, but after much messing about I've managed to send Sam a photo and get not-too-bad reception on Skype. It's fine if we don't do video, and repeat everything twice, and ignore the static.

'He is. I can tell he's hot even though it's not a brilliant photo.'

'You try taking a photo out of a frozen-up window while you're pretending to wipe off a dirty mark.' I sigh. 'He's such a miserable git. He's just totally obstructive and trying to ruin any chance of making this place good again, but I am so not going to let him win.' I'm already writing a list, with positives in one column (because this place truly is fantastic and has so much potential) and things to fix. There are quite a lot of things to fix.

'That photo on the website is his brother Ed, and he seems totally against having one of himself, though I can't bloody blame him if he's going to scowl all the time.'

'He's not scowling on this.'

'You can't see it properly. He's bawling out some poor holidaymaker who'd just got back from ski-ing. Probably telling them off for sliding down his path and leaving tracks.'

I'd been staring out of the window after he left, trying to work out a plan of attack and had watched him head off this guy who'd come zooming up the path like it was normal to be on rock hard snow. It's not. Maybe he's an alien too. Maybe me and the lovely Harris family have strayed into an alien settlement. 'I think this could be alien base camp, their nerve centre. They're going to take over the whole world, starting right here. If I don't come back you know I've been infiltrated, or brainwashed, taken over or something.'

There had been some waving of arms and body language that was something along the lines of 'you are such a plonker' from him, and 'who gives a monkey's?' from the other guy (I'm no expert at reading body language, but a moron could have worked this out). Anyway, I couldn't help but watch, then I couldn't help but take a photo. It was the perfect opportunity. I just had to do it.

Sam giggles. 'Well, they don't seem to be doing a very good job of brainwashing people or there wouldn't be so many one-star reviews on the internet! Some people must escape.'

'True. Maybe they're only interested in people who can ski, in which case I'm safe. Unless he does that long-lizard-tongue-down-the-throat thing and kills me.'

'You're thinking of kissing him!'

'I'm bloody not.'

'You must be, self-consciously or you wouldn't have said the tongue thing.'

'I think you mean subconsciously, not self-consciously. But I have no interest in snogging Will Armstrong at all.' It's just a shame I can't shake the image of his eyes out of my head, but I'm not going to tell Sam that. Whatever negatives the man has, his eyes are not one of them. He should market them, sell ice cream with them. I'd buy it. In fact, that's an idea! Not the ice cream, but the marketing bit. I could just put his eyes on the website. Or would that be banned as well?

'He went totally apeshit when I suggested we do a livestream with him in it; it's like he doesn't want anybody to even know he exists.' He'd been softening, nearly smiling, then one mention of including him in the promo and he'd hardened and thrown up the barriers, just like that. He reminds me of somebody.

I can feel myself go hot and cold.

He reminds me of me, the younger me, on my bad days.

There's more to Will than meets the eye, just as Aunt Lynn said. This isn't just careless sabotage, or lack of caring.

There's a reason for him behaving this way, and I want to know what it is.

'Whatever. But you probably shouldn't have taken his photo, if he . . . Are you listening Sarah?'

'Of course I am, but I mean, I'm not going to publish this photo anywhere, am I? So what's the harm? Lots of holidaymakers must take snaps with him hovering in the background. It's inevitable. And I had to show you what I'm up against.'

'He is quite hot, though.' She ignores my splutter. 'Let me finish! He looks quite sexy – well, very sexy – in a brooding kind of way. There's a bit of the Heathcliff about him, or Poldark.'

I roll my eyes, then remember she can't see me. 'You mean a chauvinist pig from a previous century?'

She sniggers. 'You can't say that! All he's done is given you your key and carried your bag – and anyway, I was talking about the way he looked, not anything else.'

'Heathcliff was an amateur compared to this guy.'

I have zoomed in on Will Armstrong's photo as much as I can, and I reckon, even in this snap, you can see what I've seen with my own eyes. Brooding is not the word. The man doesn't need a 'keep off' sign, you'd have to be mad to want to go within a hundred yards of him. 'Sexy? You have got to be kidding, girl. He is channelling his inner dark menace. He looks like Rufus Sewell playing a psycho-path. I mean look at him, look at him properly.'

I'm staring at the picture myself. He stares back, his steel-blue eyes sending a silent challenge. I know they were aimed at the man, this time, not me, but it sends a warning shiver down my spine. There's something about him that says he's never going to be a pushover, that says he knows what he wants and keeps going until he gets it. But those dangerous eyes have drawn me in. And I realise I want to go to battle and lock horns with him, which is a bit scary, because that look is telling me he's not the type to back down from anything.

'I can understand why he stuck with the photo of Ed on the website. At least Ed suggests this is a place to have fun. If I'd have been him I'd have done that, or replaced it with a picture of a puppy. Or a kitten. Or even a photo of snow.'

'You said Ed had a lying face, was dupli— Whatever.'

'That's when I thought Ed was Will and was sending me crappy emails and ignoring me.'

'Well, he can't have been doing both.' She says it very reasonably.

'You know what I mean!'

'Huh. Well, I think Will looks unhappy, not menacing.'

'Unhappy my arse. More like grumpy. People are expecting Santa Claus and a bit of ho ho ho, not Scrooge. I suppose he's okay if you like that type of thing. Which I don't. He's all mean and moody.' My voice falters a bit. Maybe he *is* unhappy? One minute I get the impression that he thinks this place is the most fantastic on earth, and he really appreciates how amazing it is, the next it seems like he can't wait to get away. I mean, that comment about nails in coffins was pretty heartfelt, even if it was a bit nasty. And yet, in his emails and even since I got here, underneath all the moodiness I've sensed a hint of a different Will. A funny one. A pretty squashed-down funny one, though. A bit like I used to be, in what Lynn termed my 'tricky years'.

'Mean, moody and magnificent?' The laughter in Sam's voice stops my thoughts in their tracks. Good timing.

'Not magnificent. More like miserly. And you were wrong when you said his email showed he's got a sense of humour; he hasn't. Well maybe a tiny bit. But the only real point in his favour so far is that he likes cats. Unless it was supposed to be his lunch.'

'And he likes dogs; he was bothered about his dog in that email he sent about being sued. Remember? What was it called?'

'Rosie.' I can't stop the sigh escaping. What is wrong with the man? I've got a feeling he could be quite nice, underneath all the stony exterior.

I'd quite like to just turn around and go home, but what else am I going to do over Christmas? Sit on my own, gnawing on a turkey leg with repeats of *The Royle Family* and *The Morecambe & Wise Show* on a loop? Not that there's anything wrong with either of them, but . . .

'This place is a complete disaster, Sam, it's every bit as

bad as people say in the reviews. So far a Christmas tree has nearly fallen on Poppy's head, we've been told off for wearing our boots inside, I've been flattened by a man, and everywhere is frigging freezing.'

'You've been flattened by Will—'

'It wasn't Will, it was Craig.' I decide to head her off, before she insists on filling in an accident form. 'And no way would I be kissing him.'

'Who's Craig?'

It's at that point we get cut off, which is probably a good thing. Being swept off my feet by a father of two with his family watching wasn't quite how I expected my first hour here to pan out. Or being accused of being a human wrecking ball. God, Will is being so unfair. This is his fault, not mine, even if he does have a very good reason.

I reckon it's time to finish this list and work out how to get a fire lit before we get to sample the delicious fayre. Surely the grub can't be as bad as the reviews say?

Chapter 12

'Bloody hell.' I think I'm going to die. And I haven't
even got near the food yet.

There is smoke everywhere. I can't stop coughing and my
eyes are streaming. You die of smoke inhalation, don't you,
not fire? Well, I presume red-hot flames are pretty bad for
the health, but as there aren't any flickering flames that isn't
a problem right now. But I'm sure it's the fumes that kill you
before the place burns to the ground cremating you with it.

I am wheezing like an old woman at the door to the
cabin, while trying to look as if I'm casually admiring the
view. Except it's bloody freezing. Who stands at an open
door in this weather without a coat on?

I can light a barbecue, so why can't I light a frigging log
fire? If men can do it, then I'm bloody sure a woman should
be able to. Although saying that, not all men are Bear Grylls,
just as not all women are Mary Berry. I am neither.

Aunt Lynn should be pleased though. She wanted me
to discover new things about myself on this trip, and I have
learned something new already.

I do not know how to light a fire.

I need help. God, don't you hate those words?

***

Okay, I can do this. I take a deep breath then spit it out, in one big whoosh. 'I need somebody to light my fire.' This is a big admission, but at least he's got his back to me which makes it easier to say. 'And I have a list of all the things you really need to do, after the fire of course.'

I wave my list around, to hide the fact that I don't like to admit I can't do something (especially 'man' things), and Google normally provides all the answers. But Google is not telling (don't blame Google – blame the crap Wi-Fi) and I am desperate.

'Please. I've risked freezing my bits off, and I need a bath before dinner, and this place is like, like . . .' Admitting I can't do something to Mr Will Armstrong makes it worse.

Maybe he has a secret plan to freeze me out, literally, as well as with his scathing comments.

'Wood-burning fireplace' just trips off the tongue when you read it in the brochure; it sounds romantic, lovely, warming. It is less great when you'd rather just turn the central heating on, and flick the gas fire to 'go'. I am a flicking-the-switch type of person.

He turns around and smiles, a lovely generous, open smile that warms more than the cockles (as Aunt Lynn would say) of my heart. My stomach does a plunge, in a very nice way.

'Happy to light your fire any time, babe.'

'Oh. My. God!' It might have come out as a bit of a squeal. I might be on the verge of hysterical laughter and grabbing him. 'It's you! It's really you!' I think I'm pointing and jumping about. I'm surprised there isn't a notice forbidding it.

He grins, this massive, split-face, totally-thrilled-and-happy-to-see-me type of grin that makes me feel all gooey and warm.

It's him! Well, not him as in Will. It's the one in the photo that I *thought* was Will.

'You're Ed.' I state the obvious, because I can't help myself, even though I think he probably knows who he is. But it might be worth checking, anyway.

This might be a completely out-of-proportion, over-the-top reaction, but he's the first friendly (other than the Harris family, of course) face I've seen since I got here. He's the man that should be behind reception, not take-your-boots-off Will.

I don't care if he's smug and spends too much time looking at himself in the mirror. I could hug him. I really want to hug him. Would it be wrong to throw myself across the desk and wrap him in the type of koala bear hug that should be illegal in public?

'Certainly am, and you must be . . .' He winks and runs his finger down the list of guests. 'The gorgeous Sarah.' He rests his forearms on the desk and leans in closer. He is gorgeous. Smug? Ha! I can deal with smug any day of the week.

Is it bad to snog a man you don't know?

He takes my hand in his lovely warm ones.

'What the hell are you doing?' The cold voice throws a dampener on what was warming up to be a nice encounter. I forget koala bear hugs and feel like a naughty kid that's been caught sampling the chocolate.

It is superman. And he is making me feel bad again.

Ed shrugs good-naturedly and doesn't look at all like he's expecting to be sent to the naughty step.

'I was just off to light Sarah's fire,' the grin is playing with his words and making laughter bubble up in my stomach, 'and run her a bath.' After the day I've had, this is just what I need.

'And look at my list!' I wave it about in an attempt to diffuse the situation.

'No way. You can stop right there.' I think he means the bath-running, not the looking at my list.

Oh God, I think I hate Will Armstrong, and I might have just growled. Luckily Will is totally ignoring me and glaring at his poor brother. 'You need to clean out the dog kennel before you do any fire lighting.'

This is not good news for either of us.

a. Because I may not now get a fire sorted, and
b. I was quite looking forward to seeing Ed's friendly face,

even if I did tell Sam he wasn't my type, looked a light-weight, smug, and probably only loved number one.

Right now, I don't care about being number two, or three.

And, from the look on his face, mucking out dog kennels in sub-zero temperatures wasn't on his wish list. And, c. It would have been good to get both of them onboard together, to agree on what we needed to do.

Ed winks at me and mouths 'later', then sidesteps Will and takes a step closer so he's within inches of me. 'If you fancy a bit of excitement I'm happy to provide a bit of snowboarding, first lesson free?' He squeezes my arm, and he's so close I can smell his minty breath and I lose myself in the twinkliest eyes I've seen in a long time.

He looks so bloody alive and cute it would be criminal to miss an opportunity to show off my expensive leopard-skin base layer. I mean, I didn't pay all that money to see it languish permanently under many other layers, did I? I was expecting at least some return in the après-ski arena, and Ed is definitely a serious contender.

Will, meanwhile, sees me as the final nail in the coffin. Not a good look, unless you're an undertaker.

The fact that Ed's just scrunched up the piece of paper in my hand is slightly annoying though.

'Sure.' Sugar. Why did I say sure? I've never been, and never intended to go near, a snowboard. I've seen them on YouTube videos. Ski's look bad enough, but hurtling down a sheet of ice on a mini ironing board with no brakes? You have got to be kidding me. 'I mean no!'

'No?' He looks taken aback, and those baby blues are wide open. 'Come on, tell me you're kidding! You *are* kidding, right?' He looks so earnest, then so confused, then so let down (yeah, some men can do all that, it takes practise) that I can't help but feel rotten. Okay, so it's blatant flirting on his side, and he probably acts like this with every girl that walks in, but I don't mind. I know what he's doing. He knows I know.

'Erm, I mean, I've never . . .' Ed could be fun. Men like this shouldn't be passed over. If I'm going to survive this place then I need an ally, and preferably one who's a lot of fun and a little bit wicked. I know Ed is. Ed knows I know.

'Chill.' He grins. 'You'll be in safe hands. Before and,' he leans a bit closer, 'after.'

I look down at his hand, which is still resting on my arm. It looks large and capable. Okay, I know if some blonde preppy chalet girl whizzes by on her ski's he'll be off. But my inner leopard needs the opportunity to purr. Right?

'Ed!'

I frown at Will, sending him a silent 'sod off'. He doesn't see, he's too busy frowning at Ed, who doesn't care. There's far too much frowning going on in this place.

Maybe I need a new approach, or I'll be piggy in the middle (and not in a good way) between the two guys who definitely don't seem to be sharing brotherly love right now.

'So, if you're sending him off to play with the doggies, are *you* going to light my fire then, Will?'

Ed chuckles. 'Good luck with that, darling. Catch you later!' He walks off whistling, and I'm left with Mr Grumpy again. I really need to stop calling him that, because there's a danger I might actually say it out loud by mistake.

It also isn't helping me see him in a positive light. Which I need to do if I'm going to make this work. Which reminds me . . . 'Then we can look through my list. I've got some great ideas of things you can do to get this place back on track, and it will take hardly any . . .'

Ed seems to have sped up. I don't think he's keen on lists.

'List?' I wave it at Will.

'Maybe.' I take this as a promising start. I will take any encouragement right now. 'Come on then, I need to get back and check the kitchen before everybody gets back and expects hot food.'

'You're so charming.'

He looks confused for a minute, then grabs his jacket and makes for the door. I guess I'm supposed to run after him.

Surprisingly, though, he actually holds the door open for me.

If this fire doesn't get lit soon, I've got a feeling my leopard-skin base layer might get a lot of use, but see zilch action. However cute Ed is, right now no man on earth would be able to make me glow enough to want to strip off.

***

Will has my fire (the log one, not the internal one) lit within seconds. In fact, I wasn't even concentrating, my mind was on Ed and my big pink knickers, so I haven't got a clue how he did it. It's impressive, though, and I have a glimmer of understanding for those women in love with cavemen types who are good with their hands. There's something sexy (yeah, I did apply the word sexy to Will) about watching a man do man stuff. He's just ticked boxes I didn't know I had.

I'm not sure this should be my main promotional tool in persuading people to come here for a holiday, though. Food, friends and festive cheer probably feature higher on most people's lists.

'Oh wow, cool.' I can't help myself. I'm impressed. 'You need to show me how to do that, I hadn't got a clue where to start.'

'Yeah, well, it's easy when you know how.' He shrugs self-consciously. 'Any idiot can do it.'

This is a backward step in our new, more positive relationship.

'Sorry, I didn't mean . . .'

Full marks for the recovery, though. 'How was I to know I'd need fire-lighting skills on a holiday? This isn't a bush tucker trial.'

He looks confused. 'Isn't that in the jungle?'

'Well yeah, but a fire's a fire.'

'Very true.' He stands up – he looks taller in this small cabin – and brushes his hands off on his very long legs. 'I guess you didn't expect . . .'

He actually looks slightly friendlier, more relaxed, as well as taller. So, grab your chances as they say. 'Well, no, to be honest I didn't. Shouldn't you have somebody . . .'

'We used to have somebody come in and light them ready for new arrivals.' He sighs heavily and plonks himself down on one of the chairs. 'The whole warm welcome thing.'

I nod approvingly. 'That is top of my list.' I sit down opposite him. 'And isn't it a bit stingy making people pay if they want more logs? I mean a roaring fire is part of the magic.'

'You really think we need to let people have more?' He's frowning again, but more in a worried than a cross way. In fact, he looks more knackered and hassled than angry now.

I want to hug him. But I won't, because that isn't professional, and I'm not sure he wants to be hugged. He might slam the door shut in my face.

'Well, otherwise it's like one of those hotels that offers free Wi-Fi, but then, when you get there, you find out it's only if you're sitting no more than three feet away from the main reception desk.'

'Mmm.'

'Or offering free drinks, but they just mean tap water.'

'I think you're pushing it a bit now.'

I grin. He grins back. Then goes back to looking hassled. 'It's the little things people remember, though, good as well as bad. Leave a free bottle of wine for me, and I'll forgive the fact that there wasn't a spare pillow. But stick a scraggy undecorated Christmas tree in the lobby, and . . .' I shrug, and try and soften it with a smile, then look straight into his eyes, willing him to understand that I'm trying to help here. 'You need to hit them with everything you've promised the moment they walk in.'

'The thing is, Sarah, I know we've got issues, I know that's why you're here.'

'Well, not exactly. Aunt Ly—'

'It's fine. Honest.' He holds a hand up. 'I know where you're coming from and believe me, I'm no happier about all this than you are. I hate reading all those crap reviews and answering the even crappier emails.'

I bite my tongue, I could say that he doesn't actually get round to answering many. Well, not mine.

'They come in by the droves. It's horrible, and I'm running around like a blue-arsed fly just trying to keep this place ticking over. I haven't got time to work out how to apologise.'

For the first time he looks, and sounds, genuinely upset. And hassled. Not what I expected at all, and I've got a sudden urge to comfort him, to reassure him that he's doing okay. 'You did eventually answer one of mine.' Maybe this isn't as clear cut as I thought. Maybe it isn't just a case of he doesn't give a damn.

'It was funny. I like your style.' The glimmer of a smile passes over his face, sunshine between the rain clouds and I can't help myself. I smile back. I'm beginning to think I might like his style as well. 'Come on, then, let's see the list. I know you're dying to hand it over.'

I think the folding and unfolding was a giveaway.

His fingertips brush mine as he takes it, and his gaze meets mine for a second. But it's a 'we're in this together' kind of look, not a flirty one. I like it. There's something solid and reliable about Will.

We sit in silence for the short time it takes him to scan over the sheet of paper. Then he refolds it and hands it back.

'We've got issues, major issues. I know that, but I'm not sure anybody steaming in here like some mini Alex Polizzi is going to solve anything. Look,' he runs his fingers through his hair. 'Okay,' the sigh is heavy, and comes from somewhere deep inside him that makes me lean forward, 'totally upfront? We've got massive financial problems, as in there's hardly enough money to keep us ticking over. I'm trying to do this on a shoestring, which means less staff for a start, so we've got to do this one step at a time. I can't spread myself into enough pieces to be making fires every morning and after-noon. I can't afford to be filling the cabins with logs.'

'But this is all simple stuff, just a starter. I'll help – and what about Ed?'

'Ed?' He gives a short laugh and shakes his head. I'm pretty sure he's about to say something else, but he seems to pull himself up. 'Lovely as your ideas are, it's just not possible. If you want to organise some kind of happy-clappy tree-decorating session, then be my guest. But on your head be it.'

'Not Poppy's?' I raise an eyebrow, and he actually smiles properly. Smiles! It's quite a nice smile, actually. It makes me want to smile back, and for a split second forget that I want to kill him. Or myself.

'Believe me, that tree is well and truly fastened down now, not even a blizzard will shift it.'

'And not a cat?'

He shakes his head, still looking amused.

'Chloe's such a cute name.' It's a cue; I'm waiting for him to say it wasn't him that named it.

'Well, she was a real wildcat when we found her. I called her Claw-ey, but I was kind of outvoted and everybody insisted on calling her Chloe.'

'Ah.' Not so cute. But he still has a cat, so that proves he's at least got a hint of a human side, right? 'Okay.' I'm not about to give up on this list, whatever he thinks. 'None of this needs to take up a lot of time, or money. Logs first, people want to be warm. Why not have a help-yourself log store that's a bit of a walk away? You know, supply maybe a few more for arrivals, but then say people can collect extra if they want free of charge? It would make you look generous, but most people wouldn't be bothered after the first day or two and the novelty's worn off. After a day of being out in the cold, nobody is going to want to go out again unless they need to, are they? And logs are heavy, they can only bring a few at a time.'

'Maybe.' He nods. 'And it doesn't add another job to my list. Okay. But,' the frown is back, 'I really can't spare the time to make up fires as well as everything else, and I can't afford to take somebody else on. We're stretched as it is.'

I take a deep breath and the words tumble out before I can stop them. 'I'll do it.' He looks as surprised as me.

'You don't know how to make a fire!'

'I know. But I'll help you with other stuff, so that you have time to do the fires. I'll work for you while I'm here, do the tree, check the kitchen. Stuff like that.'

Am I totally mad? Have my senses deserted me? Is this what brain freeze results in? Not that long ago I was thinking of the very cute Ed, and my base layer which really does deserve an outing, and now I'm offering to slave away for nothing alongside big brother Will.

'It's not just your business at stake here, Will. It's ours, our reputation. I want to be able to share this place with our clients – they could really love it.' I need this to work, it's my first real task as a partner in the business. But more than that, coming back here has reminded me what the place once meant to me. How magical it was. And it's also the very, very last time, the very last place, I saw my parents smile. And however much they hurt me, however much my life was screwed up, I've not been able to picture those smiles for a long time. Now I can. Here.

'And you can work miracles in a week?' He's looking amused, which is good, it's distracting me from the past.

'I'll stay longer, until New Year, if I can change my flight.' I must be mad.

'But like I said, we can't afford —'

'You can offer our agency a special discount, some kind of preferential terms. We can work something out.'

'But you don't know anything about the place, do you?'

'I've got a good idea of what people want, and I know what good customer service is. And I know what a good Christmas looks like. And,' I look him in the eye, and concentrate on keeping the wobble out of my voice, 'I have been here before, when I was little, when it was the most amazing place a child could wish for.' When there was snow every day, the perfect snow to make a snowman with. When the reindeer trotted on as I sat wrapped up in the warmest fur rug I'd ever touched. When the stars sparkled in a jet-black sky, brighter than any other stars ever had. When the husky dog trotted back to the cabin with us and was the dog I wasn't allowed to have. Just for the holiday. Just for Christmas.

'Sure. Okay then.' His voice is soft, and he's studying me. 'If it means that much to you.'

What? What the hell did I just do? He said sure. I was positive he'd laugh in my face, and yet he's looking at me as though he gets it. 'Sure?' Me and my big mouth. That's what got me here in the first place, and now it seems it has doomed me to an extra week.

'Yeah, sure. Stay. Your highly unique approach to emails might turn things round.'

'Do I detect a hint of sarcasm?'

'Not guilty.' He stands up and his smile has a soft edge to it. 'I'm drowning here, so if you're happy to help out with some PR while you're here then I'll give you a refund on the cabin.'

'Oh. Can you afford that?'

'Unless you didn't actually mean—'

'Oh, I meant it!' Liar, liar, pants on fire. 'Definitely. This week is work anyway, I came here to —'

'Spy on us?'

'See for myself why people are giving you such crap reviews.'

'The thing is, Sarah, I don't really do Christmas. I hate all the tat, the commercialism. Why can't people be happy with being in a stunning place?'

'Because they're cold and they've got kids who are excited about Christmas. They're not looking for tat, Will, just . . .' What are they looking for? What was *I* hoping for? I close my eyes and think, properly. I wanted to recapture that feeling. That happiness, that sense that nothing could go wrong, that I was in a safe place where magic could happen, where Christmas could be perfect. I don't want the bad bits, the sad bits, the bits that happened at the end. The bits that hung over my childhood. I want to remember Christmas Eve, Christmas Day. I want to be reminded of what it was to be loved and be wanted. 'Warmth, feeling wanted, hugged, hot chocolate, a bit of festive cheer.' I pause. 'Magic. People want a bit of magic, a magic winter wonderland.' He's raising his eyebrow again. 'But without the tat. And with reindeers. And stars. And hot chocolate.'

'I think you said that already.'

'It's important. And roaring fires. I'm not asking for much, am I? Just a bit of festive cheer . . .'

My words tail off at the look on his face. He's not convinced. Time for a more direct approach.

'What went wrong, Will? This place used to have all that. Why's the place got in a such a mess?'

'It's a long story.' He's at the door in double-quick time. 'If it was up to me, I think I'd ditch the place completely.'

'Don't.'

He stops dead and stares at me. I did shout it out a bit more abruptly than I meant to.

'Don't abandon it. Please. It was good once, a magic place, don't walk away from it.'

'We'll see.' He shrugs, already opening the door. 'Let me know if you need more logs.'

'Show me where they are later and I'll sort out your new firewood policy.'

'They'll need restacking if we're going to let guests loose on them. Health and safety and all that. Can't have guests flattened by firewood, can we?'

The man does have a sense of humour. Maybe I've misjudged him, maybe he's just stressed, worried. Hates Christmas. 'I'll do it.'

He raises an eyebrow.

'I'll get Ed to help me.' The eyebrow goes higher. And then with a waft of cold air, he's gone. I look down at my list. I think he needs a plan, not a list. A colour-coded plan.

Chapter 13

I blame the fondue fork. Or lack of one. We were a fork short of a fondue, to misquote Lynn, who was very fond of the 'pork pie short of a picnic' saying.

I didn't know chocolate fondue was a thing still, but apparently it is here, and it set Poppy off on a squealing spree. She's nearly as keen as me on all things (well, the definition of *all* in her case is probably slightly different to mine) chocolate coated.

'I want a fork!' Poppy nudges me hard in the ribs.

'Here, darling, I told you have mine.' Her mum Tina gets a scowl.

'Don't want yours, it's got a yellow end. I hate yellow.'

'Here, have mine. It's pink, pink is the best!' I hand her mine and get a beam in return. Sunshine after the storm. God, I'm not surprised my mother left me, if having a kid is like this. How does anybody cope? Although I did read somewhere that pregnancy hormones bear a huge part in stopping you eating your offspring just after birth. I think I'd go with gin.

Tina seems to have read my mind. She winks. 'It's true. The hormones do stop you killing them.'

'I'll go and find some more forks. We seem to be quite a few short, but at least Poppy has got one!'

I could have fought Poppy over that last one, but I reckon it wouldn't have gone down well and she might well have won the battle anyway. Or caused an avalanche with her screaming.

As all the serving staff seem to have done a disappearing act, I set off in search of assistance.

There is nobody in the kitchen. Unless you count Chloe the cat, who is cleaning the gravy pan out. I make a mental note to raise this with Will in private and settle for shooing her off the sink before I head off, tentatively, down the corridor at the back.

I say tentatively, because I can hear voices. Of the loud, shouty male kind. It is not a happy sound. In fact, I'd go so far as to say I might not dare broach the subject of the missing forks. I might go back and tackle the hot chocolate with my fingers.

But my feet seem to have a mind of their own and are taking me ever closer (on tiptoes).

***

'It's you that bloody asked me to come back!'

'Can't you just give me a break? Ease up a bit, man, you're getting wound up about nothing.'

'Nothing? *Nothing*! Have you seen what this says? This isn't one of your games, Ed. Don't you want this place to survive?'

'Says the man who was too busy basking in the glory for years to give a shit, and was more than happy to just ignore me and this place.'

'That was the agreement. This was your idea, your place. Put money in, Will, it'll be brilliant, Will, it'll make us a fortune, Will. It'll be your retirement fund, Will. Guaranteed.'

'Well, how was I to know how much everything would cost to update?'

Will groans loudly. It nearly makes me laugh, because it's a bit like the noise a whale makes. Low and pained, there is feeling in that groan. So much feeling that I have to creep closer and look through the crack in the door. Which involves screwing my head at a very unnatural angle and putting most of my weight on one leg. Dangerous stuff. I would not make a spy. Or I'd be the type that has backache and a crick in my neck and has to retire early.

'You should have found out! It's what managers do.' He closes his eyes, then opens them and glares at his brother. I know what it's like to have that gaze on you and I feel a bit sorry for Ed. 'Which you might cope with if you spent less time on the slopes, and more time studying the bank balance.'

'That's it, blame me, all my fault.'

'But it *is* your bloody fault! For Christ's sake, Ed! This was your project. Not mine.' He sounds weary now, not angry. He is raking his fingers through his hair. I hope he doesn't start to bang his head on the desk; I'd feel obliged to rush in and stop him (I can't stand seeing people inflicting pain on themselves or anything else) and then my cover would be blown, and he'd be even more furious at me for snooping around.

'You know I'm not good with money.' Ed sounds a bit sullen, like a spoiled kid. 'And you did agree we should get this place.'

'Fine. Just fine. If you can't cope, we'll sell up. Go. I don't give a shit.'

Which is a bit strange, because it actually sounds like he does. Like he doesn't want to walk away. Or admit defeat.

'Now you're just being an arse, and I know you don't mean it.' Ed sits down, and puts his feet up on the table with a heavy plonk.

'You always just expect somebody else to come and pick up the pieces, don't you?'

'And everything is always somebody else's fault, isn't it?'

'But this is your fault, this is your fucking mess, Ed, not mine.'

'You were just the same after the accident – bad snow, bad track, idiot on the course.'

'Shut up, Ed.'

'And now you can't bear it that you're some kind of cripple, and I can still hit the slopes. That's what this is about, isn't it?'

'It's about,' Will's voice is low, angry, and he's jabbing at a piece of paper on his desk to make a point, 'the fact we're being sued, the fact the firefighters say somebody set that cabin ablaze on purpose, that we can't claim insurance, that this place is going down the pan. It's about the fact that you spend all your time chatting up the guests instead of working while I'm running round lighting fucking log fires and chopping wood.' I wince at this one. 'I'll be pulling on Marigolds and cleaning flaming bathrooms next.' This does make me smile. He really will kill me if he comes out and catches me now. But the thought of Will in yellow rubber gloves tickles me. A lot. It's hard to keep the snigger in. If anybody touches me now I'll splutter. 'Because that bloody girl could start checking out the hygiene in this place.' Ah, less funny. I think I might be the 'bloody girl'. 'And any second now the bank will pull the plug and we'll be screwed.'

'Ha! That's it isn't it? I knew it. You fancy her, don't you?'

'Sorry?'

'It's the chatting up the guests bit. You never complained before, but you've got the hots for this one, haven't you?'

I probably shouldn't listen to this bit. I press my nose harder against the crack, and hope nobody suddenly slams it shut and leaves me with the type of upturned end which isn't cute.

'Ed, I'm warning you.'

'Warning me? What are you going to do? Where will you go?'

'Anywhere.' He pushes Ed's feet off the desk with what

some might consider unreasonable force and stands up. Towering over him. I hadn't realised he was quite so tall. Or imposing. Or angry. 'I don't want to be here, Ed, I don't want to be surrounded by snow and Christmas trees, and being hassled about frigging fairy lights.' I never even mentioned fairy lights, but it's an idea. Why didn't I think of them before? 'I want to be on a beach somewhere, swimming, diving, not on dry land.'

Oh gawd, I can so imagine him stripped down to his swimming trunks, wading out of the sea. Water dripping from his hair. His bronzed skin glistening. Muscular thighs rippling as he strides through the sand. I can see it, I can really see it . . . Stop it, Sarah!

'So why are you here then, Will?'

'Because you're my brother. Because you asked. You practically begged!'

There's a long silence and I think about creeping off, but I'll be heard. So I try and hold my breath because I don't think heavy breathing is going to be very welcome right now.

I also try and ignore the pain in my left calf, which I think might be cramp.

'See it through to next year, please?' Ed's voice has dropped, and he's studying the desk, and fiddling. Like a young boy. I want to hug him, but I think that's because he's perfected the 'hug me' look. He uses it quite a lot.

'That's less than two weeks, Ed.'

'You know what I mean. The end of the winter season.'

'If I stay, you need to help me, not keep waltzing off, I can't do this on my own Ed.'

'Of course, I'll—'

'No, I mean *really* help. Shift those logs like I told Sarah we would.'

'Fine, after I've—'

'Not after anything, Ed. First thing. Shift the snow off the path, mend that lock on cabin six, get the snowmobile serviced, shift the flaming logs.'

'But I've got clients with ski and snowboarding lessons booked in tomorrow.'

'And plenty more hours of daylight.'

'You're a slave-driving bastard.'

'And you're a lazy bastard.'

If I'd just walked in (well, crept up and attached myself to the doorjamb) I'd have thought they were squaring up, but instead I know this is a truce. The battle is over, and new lines drawn.

But why doesn't Will want to be here? Why live in the snow if you want to be on a beach? No wonder he's grumpy. Lynn definitely had a point. There is more to him than meets the eye.

'Now, what are you going to do about this?' Will is waving a piece of paper in the air.

'I'll go and be nice, take them to dinner. I'll talk them round.'

'They're threatening legal action, Ed; it's not something you can charm your way out of.'

'I can try.'

Oops. Looks like this isn't over at all. Definitely not the time to barge in and mention fondue forks. In fact, if I interrupt now I might get stabbed with one. Or get the whole pan of chocolate tipped over my head.

Death by chocolate is not what I want on the coroner's report, or my headstone.

I peel myself off the woodwork and take a tentative step back. I don't think I've made a noise, apart from my inward 'ouch'. It is cramp. It hurts.

There's no noise from inside the room. I take another step back.

Bugger. There's something under my foot. I freeze. Something is rubbing against my leg. Oh shit, I've been discovered, Poppy has come to find me.

My finger is on my lips as I glance down.

Angry glowing amber eyes stare back. It is not Poppy, it's the cat.

I'm standing on its tail. It's the only creature here that's enjoying Christmas less than Will.

For a split second we stare at each other and any second now it's going to yowl or jump at me.

I'm not quite sure how fast cats can move, but I'm pretty sure I match the speed, as Chloe dives one way and I sprint off in the other direction, crashing into the kitchen and sliding across the floor out of breath.

I say sprint. What I mean is do a reasonable imitation of somebody in a three-legged race, attached to an invisible partner. My calf has cramped up in spectacular style. I need to lie down. And stamp. And rub.

I limp to a stop in front of the oven.

'Hey there! Lost?' It's Ed. He's followed me. He knows.

He's humming softly, then winks. 'You'll have to excuse him, he's got issues. I wind him up, but I know the score.'

'Sorry? Just looking for forks! Fondue forks!' I fling open the nearest cupboard, which happens to be the oven door.

Ed softly shuts it, puts his hands on my shoulders and spins me round, then opens the drawer in front of me. 'Forks.'

'Thanks.'

'I'll see you tomorrow morning after breakfast, shall I?'

'Sorry?'

'We're shifting logs?'

'Oh yes, sure.'

'Then I'll give you that lesson, shall I?'

He winks again. His eyes are all twinkly and friendly.

I am all hot and bothered, despite the fact that I've just opened the door to the walk-in freezer, instead of the dining room.

Ignoring the freezer incident though, what exactly have I walked into?

Two brothers at war, with lawsuits hanging over their heads and a do-gooding visitor (me) that one of them (Will) hates, doesn't exactly make for a Happy Christmas, does it?

I think happy-go-lucky Ed might have set off a ticking time bomb that is set to blow this place into smithereens.

He's cute, but I think he might well be totally irresponsible. Nice and cute doesn't cut the ice when it comes to running a business, not when it's coupled with big-spender and fun-lover.

Poor Will. The man is so up to his eyes in stress it's no wonder he's so grumpy. It's no wonder he thinks I'm an interfering busybody. It's no wonder he is half hoping I'll be the final nail in the coffin. It would make life so much easier for him.

But not better. Better will be when we've got this place sorted. And that's just what I'm going to do. And then he can go back to his beach if he still wants. Though that would be a bit sad. But who am I to speak? I'll be back off to the UK.

As there is not a lot I can do, right now, apart from rushing in and telling him I understand, but then I'd have to explain why I was loitering outside the door, listening to a private conversation. Which is unprofessional. I make do with grabbing fondue forks and heading back to the dining room. Chocolate might not solve the problem, but it's the quickest route to happiness right now.

Chapter 14

I now understand Will's raised eyebrow. The one that shot up when I said I'd get Ed to help me stack the logs.

Ed is keener on burying me in the snow than stacking logs.

He's also just cornered me in the log store, and if I'm not careful I'm going to get completely distracted.

'Get off me, you idiot. Logs!'

'My God, you're boring for such a fun-loving girl.'

'It's for Will.'

Ed groans, and steps away. 'Eurgh, for Will.'

'And for you. You're in this together, aren't you?'

He doesn't answer the question. 'I'll do it on one condition.'

'Which is?'

'You come snowboarding. Today. Now. I'll show you what fun really is.'

I try not to groan.

There is no doubt at all in my mind that he can show me what fun is. Whether it has anything to do with snowboarding is another matter. A few days ago I'd have jumped at the chance, but now it just seems wrong. Will is tearing his hair out, and all Ed wants to do is tear the slopes up.

'It's wicked, you'll enjoy it, and you promised.' He's giving me his spaniel-eyes look.

I did, but that was before I understood what was going on here. 'I don't think—' I might have to learn how to barter. That could work. I need to turn this round in my favour.

'I'll look after you, I won't let you fall.' He grabs me round the waist then, and looks straight into my eyes. It's nice to be held, it's nice to be flirted with. Everybody deserves a bit of light relief, even if this is work. But only after he's done what he needs to do. It can be his reward. Work hard, play hard has always been a good way to live I've found.

'Youuuuuuu!'

He's shoved snow right down my back and made a run for it. 'You bugger!' I do what probably looks like a rain dance, which just shakes the ice downwards. Logical, eh? So I do what any normal person would do, a handstand against the log shed.

'Going well, is it?'

'Shit.' My arms give way and I'm in a heap at his feet. 'Will!' Oh God, why does the man always appear at the worst moments? 'We're doing—'

He hauls me unceremoniously to my feet then dusts me down, so I do a hop and skip to one side to stop him, because being belted like you're a rug full of dust hung on a line is not good. Now he'll think I'm as big a shirker as Ed, and that I don't give a damn about the resort really.

'Ouch! Bugger! Stop it!' Sugar, what is it with slippery snow stuff? I'm heading earthwards again, and he catches me by my elbow and kind of manoeuvres me upright like I'd pull the sail up on my windsurfer. Then props me up against the shed. And holds me there.

'Stop what? Hauling you out of the snow?'

'Beating me to buggery!'

The eyebrow is up, and if there was any snow left between my layers I can guarantee I've melted it now. It's not just my face that's burning up.

'There's a message from somebody called Callum at reception.' His voice has that over-casual edge to it.

'What? He's here! Hell, bugger, I mean . . . How?'

'A message, not him.' Nope, he's not casual, he's mildly annoyed. I am obviously very annoying.

'Oh, right.' Why does he find me so irritating? 'You didn't need to come and tell—'

'I didn't. I came to tell Ed that he's got a client on the ski slopes at three.'

'Aha! Great!' This is good. This means he won't have time to take me snowboarding.

'Really?' Will is now looking totally perplexed. 'Can't wait to get rid of him already? You're smarter than I—'

'Aww, Sarah, I can't believe you want to get rid of me!' Ed is giving me his hang-dog look. It's impressive, one up on the previous spaniel-eyes.

'I don't, I'm not.' I don't know which brother to talk to first. 'What do you mean smarter than you thought? You cheeky—'

'I think the pair of you need to get cracking. Moving this stuff was your idea, remember.'

Ed has somehow managed to wrap his arm round my waist possessively, Will has gone off in a huff, and I have a message from Callum. Why? I suppose it could be worse – he could actually be in reception. Although that could be better. This place is seriously hard work with these brothers. One is hard to keep at arm's length, and the other would rather have an ocean between us.

'I don't suppose you can get gladioli round here, can you?' I try to wriggle away from Ed without it being too obvious.

Ed shakes his head and laughs. 'You are one funny chick.'

'Chick? Chick? Who says chick these days?'

'I do.' He makes a grab, and before I can stop him he's thrown me over his shoulder and is striding towards his own cabin. 'Come on, forget shifting logs, we're going snowboarding. I can't wait to get my hands on that body of yours – in a purely professional capacity, of course.'

'Stop, put me down.' I try kicking and pounding on his back, but he just laughs. 'We need to stack logs.'

'Chill, babe, let's get shreddin' the gnar.'

'What?' I think being upside down is affecting my hearing, or it could be the dreaded brain-freeze. After all, my head is closer to the snow than I'm entirely comfortable with. Although the very warm hand (yes, I can feel it burning through my many layers – princess and the pea scenario happening over here) is reassuring. And distracting.

'Snowboarding.' Ed expertly dumps me (on my feet) in front of him. We are nose to nose. It's not at all like the nose to nose situation with Will, but it's nice. Friendly. I'm not frightened of him biting it off or making a run for it. 'We'll have you tearin' it up in no time.'

'Can you speak English, please?'

He grins. His eyes are blue, but a totally different blue to Will's. I'm going to have to stop this comparison to Will nonsense. It's too weird.

He pulls my hat off and ruffles my hair.

'Let's get you kitted out, lady, and have some real fun.'

'And the logs?' I fold my arms and give him what Sam calls my schoolteacher look.

'We'll do that when we get back.'

'Shouldn't you say "if we get back"? What if I break?'

'You'll be fine with me, I've got you.' And he has. Literally. Having his hands on my waist is nice and warm and reassuring. And a little bit sexy. Sam was right; I did think his photo on the website was sexy – I'd just been confused because of his antsy attitude. But that issue has been sorted. He was two people. Well, the photo was one person, him, and the attitude was somebody totally different, Will.

Sugar. Will is back in my head again. I think I'm getting a bit obsessed and need to stop.

'Good.' I might have been slightly more enthusiastic than I meant to be, in my bid to oust big brother from my brain.

'I think I'll get my hair streaked blue. It's cool.' His dimples are totally gorgeous. 'We can be the Blues Brothers, sisters, sister and brother. Whatever.'

I think the funny sensation in my tummy is very bad nerves.

'We will sort the logs as soon as we get back, though? You have got time before your lesson?'

He nods.

'Say it.' There is no way I can stack all that wood on my own, and I promised Will I'd do it. No way am I going to shirk at the first obstacle. I need him. 'Say you promise to do it when we get back.'

Ed rolls his eyes, still grinning, so I'm not quite sure if I trust him or not. His eyes are positively twinkling. Another time, another place I'd actually be more than happy to spend a little bit of time in his company, he's my perfect have-fun-no-strings kind of guy.

'I promise. God, I hope you're not going to end up as boring as my big brother. Now come on, a deal's a deal, we're going snowboarding!'

There is no way out. He's going to make me snowboard, and joking isn't helping me forget. Nor is thinking about Will.

***

'This is easy! I don't know what all the fuss is about!' I am standing upright, and have managed to move, turn and stop! Ed has been very attentive, and hardly taken his hands off me, but I've still managed it. Any second now I'll be able to tell him to let go. I can't wait to tell Will I mastered the slopes in one easy lesson (as well as stacked logs)!

'You're doing great. Ready for the nursery slope now?' Ed is grinning; he grins a lot, all lovely and dimply.

'What do you mean? This *is* the nursery slope!'

'Nooo, this is the flat bit at the bottom. That,' he points, 'is the slope.'

'You're kidding me?' Oh my God, it is all sloped. Properly sloped. And steep. 'Oh.' I try and retain the smile on my face, but the rest of me is in panic mode.

Which Ed ignores.

'We could just stay on the flat bit at the bottom?'

'Rubbish! Come on, you're ready for the next stage, you'll walk it! Even five-year olds can snowboard. It's as simple as standing on a tea tray.' He does a wobbly impression of somebody on a tea tray – his arms outstretched. I am not convinced. He doesn't give me any choice, though. I have decided he is not cute and lovely.

Obviously, I'm not five, and not in the habit of standing on tea trays. Especially if they're tiny, have no edges and are hurtling over polished ice faster than one of those thingamabobs at the winter Olympics. You know, bobsleighs. I mean, why would anybody in their right minds want to do that? It's a bit like being stuffed in a very large bullet; I'm just hoping that I don't explode on impact.

Actually no, this isn't so much bobsleigh (which is it least enclosed) as feeling like I'm one of those curling stones hurtling towards some distant target, which I might or might not hit.

So that explains why I'm spending more time screaming, or face-planting than a toddler who has just discovered he has legs. I'm better suited to sleigh rides.

Ed, however, thinks it's hilarious. If his dimples dimple any more he'll have craters in his face. He can't be in his right mind. I am beginning to side with Will, who might be stuffy, boring and grumpy, but at least he's not lost his marbles. He doesn't seem to have any interest in snow at all, apart from working out how to keep it out of his public areas, so to speak.

'You're doing fine, just er, stand up a bit.'

Stand up? Is he kidding? At least in a semi-foetal position I'm nearer to the ground.

'Look where you're going.'

'I *am* looking where I'm going – straight into that pile of slush.'

He laughs. 'Where you want to go, not think you'll go.'

'Oh, huh, yeah.'

'You'll go where you look. Bit like horse-riding.'

'I don't do that, either.'

'What do you do?'

'Surfing.'

'Well, this should be a—'

'Piece of piss?'

'Exactly. Waves move, this stuff doesn't.'

'Actually, you're wrong there – it does if you land in it.'

'Oh Sarah. I love you!' From any other man, this could be a frightening statement, but when Ed says it, and wraps me in a bear hug, it's different.

He just did it to some she-devil who snowboarded down the slope, skidded to a halt only millimetres from his nose, and kissed him before sliding away backwards. Show-off. I hate show-offs. I think it might have been Bianca, the advocaat lady.

'You're a tart.'

'I am indeed.' He is grinning, looking very pleased with himself. 'Now the golden boy has shifted his arse off the slopes, I get all the attention to myself.'

'Golden boy?' I'm happy to chat; it means I don't have to balance on a tray and try and look happy at the same time. In fact, maybe we should sit down and chat properly. Maybe this golden boy could help me out.

'Foook! Out of the way, loser!'

Something hard hits my bum at high speed and I spin round Ed, who I'm hanging on to for dear life. It is a reflex action. I don't want to be swept away down the slope. Something is clutching my knees, and as I complete my full circle it lets go.

A hobbit flies past, whooping as though this whole thing is fun.

Ed is chortling.

I'm still moving, propelled onwards by the force of the departing little person. Then I slowly slide down him. If I was doing a pole dismount, or some kind of slithery ice-dancing move, I'd get a ten.

He looks down at me, the heap at his feet.

'Good on you, you stayed on your feet, er, most of the time.'

'I didn't have any choice! That, that, that thing had me in an ironman grip.'

'She's seven years old.'

'Not a hobbit?'

'A kid, I gave her her first lesson yesterday. Fearless.'

'You just said that as though it was a good thing! I need to get out of here before she turns eight and amputates me at the knees.'

'At least she wasn't going fast, it's a nursery slope.'

'Feels bloody fast to me.' I'm not sure seven-year-olds should be on the same slope as me (my problem) and shouldn't be yelling fook (her parents' problem). 'So, who's this golden boy?'

He raises an eyebrow in a 'don't you know' kind of way. 'Big brother, of course.'

'Will?' Maybe he has another big brother. I didn't have Will down as gold, or silver, or bronze.

'The same.'

'But he doesn't like the snow, does he? Why doesn't he ski? He's scared?'

'Scared that the hero worship will have gone, more like, now he can't do the tricks he could. Look, can we go back to talking about me?'

Tricks? Hero worship? I don't want to talk about Ed, I want to know more about this side of Will that I had no idea about. If he isn't scared of snow, why does he hide away inside when he's got all this on the doorstep?

'Hell-o?' He stretches the word out and does a funny dance.

'Idiot.' He's a complete attention-seeker (unlike some-body else I know), but I can't help but grin back.

I throw snow at him. He dodges and throws some back, and before I know it I've been expertly rolled down the slope and we're in a tangle at the bottom. I quite like rolling and tangling, much easier than tea-tray stuff. Where you just look silly and incompetent. I like to be able to do things. I'm not into being pathetic.

He looms over me. Staring at me with those clear eyes of his.

'To be brutally honest, you're rubbish at this, aren't you, Ms Hall?'

'Totally.'

'I bet après-ski is much more your style. Come on, let me show you some real Canadian hospitality.' He's on his feet and whisking me up while I'm still wondering if this is a good idea.

***

There are two messages at reception when we get back. One for me, and one for Ed.

Hi sexy legs, (this is the one for me), *on my way to Bali with Daz for some Chrimbo surfing. Thought I better wish you a Happy Christmas now, in case reception crap when we get there. Miss you, my little snuggle monster Smurf. C xxx*

'Snuggle monster Smurf?' Says a voice in my ear.

'Hey, this is private. You better show me yours, now you've seen mine.' I give Ed a shove and hide my hurt with indignation. I don't regret splitting with Callum, I know it was never going to work, and it was best to do it now. But I do miss him. And surfing in Bali sounds so much more 'me' than sliding down slopes on a snowboard. It would be nice to think I could go home and we could just be mates. Nice. But maybe not possible. Or fair.

'Mine's much more soppy.'

He hands over the slip of paper, a handwritten note in sharp, spiky writing. It is not soppy.

Had to go into town. Don't forget to check supplies at the Halfway Cabin and the snow conditions once you've stacked the logs. W.

'W?'

'Big brother. Shit, I forgot about the supplies. Wanna come?'

'Come where? And what about the logs?'

'We'll do the logs when we get back. It's a cabin in the mountains where we keep spare kit and stuff tin case of emergencies, and we use it in the summer for long expeditions.' He grins, a very naughty grin. 'Very secluded and cosy. Fancy a mini excursion?'

'Yeah, right, and the only way to get there is on skis or snowboards?'

'Aha, and that is where you are wrong, Smurfy legs. Come this way, your chariot awaits.'

It's hard to say no, and I am quite intrigued about the whole chariot thing, and okay I admit it, the cosy thing. It might give me some ideas for cosying up the other cabins.

He screws up the note, and expertly throws it into the wastepaper basket, then grabs my hand and heads off outside. Past the log store (which unfortunately isn't stacked with logs yet). Past the kennels (which looks cold, so its handy I got a cabin and didn't insist on staying there) and to a store shed.

'Well, is this more your style my little Smurf?'

'I'm not your Smurf. Oh wow!' It is big, it is black, it is gleaming and shiny. 'That is so cool! Can I drive? Please?'

'Have you ever driven a snowmobile?' He dangles the keys, just out of reach, I resist the urge to childishly grab them. Although Ed does bring out my childish side. Unlike Will. I still haven't decided what side he brings out.

'Never! It can't be much different to riding a motorbike, can it?'

'And you've done that before?'

'Are you kidding? Aunt Lynn got me a moped when I was sixteen, then a bike as soon as I was old enough.'

'Aunt Lynn sounds cool.'

'Totally. Keys?'

'You're like a kid on Christmas morning.'

'This is way better than Christmas morning.' I grin. I can't help it. 'Nothing can beat a big throbbing beast between your legs, can it?' Ed raises an eyebrow. 'Sorry, did I say that out loud?'

He's laughing as he hands me a helmet and gloves, but I don't care. 'We'll take it easy on the track first, then head uphill, maybe even go on the lake if we've got time.'

***

The cabin is the perfect hideaway. It's also cosy, as in snug, as in not-enough-room-to-swing-a-cat without the RSPCA getting cross. And it's hard to avoid being up close to the gorgeous Ed.

'Well, do you like it?'

I'm not sure if he's talking about the cabin, or the way his hand is stroking down my spine and over my bum in long steady strokes that are making me go all goose-bumpy. I swallow hard. 'Love it.' I do. On both counts. Specially the squeezy bit which just brought an involuntary 'oo' to my lips.

We're hip to hip, and practically nose to nose and he really is the most gorgeous guy I've been this close to for a long time. My heart is hammering, and my body is humming with anticipation as he leans in even closer.

184

He's my kind of guy. He is. I think I'm trying to convince myself here. No strings, no expectations, just fun.

'The cabin, I love it.' Why did I need to qualify that?

'You're not so bad yourself.' He's grinning, but also studying my mouth intently. I bet he's a great lover. Fun, considerate, experimental. A shiver runs down my spine, my mouth has gone all dry with expectation, and my stomach is hollowing in anticipation of his kiss. He's so close now, I can feel the heat of his body. Smell the faint ting of aftershave. Feel his capable hands caressing my body.

I close my eyes.

'No.' It comes out as an indignant squeak. Some part of my brain trying to tell my vocal chords what to say. But they don't want to say no, my body is well up for this. It needs this. To be wanted. To want back.

'No?'

I open one eye. His lips stop a few millimetres short of their target. His warm breath fans my mouth. I swallow hard. What's wrong with me? No? I lick my dry lips, and his gaze fixes on my mouth again.

'Or yes?'

'No, as in no, no, not yes.' I must be mad. He's totally cute and fanciable, and I've just said no to a snog and a wonderful roll on the cosy fur rug. Although it would not have involved total abandon, as elbows and knees would have had to be contained to avoid accidents. It really is that 'cosy' in here.

Gawd, this is odd and embarrassing.

'I got this wrong, didn't I?' Ed grins, not letting go, totally cool with it. Unlike me. I wriggle a bit. I'm confused. He didn't get it wrong, five minutes ago I would have said some tonsil action with this hot and hunky guy was just what I needed. 'Your Callum must be special.'

I nod. This is the point when I should say he's not my Callum now, and he is special, but not in that way. But if I say that, how do I explain the 'no'? I can't even explain it to myself. Something just doesn't feel right and, for once in my life, I don't want to dive in to something, even if it is string-free. Maybe it's easier to stick with the Callum excuse?

'Don't panic. It's cool, come back next year when you've ditched him, eh?' His eyes are twinkling, but his hands have dropped to his side, and although he's still grinning, it's game over. 'Come on then, Smurfette, we better get back and stack those logs.'

We get back, and this time he drives. I don't get to go on the lake and it's not as exhilarating, it doesn't make me yell or whoop. I just press myself against his back.

Maybe I'm depressed, or the cold is affecting my brain. Or, which is totally scary, maybe this means I'm growing up.

Or I've hit a very early menopause. You can go off sex for a bit, can't you? Aunt Lynn called it the solo years, she said that if *she* couldn't make her mind up what she wanted, a man wouldn't have stood a chance. And who wants to sleep with a woman who makes a tropical rainforest feel dry, and might kill you afterwards if you want sex?

Oh God, no. I'm not ready for any of that.

What if I've used up my quota of sexy hormones and there aren't any left? I am never again going to experience lust, the total need to jump on a man and forget the rest of the world exists.

Or, and I close my eyes at this one, maybe it's because I feel guilty. I promised Will I'd help him out today, I promised I'd do stuff, and I've wasted a good part of the day gallivanting about with his very cute, but very lazy and irresponsible brother.

Will is trying his hardest to sort this place out, and the person who is responsible for the mess is the one who doesn't seem to care.

I can't just say yes all the time to everything and everybody. Saying yes can be ace, and fun, but why bother keep saying it to the wrong people, the wrong things?

Hell. I think I need hot chocolate. Lots of it.

Chapter 15

This place is going to kill me. I've got used to the cold, and I'm actually falling in love with the snow (as long as I can handle it at my own speed, or on a snowmobile). When the sun is on it in the day and it's all shiny and sparkly and verging on stark in a bright-light kind of way. But in the evening there's a magical shimmer. It's hard to describe, but in the quiet stillness, with clean, dry, ice-cold air biting at my cheeks, it's incredible. I hold my breath unconsciously, as though my body is trying to tap into the moment.

This is what Will was trying to explain to me; this is the amazing, beautiful place he sees, without all the baubles and tinsel, the glitter and man-made magic. And now I'm seeing it for myself.

I've never known anywhere so totally suspended in time, and it wraps itself around me, curling deep inside me and bringing a peace, an equality I didn't know existed. In this instance I can like, well not exactly like, more accept, myself. I'm good enough, as good as I need to be. I'm not a little girl who nobody loved. I don't have to try and guess which part of me makes people leave: here I can be whoever I really want to be.

There's no intrusion, nothing else exists, which is heavy stuff for a girl who surrounds herself with noise and doing.

There's just me and the world.

I never normally stop. I never let myself experience nothingness. Because if I do then I'll start thinking. I'll leave space for the memories I don't want, for the questions that I long ago squashed down and blocked out.

Out here though it seems kind of okay. Natural. I've wrapped myself up warm and come out in search of the place that I've avoided so far since I've been here. I've come in search of the huskies, Rosie. Well, to be more precise, the kennels. Bear Cabin.

My heart aches, a steady heaviness in my chest that's in tune with the rest of my tired body. Maybe that's why I want to do it right now. I'm one big blob of achiness. My arms are heavy from lugging about logs this morning, and then again after Ed had gone to do his three o'clock lesson. My legs are wobbly from trying to balance on that bloody board. Ed had offered a steaming bath and massage oils. He'd said it with a definite glimmer of hopefulness. But I'd said no. Again.

I'd looked at him, and ached for my normal escape, but a tiny, bloody, obstinate, *empty* bit inside my heart had told me no. At the time, I didn't know why I said 'no' in the halfway cabin, but on the journey back it hit me.

I don't need to play games with Ed. I have got people who love me, people who mean a lot to me. Even if they aren't here.

It's not about playing hard to get, or not wanting. And it's not just guilt about letting Will down. It's more complicated, and I don't think I've got my head round it yet. But maybe coming here *without* the people I love, is making me realise that sometimes just having me is enough. Being alone doesn't have to mean lonely. It doesn't have to mean nobody wants me. It doesn't mean I'm not good enough to play.

I've always grabbed what fun I can; it's what has made me, me. But maybe it hasn't. Maybe it's stopped me being the real, total, me.

So, with profound thoughts in my head, I'd added a very un-profound stripey bobble hat with a very big snowball-sized bobble, and another layer, and trudged round here to the spot I'd seen when we'd restacked the logs. The place I'd very deliberately turned my back on.

A giant bear-like dog wanders over, sniffing the air.

I can feel her warmth even though we're not touching, and I long to wrap my arms round her. Bury my face in her fur, feel the steady breathing, the heartbeat of another that tells me I'm not completely alone.

She wags her tail, as though she understands.

'You can go in if you like, she won't bite. She likes company.' The soft male voice makes me jump, and I realise why she was wagging. She wasn't pleased to see me. She was pleased to see him.

Will.

'I thought snow was supposed to be crunchy? It stops murderers creeping up unannounced, and committing murder!'

'Wrong type of snow.' He grins, slightly self-consciously. 'Come on.' He unlatches the gate. 'It's warmer in here, but you still get to see the stars.'

The moment we get in there, the dog that came to see me reaches up and licks my cheek. And I'm right back to being a little girl again, with the husky that followed me round – the dog that I hadn't been allowed to have at home. I close my eyes and for a moment it feels so real, the dog licking me until I giggled, nudging me with her big, wet nose for attention, tickling my cheek with her fur. Dad had stroked her with his big, strong hands until she'd rolled over onto her back, begging for tummy-rubs and Mum had laughed with me.

He'd laughed, his big, rumbling laugh filling the cabin. Here, on this very spot. A laugh I'd completely blocked out of my mind until now.

Rosie's tongue is warm and I suddenly realise she is licking away the tears I hadn't even known were there.

'I wasn't checking up on you.' Will shrugs, looking awkward, not really meeting my eye. I bet crying girls aren't his thing. Though they're not mine, either. I want to tell him it's the cold air that's made my eyes smart and water.

But I don't. 'I always come and check the dogs are okay before I go to bed.' He sits down in the straw, stretching his impossibly long legs in front of him, and one of the dogs immediately settles its head in his lap.

'It's me that should apologise, and I wasn't snooping . . .'

'I know.' The voice is velvet soft. As gentle as the hand he's using to stroke the dogs ear. The first time I've heard him speak without an angry or frustrated edge. 'We all need our down time now and again, eh? I come here. Dogs understand.' He nods towards the dog that is now sitting in front of me. 'That's the infamous Rosie. She likes a hug as much as the next person.'

This is so not me, the dampness of tears still on my face, sitting in a dog kennel with a giant furball trying to lick my face off.

Me is working in the travel agency, joking with Sam, selling exotic dreams and Ibiza raves. Wearing funny T-shirts, not so many layers I'm the size of a polar bear.

'We all need a hug at some point.' His words are soft enough to let me ignore them if I want to, and he's gazing at me steadily, which is slightly harder to ignore. So I wrap one arm round the giant woolly dog that is Rosie, and hold my other hand out for her to sniff. She sniffs, then settles in, thumping her head down on my knee and stretching out on one side, lifting her leg slightly. Inviting me to stroke the huge, soft tummy.

'I came here quite a lot after the accident because the dogs just accepted me as I was.'

'Oh.' I don't know what else to say. 'Is that what caused the, er, limp?'

'You noticed.' He gives a wry smile. I think he's trying to lighten the atmosphere. 'Yeah. Had a bit of a wipeout.'

'Wipeout?'

'Crash.'

'Car . . . ?'

'No.' He smiles. Gently. Most of his attention on the dog, the occasional glance my way. He inclines his head towards the mountains that rear up at the back of the resort. 'Snow.'

'But I didn't think you liked snow!' I blurt it out before I can stop myself. Shit. Now he'll know I've been eaves-dropping. How else would I know?

'Not now I can't snowboard, no, it kind of put me off.'

Oh God, he's scared. He's scared of the ice and snow, just like I am. That's why he had a fit at Ed about clearing the paths. 'That must be terrible.' It comes out a bit squeaky, but I'm genuinely sorry.

It explains so much.

One day he's happy messing about like Ed, the next he's got a gammy leg and daren't try it again. 'I'm sorry. Have you tried just going on the baby—' He's kind of glaring at me now, except I think he's actually trying not to laugh. 'I mean nursery bit, slope. You know, build up the confidence again?'

'It's not about confidence, more about being capable. The leg just won't take it.'

He's gone back to looking at the dog. Okay, I get it. Big

strong he-man who chops wood and lights fires, he's not going to say he daren't even venture out with Poppy and her mates, is he?

'I'm not so keen on snow, either.'

'Really?' I'm getting used to that dry edge in his tone. It's kind of nice. Goose bumpy. 'I'd never have guessed.'

'Stop laughing at me! I bet I could beat you on the surf any day.'

'I might hold you to that, though you're probably right. So.' He pauses. 'Bear Cabin?'

'It was where we stayed last time I came, with Aunt Lynn – she's the one who owns the travel agency.' I look around. 'No straw on the floor last time I was here.'

'Ah.'

'And . . .' I take a deep breath, my face buried in Rosie's fur. She's warm, smells all doggy and lovely. Safe. 'I came with my parents.' Rosie wriggles free of my grasp, but she doesn't go like I expect her to. Doesn't abandon me. Instead she moves closer, licks my chin. 'It was the last time I saw them.'

Will has gone pale under his tan. I watch as his Adam's apple bounces convulsively. 'Ski-ing accident? Avalanche?'

'Oh no, no. They just left.'

'Left?'

'Walked out. I hardly knew Aunt Lynn; she was my mum's sister and she came here hoping to change their mind, but it didn't work.' I gaze into the dog's brown, almond-shaped eyes, and Rosie gazes back. It's easier talking to a dog. Maybe I need to get a dog when I'm home. A hell of a lot cheaper than a therapist and guaranteed to be nonjudgemental. 'They didn't want kids, I guess. It messed up their lifestyle. When I was tiny and portable it was fine, but I was getting to the age where I needed nursery school, friends.' Rosie nudges my hand, and I realise my fingers have stilled. I go back to stroking her, and she drops her head, resting her chin, but still gazing up at me.

'And you've never tried to find them?' He lets the question hang in the air.

'It's complicated.' I can't share any more right now. If it had just been me and the dog, maybe.

I half expect him to push it. But he doesn't.

'I'm sorry we knocked the cabin down.' He sounds like he really is. 'There was a fire and—'

'I'm not sorry. It's better like this.' To come back to the place just as it used to be would have been wrong. And a dramatic change like this is far easier to cope with than if it had been basically the same. It's moved on, like I should have done. 'Things change.' I wriggle. Suddenly shivering.

'You're cold. We should get back.' Will struggles to his feet, then holds a hand out. I take it. It's strong and lean. Capable. He hauls me to my feet effortlessly and we stand there a few feet apart slightly awkwardly until Rosie nudges me in the back of the knee and I lurch forward.

'Stop it, Rosie. You're a bugger. She's after treats.' I'm caught and bounced back on to my feet before I can even reach out and touch him.

Ah, so not some cupid dog trying to throw us together. It all comes down to food.

'I better let you lock up, check them over. I'll, er, get back to—'

'Hang on. I'll walk you. I know you don't like ice.'

'Really, am I that easy to read?'

He laughs, a blood-warming, full-hearted chuckle that seems to come from deep inside his chest. 'You're funny.'

'As well as a pain in the arse and scared of the snow?'

'Yeah, total pain in the butt.' He's still smiling, but his gaze has stilled. 'You had a good time snowboarding with Ed, though?'

'Truth? Terrible. Horrendous, worst nightmare e-vah! You ever seen a cat chasing fish on a frozen pond? That was me.' I feel on more of an even keel now I'm on my feet, now we're talking about something else. But I'm glad I came here tonight; maybe I really am ready to move on.

'Interesting comparison.'

He's got nice white teeth. I like good teeth. When I do move on properly, somebody like Will might be a good bet.

'I only say that,' I put on my haughty tone, 'because cats are normally graceful and agile. I am a superior streamlined feline under all this clobber.'

'I bet you are.'

The steel blue of his eyes has softened in this light. He's not looking stern and serious tonight, he's more like the huskies that are piled around us. Watchful, patient. All-seeing. Which sends a shiver down my spine.

197

'I could take you out with the dogs if you want, some-time? Safer than a snowboard.'

'In a sled?'

'Yep, you can't come to Canada and not go dogsledding. You'll like it.'

'I will?'

He nods, and I believe him. 'Come on.'

With him at my side I don't mind the slippery path as much. When I slide he's there, a steadying force at my elbow, a light but strong touch in the centre of my back.

You know when people describe their partners as their 'rock'? Yeah, it's that. He's rock-like. Solid. But obviously not my partner. I guess Will is one of those guys who takes his responsibilities seriously. Which is why he's a bit grumpy most of the time. But I think he's kind. Considerate.

Complicated. Like Aunt Lynn suggested.

I guess that's why he's here, when he doesn't really want to be. Trudging through the snow that scares him, propping up the brother who isn't very good at managing money.

But he probably needs to lighten up a bit every now and then.

I'm ultra-aware of his body next to mine, of the slightest hitch in the rhythm of his steps, and wonder if there's ever been a Mrs Will. If there is, or has been, she's probably very serious, just like him. Steady. Clever. Not at all like me.

She can probably ski like a demon and looks totes amazing swaddled in a puffa jacket.

'Sarah?'

'Yes?' I'm doing the holding breath thing again and leaning in, I can't help myself. He's looking at me, and I'm thinking that maybe a kiss wouldn't harm. It's his eyes. They've not got that playful, black-eyed lust thing going on, but they're so intense. So, so . . . well, so *honest*.

Maybe we both need something after all that intensity. A soft brush of our lips. My hand goes up to my mouth automatically, as though I can already feel his touch. A goodnight kiss, that's all I need.

'Feel free to go down to the kennels any time, if you feel you, er, want time out. The dogs know you now, they'll be fine.'

'Good, er, thanks.' His hand is still resting lightly on my arm. His lips look soft, inviting.

'And we can go sledding tomorrow if the weather's fine. If you want to, of course.'

'Great. Sounds fab.' He smells of coffee, of the outdoors.

'Right, then.'

That had a kind of finality to it. A 'bye, see you later'. He's not going to kiss me. And I'm right in his face. This is awkward. What do I do now to avoid unwelcome lip action?

I do a kind of sidewards tilt and step at the same time, trying to casually put some space between us – and forget all about the ice. Mistake. Word of advice – don't throw all your weight one way, cos sure as eggs is eggs your feet will go the other.

Mine do, anyway. 'Fuggering hell!' I grab his sleeve, he

grabs and gets a bunch of jacket that's been innocently nesting between my boobs. We're nose to nose. Closer than before. I could kiss him anyway. I can't not. Not when he's looking at me like that.

I've not even puckered up, and I reckon it's nostril contact at best, or his eyelashes flutter against mine briefly cos it's like an alarm has gone off inside and he jerks me upright, turns his head like he's been burnt, narrowly avoiding giving me friction burn from his stubble, and we're a good foot apart before I can blink. Wow! This is one dude who is determined to avoid contact sport at all costs.

'You need to get in, you'll get cold standing around.' It's gruff, but verging on friendly.

I swallow hard, my head still trying to work out what just happened. 'True. I'll sort the Christmas tree tomorrow, shall I?'

I notice he's put another twelve inches or so between us; even a lizard-tongued alien couldn't cope with this kind of distance. To be honest, I don't know what I was thinking. What *was* I thinking? Honestly, this is sad, I'm not some kind of sex maniac. It was just a moment. An intense, good-job-it-didn't-happen moment. I don't even much like the man. He's so not my type it's unreal.

I've just spent half the evening telling myself I don't need to say yes, and before I know it I'm in there before there's even an invite.

It must be that brain-freeze thing he mentioned. I've been out in the cold too long and short-circuited. Or my brain has expanded as it's frozen and is banging against my skull and needs an outlet. Or it could be the total hurrah! feeling cos I've just realised my well has not run dry, that lust has not deserted me, and I am not going to be dried up and old before my time. That's what it was. Relief.

'If it'll make you happy. If I'm not around, then Ed will show you where the decorations and stuff are.' Which I take it means he doesn't intend being around. So bang goes the dogsledding. Which could have been lovely. I'd definitely been warming to the dogsled idea. Dashing through the snow and all that. 'Goodnight, Sarah.'

The last notes of the song, which I've been on the verge of humming, grind to a halt. Die away for ever. The words 'One dog open sleigh' didn't work anyway.

'Night.'

And Will slips away into the night. Not even a peck on the cheek.

Phew, that was a lucky escape. If I'd have kissed him, how weird would that have been?

Chapter 16

'What the hell is that?' Will is staring at me like I've got two heads. Or maybe he just hasn't noticed my blue hair before. There's a lot of hat wearing goes on round here. I'm ultra-glad I got a pixie cut though, ear-warming it is not, but wearing cosy hats all the time gives you helmet-hair. Believe me, I know how bad this can be. I spent three months backpacking round Spain on a scooter. Neither my flat hair nor my numb bum has ever fully recovered.

'What?' Maybe he's just spotted the piece of sticky pancake that went missing at breakfast. I think I've started a love affair with maple syrup.

I might not be getting any man action, but I'm seriously making up for it on the chocolate and syrup front.

'That!' He's not staring at my hair, he's pointing just to the left of my ear.

Aha!

'That.' I smile triumphantly because it took a lot of doing and I am proud of my achievement, 'is a spreadsheet.'

'I can see that, but why have you just pinned it up in my office?'

I have an inkling that I may have overstepped the mark. That when he said, 'feel free to make suggestions' he didn't mean 'plan out my life'. It's just that although people often think I'm a bit flaky and disorganised (this isn't just me being paranoid, this is what several people have said.) which I am, I like a plan as far as work goes. Life equals no plan at all, suck it and see (literally sometimes). Work equals structure. I structure it to death.

And I realised as I worked my way down my initial list, that it just wasn't going to be enough. Ticking off the items on there was just the start; what we needed was a rolling plan.

'It's all about organisation.'

'And money.' He looks like he is fighting a losing battle not to fold his arms or push me out of his office.

'Yes, and money, but,' I'm not going to let him put a dampener on my plan, 'time management is the biggest prob if you haven't got any dosh, isn't it?'

He raises an eyebrow and sits down heavily.

'Can you groan a bit quieter please? And pretend to be interested. You know yourself that you can't get everything done. You said so.'

'I need coffee.'

'Will, I said I'd help you and I want to. Decorating Christmas trees is one thing, but if you think I'm just going to wander round aimlessly looking for stuff to do, then you've got it wrong.' This was the other thing I decided last night. Not having decent phone reception means I have to fill my head with other thoughts. Some good, some less good.

'I've got lots of things wrong lately.' He gives in and folds his arms. 'Go on then, Catwoman.'

He's not been spying on me and spotted my base layer, has he?

'Can I be Superwoman instead?'

'It was you that said you were an ice-skating cat the other night, and you're actually quite like Chloe.'

I wait. Slim? Poised? Elegant? I hope I don't have to wait much longer because my brain has moved on to cunning, detached . . .

'Strike first, ask questions later.'

Didn't see that one coming. Claw-ey. Hmm. 'I don't—'

'I like it.' His mouth is doing that quirk thing, and his voice has slowed. 'It's refreshing.'

'Stop teasing me! Who's being cat-like now? I know just what you're up to; you'll lull me into thinking you're taking this seriously, then pounce on my spreadsheet and rip it into shreds.'

'Oh, come on, Sarah, be fair. I want to get this place back on its feet as much as you do.'

'I doubt it.'

He ignores that. Luckily. 'But a spreadsheet? I thought girls hated spreadsheets, that it was a man thing. Though obviously not mine.'

'Obviously. But obviously you have spent time with the wrong kind of girls.'

'Well, we're on the same page for at least one thing, then.'

I decide not to ask about the girls. Though I am tempted. Very. But I am practicing my new self-control and concentrating on me. Not other people. 'You need to work out what you've got time to do, and I need to work out what I need to do to help. It's all about prioritisation.' I unpin the list and put it on his desk. 'It's no good you being up until three in the morning every night.'

'How do you know what time I'm up to?'

'I couldn't sleep and saw your light.'

'How do you know I didn't forget to turn it off?'

'You're trying to save money.'

'So you did this spreadsheet? Bit hypocritical on the working late thing, eh?' But he's smiling.

'I figured that if a spreadsheet wasn't boring enough to send me to sleep, then nothing would work.'

'I do appreciate this.' His finger touches my hand. Briefly. Maybe he didn't get enough hugs as a child? Although Ed more than makes up in the touchy-feely department. 'But don't stay awake on my account.'

It actually hurts a bit, which is strange. Why should I care that the man can't bear to touch me for more than a nanosecond? 'Don't flatter yourself. You're not that important Will Armstrong.' I don't know why I said that. It was a knee-jerk reaction. One, to stop him thinking I could possibly have any interest in him (as he obviously has zilch interest in me, or my spreadsheet skills), and two because no way do I want to start thinking about what is really going on in my head.

My parents. They seem to be sneaking into my head more and more often. Partly because I have an empty head, due to lack of phone app activity. And two, because I'm here. Ground zero.

He sits back in his chair and puts his feet on the desk.

'You won't be able to read it from there.'

'Tell me what it says then.'

'It's a rota, you, me and Ed.'

'Ed?'

'It's up to you to make sure he sticks to it.' That's telling him. 'Right, I've got log chopping.' I tap the relevant square.

A raised eyebrow again.

'How do you know how often we need to do that?'

'I counted how many we—'

'You counted the logs?'

'Well, I had to bloody stack them, so I knew where they were. I went and counted them.' It was a displacement activity, before I went to the kennels.

He makes a funny harrumph sound, which could be a stifled laugh, or incredulity. I don't care which. 'Honestly?'

'Well, how else would I know when you're going to run out?'

'Mmm, I always work on the theory that when it's only a quarter full it means I need to chop logs.'

'Huh. And what if you forgot to look?'

'How can I when I'm collecting the bloody things every day?'

'Well, it's not just you now, is it? Other people are getting them.'

'I knew that was a bad idea, letting people help themselves.'

'Which would you rather do, run out of logs quicker, or run out of clients?'

'Well, now you're asking . . .'

'Don't answer that. Anyway, I looked at how many cabins are occupied, and worked out roughly how many logs I've used, and—'

'Enough, stop woman, I believe you; I trust you've worked it out.'

'Then there's mucking out the dog kennels, cooking food,' I'm not sure they should be side by side on the list, 'cleaning the cabins, making up the fires, which,' I look at him, 'you have now got time to do.'

'Yes, ma'am.'

'And the welcome packs.'

'Welcome packs?'

'I'll come back to that in a bit – they've got the entertainment listed in them.'

'Entertainment? No way! If you think I'm acting DJ or running a kids camp you've got another think coming.'

'Oh, don't be daft, not that kind of stuff. That's more Ed's style. I was thinking you could run a yoga or step class, or Zumba. You'd look good in the right gear. Have you got a room with a big mirror? No? No probs, I'll work round that.'

I can tell he's not sure if I'm kidding or not.

'You can do a kick-pivot? Yeah, piece of piss for a fit guy like you.'

His mouth has dropped open.

'You'll need shorts.' I eye up his crotch. 'Or something with Lycra in, you know, that'll stretch. And a headband would look cute. You will totally rock that kind of look. We can spike up your hair with gel.' I spike my own up, though I do think he's smart enough to get the picture without a demonstration.

'You're having me on, aren't you?'

It's my turn to raise an eyebrow and lean on the table. 'Will, you do want to turn this place round, don't you?'

'You're winding me up! Tell me you are.'

'You're not telling me you don't like Zumba? Wow, it is just so awesome. I mean, the moves, the music – you can really do your thing. I can get something really hip and Christmassy and we can have bells and baubles.' I might be getting a little bit carried away. I definitely am when I prance round in a circle like a Morris man on speed.

He's looking seriously worried now.

'Here, I've got some music on my phone. Come on, come on, get up and we'll try some steps.'

He stands up. Bugger. He's called my bluff. But he's not going to out-Zumba me, I am the queen of hip-wiggling.

He ventures out from behind the desk. I'd forgotten how

big he is and I seem to be gawping up in admiration. Which I have to stop.

I put a track on and feel a bit like a pole dancer, or stripper. Any minute now and I'll be stripping the seven veils (or layers as they call them in this part of the world) off.

'Stand there.' I position him. Being businesslike and bossy helps. 'Now, get into the rhythm and do what I do.'

'Honestly?' But he does, and I'm already mesmerised. This guy has rhythm. The real deal. And snake hips.

'Ohhhh sugar . . .'

'Ohhhh sugar. I take it I sing along?'

'No shit, sugar. Shut up, arghh that was pain, I think I've strained my groin or something. Buggering hell. Stop, stop.'

I've never seen a man nearly collapse with laughter before. He's got his hands on his knees and his whole body is shaking. I almost forget the pain between my legs. If he'd not been wiggling so much this wouldn't have happened. I'd have been concentrating rather than trying to get into a groove I'm not fit enough for.

'So, I take it you're not doing the classes?' He's still laughing.

'I will be doing an inventory of your food supplies. While you do the classes.' I'm not sure I'll ever be able to walk again.

'Are you okay?'

'Sure.' I think, if I move very slowly, I will be able to

stand upright. Something deep in my groin is on fire in a totally unsexy way.

'Definitely? You wouldn't like something to put on that?'

I don't think he's offering to apply anything. So, no. 'I'm fine.'

'You aren't serious about me doing that? I don't think my bad knee would be up to it.'

I'd forgotten about his gammy leg. Though even with a bad leg I reckon he's better at strutting his stuff than me.

'Maybe. Well, nix the Zumba. But I do have activities planned.'

'Go on then, hit me with them.'

Ha! My strategy has worked; I might not be able to walk properly later, but he is listening. I have his full attention *and* dogsled rides, Father Christmas, and a quiz night will seem like a walk in the park after the horror of Zumba. He'll fall like a pin in a bowling alley. Result!

'Here.' I show him the list.

He doesn't fall.

'No.'

'What do you mean no?'

'No dogsledding. The team are too old now, with the exception of four dogs, and I'm not working them to death to amuse holidaymakers.'

'Nobody is saying—'

'They're not machines. They're animals, pets – you've seen them yourself. I'm just bringing Rosie back into work after she had the pups and I'm not rushing anything. Next year, maybe, but not now. Definitely not.'

'Okay, you don't have to keep saying it. Can you get hold of a reindeer? No? Little pony? Okay, that's a no then. Father Christmas, then.'

'I am not—'

'I was thinking of Ed. People like Ed; he's, you know . . .'

'And they don't like me?'

'Well, you're a bit . . .'

'A bit what?'

'Er, stand-offish? Nowty.'

'Nowty?'

'Moody?' I shrug, trying to soften the blow. 'I mean, I know you're under tons of pressure, and I'm sure you're not usually.'

'He is!' The loud voice makes me spin round. Not advisable in my fragile state.

'Bloody hell, you made me jump!'

'Oh, I'll catch you if you fall, darling.' Ed has his hands on my waist and has dropped a kiss on my cheek. It's a good job he didn't turn up ten minutes ago in the middle of Zumba.

'Sarah is planning our work schedules, so let's look at what you're supposed to be doing right now, Ed.'

Ed lets go as though he's discovered I'm on fire and stops nuzzling my cheek.

It's as if Will has found a magic off switch.

'No, no sorry, don't mean to be rude, just came to tell

you I'm off to take the Liddle kids onto the nursery slope. Be back in time for tea. Catch you both later!' I have never seen a man move so fast. Not even Will when he saved Poppy from the crashing Christmas tree. Ed is out of the door and down the corridor before I can even say what his next job is – and I do know them all off by heart. This spreadsheet is deeply ingrained.

'You told him about the schedule to get rid of him, didn't you?'

Will shrugs. 'I know you've fallen for his charms, Sarah—'

'I have not.'

'Everybody does, it's fine, People like him, he's not nowty.' He shoots my own words back at me and it feels horrible.

'I didn't mean . . .'

Will holds a hand up. 'It's fine, but just be warned, he doesn't like hard work. Ed likes to play, he likes to be on the snow, he likes to be wining and dining.'

'Are you warning me off?'

'Oh, don't be daft.'

'I'm quite a big girl now.' Even bigger than normal in my winter wear. We're both rocking the arms-folded, keep-off look.

'I can see that.' His tone is dry and I'm not sure if it's an insult or not. 'I'm trying to say he might not stick to a schedule.'

'Well, you'll have to make him, won't you?' I give him what I hope is my brightest smile. 'And for your information, I'm quite capable of looking after myself and making my own decisions about people.' God, one minute he's making me feel guilty, the next he's warning me off about jumping into bed with his brother. What does he think I am?

'I'll leave this with you, shall I? You should be putting welcome packs in Moon Cabin and Big Bear right now – oh, and don't forget to muster up some elves.'

'I know exactly who can do that.'

He's got a glint in his eye I don't like.

'I'm a guest, and an observer.'

'You're a member of staff, and spreadsheet assembler. If Santa's coming to town, then you're playing a part, however,' he pauses, 'small.'

'I don't know how Ed puts up with you.'

'And I'm not surprised Lynn decided to get you out of her hair for a bit.'

'Touché.' We stare at each other. Both shocked at what we've said. But it hurts. It bloody hurts. How dare he say she wants to get rid of me? How dare he say that the one person who truly loves me doesn't actually want to be with me.

'Her friend was dying. She had no choice.' I'm gritting my teeth so hard my jaw aches.

'Sorry. Look, I'm sorry, I shouldn't have said that. You just got under my skin.'

'Christ, you really are a miserable sod, aren't you? Ed was right, it's always somebody else's fault.'

'Sarah—'

'I've got things to do.'

'I'm sorry. Truly. Come out on the dogsled with me.'

'No.' I wipe my arm across my face.

'They need a run. Rosie needs to get back into work.'

'I've got work to do, so have you.'

'It'll wait.'

'I thought you were the conscientious one, trying to sort this mess out?'

'We all need time out sometimes. Please come with me?'

'I've got the tree to decorate.'

'Do the tree tomorrow. It's perfect sledding weather, and it's due to change soon. If we get a blizzard we'll be stuck inside. It's fun.'

'No.'

'I dare you.'

Bugger, how did he know I can't resist a dare? Now I'm going to have to say yes.

Chapter 17

I've never seen dogs get so excited. You'd have thought we were offering them raw steak with a side of chicken, or whatever it is that turns them on. Instead, Will has a handful of leather straps and harness bits, and I have an extra big pair of warm boots, and some supersize gloves which he insisted I wear. He told me that my chain-store cheapies were only good for looking pretty. I took the pretty bit as a compliment – you have to take what you can with this man. I also informed him of the hefty price tag and the wow factor I have invested in. I skipped the bit that it was about creating the right impression. Because it obviously hasn't. The man is immune to impressions, apart from bad ones.

'Looking cute and sexy,' okay, this is positive, except I was after *businesslike but still me*, but I won't spurn cute and sexy, 'is all well and good if you're just taking a quick trip down the slopes, but you'll get cold on the sled. This is the proper gear, the stuff the guys who live here wear.'

I no longer feel quite so cute and sexy. I feel like I've

been parcelled up and am not authentic. Now all I need is a red bow on my head. Except this man doesn't do ribbons.

He straightens the hat on my head, and pulls it down over my ears. Then tucks a wisp of hair in, which is strangely sexy coming from a man with big, work-roughened hands.

This is the bit where he could kiss me on the nose (I reckon Ed would), but he doesn't. He's not Ed.

He's driving me mad. We have this love-hate thing going on. One minute I want to hug him (except let's get this clear, I'm not really a hugging kind of girl) because he seems kind of vulnerable (in a brave man kind of way), the next he's taking the mickey, or having a go. Totally contradictory, if you ask me, and I'm an expert at that kind of thing.

It's not that I want him to kiss me. This is business. I don't fancy him. At all. But we could be friends.

When he touches me, or stares in that way he has, it makes me feel squirmy. And I don't like feeling squirmy, unless it's because things are about to get hot and it's lustful anticipation. Then he'll jump away, or scowl, which leaves me feeling empty inside. Rejected. Which is ridiculous.

I obviously have to do more work on the feeling valued for who I am front.

'Okay?'

'Sorry?' I lift a flap. I'm quite glad I've got my ears covered, because, boy, can these dogs bark. Last time I saw them, they were big, floppy gentle giants cuddling up in the straw; now they're musclebound bouncing machines.

'Hold Rosie, or they'll be off before I've got them all hooked up.'

Rosie's eyes are positively glowing. She looks way bigger than she did in the kennels, her fur brought alive in the cold air, and she's dancing on air, eager to go. Her warm breath is hanging all around me, like a ghostly halo, and the excitement is catching. How could I have said no to this?

Will moves around as though he's been doing this all his life. He probably has. I know absolutely nothing about him, apart from that he had a bad fall on the slopes that left him with a limp and he's scared of going back, and he's got a brother who is different in every way.

His movements are economical, despite the clumsy thick clothing, his voice low as he murmurs and steadies the excited dogs. For the first time since I met him, his limp is barely noticeable, and his moodiness isn't weighing heavy on his shoulders.

He holds out a hand, whisks me aboard, and then we're off before I've barely caught my breath.

We head down a path I'd never really noticed before, at the back of the resort, a track that plunges into a forest and soon we could be a million miles from everywhere.

'Wow!'

'It's good for the soul.' Will's words are soft, his eyes fixed on the trail ahead, but I hear him. And I know what he means.

There's a hush in here. I can hear the dogs' paws, the

jangle of their collars and the harness, but apart from that there is only silence. Stillness. It's as though we're floating, gliding through the air, and nothing else matters.

My cheeks are burning from the bite of the cold air whizzing past us, but it doesn't matter. Inside I want to laugh, shriek. Instead, I settle for a grin, and glance Will's way, just as he looks in my direction.

'Okay?' He mouths the word and I nod. It's weird – it's like the most intimate moment I've ever been in with anybody. And we're fully clothed, with a pack of dogs for company, and he daren't even touch me. But it doesn't matter. It's more important than that, this shared experience, this short moment in time.

I feel as though he's let me in on a secret.

Christmas has come early, and not the noisy fun type. This is like a precious gift.

To the left are snow-covered mountains, ahead picture-perfect trees that are dusted with snow from top to toe.

One soft word from Will and the dogs seem to find another gear; barking with excitement they throw themselves forward with an enthusiasm which nearly upends me. I squeal and grab his arm.

'Love a duck!' We're galloping. The dogs are barking, my eyes are streaming, but all I want to do is whoop. 'This is amazing! Can we go faster?'

We go faster, the freshness of the air making my whole body hum from my burning toes right up to my tingling scalp, and I get this. Totally. It's just us and the dogs tearing through this surreal landscape with only a tiny sled keeping us all together. This must be the closest you can get to flying. I'm laughing, I'm crying, I'm hanging on and grinning at Mr Grumpy like a loony, and he's smiling back. Not in quite such an unhinged, unselfconscious way, but he looks happy.

I hadn't noticed how much tension he held in his body until now, when it's gone, when his shoulders are relaxed and his body is moving with the motion of the sled.

We slow down and I can catch my breath. Will's eyes are gleaming.

I ease my grip on everything and hope I haven't left indelible fingerprints on his arm.

'Did you say love a duck back there?'

'Er, yes. It's olde Englishe – to be used for special occasions.'

'Honestly? You're not kidding me?'

'No joke. You love these dogs, don't you?'

He shrugs. 'I'm pretty close to them. I used to go skijoring with Rosie's grandad when I was a kid.'

'Skijoring?'

'Cross-country skiing, with the dog pulling. It's how I got a taste for speed, we competed. He was a fast one, that dog. It was wild.' He's smiling. It's the type of smile you can't resist, the type that brings a smile to your own face – one that will pop up however hard you try and stop it. It's pure pleasure. Contagious. I can't stop looking. It's getting to the point of rudeness, but I don't think he's noticed. 'Some people do it with horses, but I like dogs. You can feel their excitement.'

'You're a bit of a speed merchant.'

'I am – or rather, I was.'

There's an awkward silence.

'I'm sorry.'

'Don't be. These things happen.'

The dogs pull up, and I stare across the lake.

'Here.' Will leans in close. Wraps a blanket round me. Pauses for a moment.

This is the bit where he pulls away. But this time he doesn't.

'Sarah, you don't have to do this you know. Help. Stay.'

'I do.'

I think it's him that moves first, but it could have been me. Or the dogs might have jolted the sled, or . . . who knows?

His lips are firm, dry. His breath smells of coffee and mints. I close my eyes and all I can hear is the jangle of dog harnesses. All I can feel is the warmth of his hand as it cradles my face, the soft heat of his breath, the feeling that this is right, natural, and then I know when he pulls away that he's staring. That he's going to spoil it.

I open one eye, just the tiniest bit.

'I'm sorry. I can't do this, I shouldn't . . .' I don't say anything. For the first time in my life I don't impulsively grab him, so I can change his mind. 'I'm bad news, I shouldn't . . . It's not you, it's . . .'

'Oh, for heaven's sake, give me credit. You either want a snog or you don't. Why not just say you changed your mind?' I open my eyes properly because I know he's turned back to face front and is stirring up the dogs.

He doesn't say anything. So I do, because I'm frustrated, and put out, and rejected. This wasn't like with Ed: I *wanted* Will to kiss me. Needed him to get on with it, rather than all this near-miss stuff.

'It was a snog, not a bloody relationship. Jeez.' I mutter it into my many layers, for my own benefit, not his, and try and act like I don't care. But I do. I want to kiss him more than I can ever remember wanting to kiss anybody. Ever. And now he's pushed me away and my stomach is churning for all the wrong reasons. And I've got a horrible feeling he heard. And this is all over before it even began.

Chapter 18

'Look, look, I'm decorating Chloe!'
I look. Poppy has got the cat firmly wedged between her legs and is wrapping a piece of gold tinsel around the startled animal's neck.

The cat's pupils are so wide her eyes are almost black. She looks wild, and not in a good way.

Christmas Day is fast approaching, and I have decided to rally the troops for one final push. This place is going to look festive on a shoestring budget if it kills me. It's looking like Chloe thinks she's the one about to expire first though.

Ed managed to find a giant box of decorations (which I'm sure I recognise from my last visit), and Will has shocked me by returning from the general stores with new lights, candles and a blow-up Santa.

He also sheepishly handed over a box which was full of pine cones, holly and other delicious smelling natural stuff, which was really touching. I was just about to come over all gushy, when he spoiled the image I had of him hunting

225

and gathering by saying he paid two local kids to forage for the stuff, and backed off quickly as though he was half expecting me to leap on him with gratitude. And kiss his face off.

I wasn't. I don't go where I'm not wanted – even though a part of me would still really like to. But it was cute of him to get the box of goodies, and it's the thought that counts, even if he didn't do it himself, yes? Unfortunately, I can't help but like him a little bit more each day, even if he makes me want to scream in frustration. Which I'm not going to do. I'm bigger than that. I hope.

It's not just his amazing eyes, the ones that caught my attention on day one, or the rather gorgeous, lazy smile that lights up his whole face when it makes a rare appearance, it's him. The man inside. His quiet determination to fix this place, despite Ed's total lack of commitment and slightly disruptive behaviour; his love of this special spot in the world, despite the fact he's obviously fighting some demon I've not really managed to get to the bottom of yet; the way he watches me when he thinks I'm not looking.

But I'm trying to ignore that. He's already flashed up a no-entry sign. So I try and concentrate on the job in hand. Not the job I'd like to have in my hands.

The tree is my first target, followed closely by the dining room and lounge area, then the reception. I'd really like to cosy that up, but as we've all been 'received' we've kind of lost the need for an immediate wow factor.

'I'm not so sure she likes that.' The words are barely out

of my mouth, when Chloe goes ballistic and does the kind of double flip only a cat can do. She looks like she's trying to turn herself inside out. When that doesn't release her from the deadly tinsel grip she yowls indignantly and makes a dash. Straight towards the fireplace, and she shoots up the chimney before anybody can stop her.

There is the sound of frantic scrabbling, that lasts all of three seconds. Then luckily she falls back down with a plop. Unluckily, she is now covered in soot. I don't know who is more shocked. Us or the cat.

'Bloody hell.' Will chooses just that moment to appear at the door. He has been noticeable by his absence ever since the kiss that shouldn't have happened. I reckon he's a Christmas elf and does all his work at night when everybody is asleep.

He is not amused.

'The cat apparently does not like being decorated.'

'I can see that.' He makes a dive towards Chloe, who instantly decides that she's in trouble and skitters across the room, the tinsel flying behind her and leaving dirty footprints in her wake. 'Don't say anything.' He waves a hand dismissively in my direction.

'I wasn't going to.' I was, actually. I was going to say that if he hadn't chased her it might not have been so bad. But sometimes it's better to keep your mouth shut. Even I know that.

'I'm off – and I'm not coming back until the mayhem is over and things are back to normal.'

'The second of January then?'

He is even less amused, and stalks off towards his office. If there was any doubt before, I think I've now totally blown it on the snogging front.

'I'll go and find a mop.' Tina sidles off towards the kitchen.

Undeterred, Poppy has dived into the box of decorations again.

'Where's the fairy?'

Fairies just don't feature in my thoughts right now. My plan involves flinging baubles and tinsel around and hoping they land on the tree, and not the cat (if she ever comes back). That is how Aunt Lynn taught me to decorate the tree. Finesse is for cissies.

'I don't know if there is one, Poppy. How about a star?'

'Stars are boring.'

'They're also the guiding light, or something.'

'This isn't,' she says, with all the solemnity she can muster, 'the Baby Jesus in a manger; it is the *tree*. It's different.'

'Oh. More tinsel?' I can't remember having this sort of conversation with Lynn when I was younger, or ever. I was more interested in scoffing the candy canes on the quiet.

'We can make a fairy.'

I don't like the sound of 'we'.

'How about we all make snowballs instead, darling, and ask Will or Ed about the fairy later?' Tina has returned, armed with a mop and various cleaning clobber to rescue me just in time.

'Snowballs? Honestly Mummy, don't you listen? We have to stay inside cos of the buzzards.'

This is a new one on me. Are we about to get swooped on by man-eating birds, and dragged away into the mountains?

'Blizzard,' Tina corrects.

'What's a blizzard? I thought it was lots of massive birds that would eat us.' Poppy and I appear to be on the same wavelength. I'm not sure if this is good or bad, but you should never knock childish enthusiasm at Christmas. She has her head in the box and is throwing baubles and paperchains that look like they come from the same era as the reception room décor in all directions.

I wish I was a child again, life is so much simpler, but more exciting.

'These are cotton-wool snowballs, darling, and we put presents inside them, for Christmas Day.' Tina looks at me for support.

'Sounds fantastic.' Stuck inside with Poppy and cotton-wool snowballs hadn't been quite what I'd planned for the day, but Will had been right about the weather changing. Skiing had been halted so the reception area had turned into a children's activity den, and I had somehow got cornered, surrounded on all sides by kids and their parents, and Ed hadn't helped at all when he'd dumped the tree decorations at my feet and cheerily declared, 'Line up, Sarah's in charge!' Damn his twinkly eyes and dimply smile. He'd winked. 'Will put it on the spreadsheet!'

'No!' I nearly broke my neck and ended up in the box of tinsel as I headed down to the office.

'Christmas decorations' had been tipex'd out and 'entertain the masses' had been neatly written over the top. I put an arrow up to the margin and added 'they're called guests'.

'How about I blow up the balloons.' The man in question, Ed is whispering in my ear.

'Well, you *are* full of hot air.' I jump about a foot away from him guiltily as Will's dry tone unexpectedly rings out right in the gap between us (not that there was much gap).

Ed holds his ground; in fact, I think he moves closer to me. I reckon I've gone the colour of a ripe tomato, and try to move away, which leaves me dangerously close to shoving Poppy into the basket of logs. She sticks a bony elbow out. That kid is going to go far: nobody is going to push her around. I love her.

'How about you do what you promised you'd do and get some logs in the cabins, Ed?'

'I thought Sarah could do with a hand, the logs can wait.' Ed has followed me over towards Poppy. We're all going to end up shuffling into the tree at this rate.

'Until the cabins get cold?'

'Jed can do them.'

'He's gone home, so he doesn't get snowed in.'

Ed has been cornered. Well, not literally, that appears to be me. So he whisks me into his arms, plants a smacker on my shocked mouth, then deposits me back on my feet and winks. 'Catch you later, snuggle monster.'

All I can do is a fly-eating frog impression as he saunters off. Where's a singing fish to lighten the atmosphere when you need one?

'I, he, we.'

'I think you better stop, you're making it worse.'

He's right. 'I thought you were tidying the store, Will.' It's on the spreadsheet. If in doubt, be business like.

I am actually pleased he came back, but not pleased that he's chased my helper, Ed, away and might do another of his disappearing acts any second.

'It can wait. I reckon I owe you an apology.'

'Really?' Is he going to say he wished he'd snogged me properly?

'I might have overreacted just now when I saw Chloe come down the chimney.'

'Ah. I suppose it was a shock.' We look at each other and accept the truce. It could be worse; he could just be apologising about writing on my spreadsheet.

'I've got time to give you a hand with these balloons.' He picks one up, the corner of his mouth quirking.

I think my mouth is wide open. I shut it.

'I can do that, Sarah. No probs.' Craig grins and grabs a handful. 'I'm used to this type of thing, what with having two kids.'

'Huh. You've never offered to do that at home.' Tina thrusts baby Jake into his arms. 'If you're at a loose end you can look after your son. Now leave Sarah and Will alone. Honestly.' Her eyebrows are sky high, and she's wheeled him round and is pushing him away before I have chance to tell them that Sarah and Will do not want to be left alone.

Well, Will definitely doesn't want to be left alone with Sarah.

He stretches a balloon out.

'So why are we doing this?'

'Well, I've been told we cover them in flour and water paste and shredded newspaper, let them dry, then burst the balloon and cover them in cotton wool.'

'Really?'

'Really.'

'Is this some strange British custom?'

'We don't get much real snow. We rely on cotton wool. You don't have to do it.'

'I want to.'

Will is actually good at blowing up balloons. The first one is up before I've even got mine out of the packet.

'Wow, so who was it that was full of hot air?'

'Watch it, lady, or I'll have to sort you out.'

'Oh yeah? You and whose army?'

'I've always been able to sort out girls without an army.'

'But you've never met a girl like me.'

'Now isn't that the truth?'

'Reckon you're up to the job? Men make poor losers.'

'I don't lose.' He grins. 'Reckon you're up to being the underdog?' He's meeting my eye, and it's me who looks away first. This jokey Will is hard to deal with. Especially when he's looking at me so intently.

Being the underdog actually sounds pretty damned tempting. Tempting enough to dry my mouth out. This is *wrong*. Will is *not* tempting. Will is just trying to be nice, to show me he's not the infuriating stick-in-the-mud inflexible jerk Ed accused him of being.

He's holding his hand out. Is this some strange Canadian thing I don't know about?

Do I grab it? In front of children?

'Balloon.'

'Wha?'

'Pass me another balloon. First to ten and I'll give you a handicap of three.'

'Nobody is handicapping me, mate.'

Okay, I might have cheated. I may, just may (not admitting to anything here) have given him a balloon that I suspect might (just might) have been pierced with one of the drawing pins we'd used to put the decorations up.

Well, he was six up, and all is fair in love and war, as they say.

Chapter 19

After all the excitement of yesterday, things feel kind of flat. An anti-climax. Everywhere is decorated, the tree a chaos of bright colours and the blow-up Santa looks like a bondage extra at the front of reception. Apparently, the wind can get up and Ed decided it was better to be safe than sorry. Well, that was his story, I think he's done it on purpose.

Poor Santa has his wrists and ankles shackled and appears (from a distance) to have a gag. Ed said he didn't want him to start headbanging if there was a breeze, which I agree is inappropriate, but he certainly won't be up to saying ho ho ho this year.

The smell of holly, cinnamon and pine cones drifts through every room and candles shimmer in all the dark corners, sending a warm glow around the walls. And outside the snow is glistening. The cabin roofs have a dusting that's more perfect than any icing on a gingerbread house, and when the moon and stars sparkle in the dark night sky the place truly does look magical.

It looks perfect; I should be happy, and on the outside I

am. I'm excited, and yet a tiny bit inside of me feels like a festive wasteland. Because it's as amazing as it was when I first set eyes on the place, all those years ago. When the happiest of Christmases ended in a nightmare I could never have imagined.

It has suddenly hit me, hard, that I'm almost back where I was then. I'm older and wiser, but inside I'm still a little girl who hurts. Blocking things out has been my coping mechanism, but right now I can't.

The place is also deserted, so there are no distractions. Everybody, it seems, has gone out. Will has gone to pick up food, and Ed is out on the slopes supervising.

They're all working up an appetite for Christmas and I feel a bit deflated. Flat. Everything is ready. Even the vegetables have been prepped for tonight, and a lot of the staff have been given time off to go and do Christmas shopping.

All the cabins have a good supply of logs, the papier mâché snowballs have been appropriately stuffed (with alcoholic miniatures for the adults and chocolate for the children), the crackers are made and the presents are under the trees. Except I haven't got any to put there, nobody to share with. Which could be what brought on the dull weight in my chest.

There's nothing left that needs doing.

I am redundant.

My spreadsheet has served its purpose, and I should be feeling triumphant. People are happy. Even Will and Ed seem to have made a temporary truce, and all threats of court action have been put on hold.

But the flurry of messages that arrived an hour ago from Aunt Lynn made me realise just how much I miss her. That's the trouble out here; my phone seems to give up trying to receive messages, then there's a glut. Some of these were sent two days ago.

Looking at all the brightly packaged presents didn't help either.

Christmas has always been about me and Lynn, about family and friends.

On the last Friday before Christmas, we'd normally shut up the travel agency at lunchtime, go out for a boozy lunch with Sam, and then do some last-minute shopping, because you can never have enough baubles, and silly little gifts, and bows and ribbons to wrap them up in.

Then we'd settle in for the evening with a bottle of bubbly, peel sprouts and wrap bacon around tiny sausages. We'd be laughing. Having fun.

It is then, on cue, that the phone rings.

'Happy Christmas, darling!'

'But it's not—'

'We're having it early, isn't that fab? We're just about to make breakfast then open the presents! We're off in Ralph's camper van for a few days on a trip down memory lane, and I'm not sure if the phone reception will be any good, and there's no room for a tree or presents because of the dogs and the barbecue. What was that Ralph, darling? Oh yes, and my wine, lots of wine! So we're having my proper English Christmas Day today, and then doing the Australian beach version on Monday. Isn't that lovely? We've got a tree and everything. Have you got a tree? Oh, of course you have. They grow them there, don't they? Are you enjoying yourself?'

I don't know whether to laugh or cry. I am quite glad I can't get a word in.

'Have you opened your presents? Have you found the one I sneaked into your bag?'

'I haven't opened anything, Aunt Lynn; it's only Friday and Christmas Day isn't until Monday!'

'I know it's very early, but it's definitely Saturday, love. You must be having a very good time if you're confused! It's Saturday, not Friday, and we always do things the weekend before Christmas, don't we? It's the same day everywhere, you noddle.'

'Except that in Australia you're hours ahead of us here. It's still Friday.'

'Is it? Are you sure? Oh. What was that?'

'I told you, you daft bat.' I can hear a voice in the background. Presumably Ralph.

'What day did you say it was, Sarah?'

'It's Friday, and it's only . . .' I check my watch, even though I know what time it is. Today has passed in super slow slow-motion. 'Two o'clock in the afternoon.'

'Really? Ralph's right then, we're sixteen hours ahead of you! Would you credit it?'

For a woman who has made a living out of travelling to different countries, Aunt Lynn can be a bit odd at times.

'Well, anyway, we're off on a little road trip and it might

be hard to call you, so I thought I'd ring now. You're so hard to get hold of. I've sent umpteen messages, haven't I, Ralph? I thought, what with our dodgy internet, and you gallivanting about and enjoying yourself, we might not get a chance on Monday, which will be Sunday where you are anyway! I mean which day do I say Happy Christmas on?'

'I've not been gallivanting. I just didn't get your messages until an hour ago. The reception here's terrible. They all came through at once and I was just reading them.'

'Oh well, never mind, dear. But I did want to check you were okay.'

'I'm good; I've done exactly what I needed to and the place looks brilliant. You'd be impressed!'

'Oh, I'm sure I would, darling, but not surprised. You always do a good job of whatever you set your mind on. Send me photos – I'd love to see if it's how I remember it. I'm going to take the present from you with me, but did you find mine?'

'What present? We've already swapped presents?'

'Just a little something, dear. I put it in that pocket on the end of your bag, inside the zipped up bit where I put your fizzy tablets.'

'Fizzy tablets?'

'For the hangover on Boxing Day. I was sure that way you'd find it! Oh well, I better go. You will ring, won't you, and wish me a Happy Christmas properly? I mean, you might not be able to get hold of me, but Christmas won't be Christmas if we can't at least say Happy Christmas, will it?'

'It won't. Of course I'll call. I'll try on Christmas Eve, before I go to bed, because it'll be Christmas Day there.'

'Lovely. That's all I want, Sarah. Bye for now then, darling.'

'Have a lovely day.'

'We will, dear.'

I don't ask how Ralph is, because he's obviously there, listening. And if you're dying you don't want to listen to people talking about it, do you? Especially on your pretend Christmas Day, when you've been reunited with your long-lost love. At least, I think that is what Lynn is.

'Has everything worked out okay there, darling?'

There's a question in her voice. I can tell she'd been undecided about asking, then couldn't help herself.

'It's great. I mean, Will is a bit of a grump, but quite nice underneath when you get to know him. And his brother Ed is a real womaniser – you'd love him, he's cute, too.'

She laughs that lovely throaty laugh that I've missed.

'And you're all right? I'm sure it's been a bit strange, you wouldn't be human if . . .'

'Of course, I'm all right! I told you, it's perfect here now; we'll soon get people flooding back and loving the place.'

'Sarah.' Her voice is soft. 'I'm asking about you, not the resort.'

'I'm fine. Honest.' It comes out slightly too bright, but luckily she doesn't comment.

'Well, good. You can always call me, you know.'

'I know. I will.'

'And do send me some photos, won't you? I'd love to see

what the place looks like now. Is Bear Cabin just the same?'

'Not quite.' I haven't told her about the kennels yet. 'But the rest of the place is – I don't think some of it has been changed at all since the seventies!'

'Oh, how wonderful! Well, I better say bye for now, darling, have fun tonight, don't do anything I wouldn't!'

'Miss you.'

'Miss you too.'

So this is it. My first Christmas without Aunt Lynn, and she's started without me.

The place is looking much more like I remember it now, cosy and inviting. Beautifully festive. So it makes it even more strange that I'll be spending the day on my own. Well, not on my own. Tina and her family are lovely, and Ed is funny, and Will seems to have lightened up.

But I need to get out. Just for a little while. I need to be able to see this as a new beginning. I've not exactly gone back in time, but it's all a bit déjà vu and it's up to me to make sure that when I leave this time, I do it my way.

Aunt Lynn was right, she always is. I need to face up to the past before I can draw a line under it, not just block it out as I have been doing.

Except I'm not quite sure how to do that, I'm not sure I can ever find peace with one particular part of my past. I'm not sure I want to.

I grab my snow-boots. I have a job to do. Aunt Lynn wants photographs and she's going to get some. I'm going to make new, sparkly, happy memories. My way.

Chapter 20

'What do you think, Rosie?' Rosie licks my hand. We're mates, she understands the unspoken words. If I knew how to harness the dogs and sled up and had somebody to hold them until I was ready, and knew they wouldn't charge off without me, and could remember which order to put them in, and how to stop and start them, then a ride would be perfect.

I know none of that, though. I wasn't concentrating when Will did it. And I'm pretty sure that if I try I'll either end up strangling a dog, being dragged off up the track on my bum or suffering a nasty death by garrotte. Not a pretty sight for any late-afternoon skiers who might find me.

I glance over towards the shed. The one that houses the snowmobile.

It twinkles at me in the sunlight. Offering an invitation. Come and have fun, I'm your friend!

Ed let me drive when we went out the other day. The man is a bit of an adrenalin junkie, which suits me fine. On a snowmobile I can cope; it's a bit like a motorbike, but more fun. On a snowmobile I feel a bit like I do when I'm surfing, totally free and unencumbered. Which is definitely not how I feel on skis or a snowboard.

It's what I need right now. To go fast. To head down a path of my own making. And taking a few photo's here is one thing, but I think I've exhausted the cute cabins and snowdrift theme, and I want to take shots inside this evening when all the candles and fires are lit, and there's a hot chocolate at hand.

I raid the shed for boots, snowmobile suit and helmet, and leave my mobile on the side. The reception is pretty crap round here anyway.

I pat my pocket, check that the small package is in there. It's the present from Lynn, and I really want to open it today, on my own, not when I'm sitting around a Christmas tree with friends I've only just met. That way I'll feel like I'm sharing her early Christmas Day with her.

Rosie barks as I start up the engine, then puts her head on one side and whines.

'I won't be long. Promise.' She paws at the ground, then lies down, her gaze never leaving me. 'Shh, don't tell anybody.'

I set off up the track slowly, not wanting to disturb the peace, and wanting to take in my surroundings properly. Let the breathtaking scenery work its magic on me. The trees are heavy with snow, the air clean and crisp, and as I head up higher the layer of sadness starts to lift. It would have been nice to share this place with Aunt Lynn, though. She'd love it.

I draw to a halt. The heavy snowfall finished some time ago, leaving the ground new and untouched. All around is a beautiful blanket of untouched, sparkly whiteness that takes my breath away, even though I am feeling down.

Living in a place like this must be incredible. I can understand Will's frustration that all this splendour isn't enough for the people that come here. That they want entertaining. But it's all about expectations, isn't it? Sometimes we can't see the beauty in the things we haven't asked for, we only look for what we expect, what we thought we were promised. And our disappointment at the little niggles clouds over the wonderful parts of life until we can't see them.

Where do I go now? Ed took me to the Halfway Cabin when we were out, a place where they stored some gear in case of emergencies, when they were taking more experienced snowboarders and skiers further up the mountain. It wasn't too far, and I know roughly the direction, so it will be easy to find. There were blankets there, and I know that's where I've been heading, even if I didn't admit it to myself. I can sit and get my head together and get myself in a festive mood. Then it will all be splendid when I come back and join in the Christmas celebrations. I'll have blown away the storm clouds and will be able to appreciate the glimmers of sunshine.

One thing with this place, it's dead easy to get your

bearings. There are landmarks of the lake, certain mountain ridges, copses of trees. So I know exactly where I'm heading.

When I came with Ed, I started out at a potter, feeling my way, until I could speed up, pushing myself to the limit, whooping as we carved a new track through the snow, letting the adrenalin course through my body. But today I feel the haunting beauty of the empty space, a nothing-ness that reflects what I feel in some little bit of me, deep inside. I hate the feeling and being sorry for myself. It's stupid, it's a waste of energy, a waste of life, but sometimes it creeps up on me, settles in my gut, and I don't want it to. I want to escape. Find a way of leaving it behind. Which is why I've always tried to fill my life with work, friends, happiness.

The feeling's still niggling in my gut, but I'm leaving the resort behind as I climb the slopes, the snowmobile carrying me effortlessly until I slow right down to a stop and catch my breath, gazing down at what I've left behind.

The Shooting Star Mountain Resort nestles below. I can pick out the kennels, the cabins – my cabin – and the place has a weird pull on me. I like it. I didn't expect to feel like this when I came back; I expected to feel sad, or angry, but I don't. The place itself is beautiful. It's just me that isn't.

I'm the one who wasn't good enough and was left behind. The one who doesn't belong even now. Would my parents love the grown-up Sarah more, if they came back now? Would they be proud, like Aunt Lynn is?

Maybe I just need to believe they would; maybe I'm

heading to the Halfway Cabin because it doesn't hold those old memories. Mum and Dad never visited there. Maybe it's the place I can face up to what happened and make a fresh start. Maybe Will and I have more in common than I've realised, both working hard to paper over the hurt rather than facing up to it. When I see him backing away from me, it hurts, but maybe that's what I've been doing. Avoiding any kind of relationship that might hurt me, where I might get rejected.

And Will saying no hasn't finished me off.

Maybe, just maybe, being here on my own has made me realise that being me is enough.

So many maybes.

I turn back and start up the vehicle again. Except I don't. Or rather, it doesn't. It splutters and dies. Then ignores me when I try again. It ignores me even when I jump up and down and kick it.

If I had one of Ed's tea trays I could just sale down the slope, ha ha, except I don't want to anyway. I want to go to the tiny Halfway Cabin.

It's where I have to be. It's my new start.

I am not going to let this place beat me. Jumping off the snowmobile doesn't go as well as I'd hoped, though, I'm swallowed up by a snowdrift nearly to my knees.

Oh, my God, this stuff is deep! I'll be swimming in it soon. Actually, a bit of front crawl might be the way forward, except somebody might see and that would be a bit embarrassing.

I look round. Nobody. Total silence, total whiteout.

I probably should have brought a snowboard, or skies, or at least ski poles.

I think I can see the Halfway Cabin in the distance. Or it could be a pile of snow. Or a bear covered in a pile of snow. Or just a white bear. That gives me two reasons to turn back, and one to keep going. I never was very good at the whole head over heart thing. This might or might not mean I will get eaten by a wild animal before I reach my next birthday – which is not usually a problem at home.

***

It might be not much bigger than an outside toilet, but I have never been more pleased to open a door in my life. Luckily, it is not locked, something I did not think about before setting off. Although thinking about outside toilets, which I shouldn't have, what if I need the loo? That does not bear thinking about. So instead I shove the door shut, pull my boots and gloves off, and explore the place properly. I didn't really get a chance to look round last time, as Ed had a different type of exploration on his mind.

I am on my hands and knees, head deep in the small cupboard in the corner, when there's a noise. I freeze. It's a shuffling, panting noise. When you're in the middle of nowhere, you notice stuff like that.

What if it's a yeti? Or a wolf. If it gets in here, the first thing it will see is my bum stuck out, like an invite to a picnic. Oh, bloody Nora, what if it's a polar bear? People come to Canada to see polar bears – Lynn added a great new resort with tours and everything not long ago – though why would you want to get up close to a man-eating woolly mammal?

It might maul me, rip my leg off like a student in KFC after six pints and a boogie. I'll never see my new tattoo (which cost a lot in terms of pain and cash) ever again. Or my leg.

Maybe I need to get out of this cupboard and find something to fend it off with. Though I'm not sure a flurry of soft furnishings has ever put a big mammal off its lunch.

Sugar. I haven't even got any buns to throw at it. All I've got are a pile of furs, which it might think are its relatives. Throwing what remains of its dead Uncle George at it won't go down well.

Oh bugger, it's getting closer. Maybe I can hide in the cupboard.

It's banging on— No, wait, it's opening the door. Bloody hell, this isn't just a smart bear, it's evolved into one that can cope with door handles.

'What the hell are you doing here?'

It's not a bear, though it isn't much smaller than one to be honest. It's a man. And a dog.

I recognise the dog first, because she is not wearing goggles and a snowsuit.

She also looks happy to see me. Her mouth is open and her tongue is lolling as though she's smiling.

'Rosie!' I have never been so pleased to see a dog in my life. I didn't even know they were my most favourite animal in the world until now. I'm so pleased, I forget I'm half in a cupboard and bang my head on the way out. But two paws on your shoulders and big sloppy dog kisses more than make up for mild concussion.

The man stops stamping snow from his feet and pushes his goggles up. He has steely eyes. I preferred it when they'd stopped being steely.

'I said, what the hell are you doing here?'

'Having afternoon tea with the snow leopards!' I don't know where that came from, but it's stopped him dead.

There's a long pause. 'We don't get snow leopards here.'

'Well, that explains why they didn't turn up.'

'Have you banged your head?'

'No, I bloody haven't. Well, I have, but . . .'

'Where've you been?'

'Nowhere!'

'Nowhere?'

'Well, here. What do you mean, where have I been?'

'Haven't you got the faintest idea how worried we were when nobody could find you? You're a – a liability.'

'I'm not a liability!'

'You disappeared!'

'I went out. You're not my keeper; you went out and I didn't have a hissy fit.'

'I told you where I was going, and that's different.'

'No, it's not. I can do what I want and I've only been gone a couple of hours. I would have thought you could manage without me for that long.'

'You can freeze to death, get buried in the snow, injure yourself, die,' he's glowering at me, and close to shouting 'in less than a couple of hours, and it's been more than that.'

'Well, I'd only planned on a couple of hours, then the snowmobile wouldn't restart, and I had to walk up here, but I got a bit lost. I thought I knew exactly where it was, but . . .'

'How on earth can somebody like you—'

'What do you mean, somebody like me?' My eyes are burning, and I'm shaking, adrenalin still rushing through my veins. 'Some stupid girl? Somebody who hasn't got a clue what they're doing?' I think it's the shouting that's really got to me. I've never heard Will raise his voice like this.

'I didn't mean that.' He's glaring now, all cold and businesslike. 'I meant somebody who doesn't know this area. Doesn't know the weather conditions.'

'The weather is fine, it's not snowing! I'm fine, I don't need rescuing, so why don't you go and shout at somebody else?'

'You stupid—' He stops short at what I guess is a look of horror on my face. It's probably more a screwed-up, about-to-cry look. Because that's how I feel inside, all tangled up. 'It's stopped snowing, but it's prime avalanche time. You haven't got any idea, have you?' His voice is softer now, but not particularly nice. It's got an almost scornful edge to it.

'But the snow stopped ages ago. I thought—'

'You didn't think at all!'

'I just wanted to go for a walk, I wanted to get away from you and your bloody grumpiness, and all the Christmas stuff and—'

'But you like all that stuff, it was your idea!'

'I just wanted . . .' I don't know what I wanted. I did want Christmas, but now it's all too much, and all the people I love aren't here. And what's Christmas if you're not sharing it with the people that mean the most to you? I'd thought Christmas was about tinsel and ribbons and turkey, but it's not. I want to be with the people I love.

'And why did you scream when I came in the door?'

'I thought you were a bloody bear and I wish you had been! I'd rather be eaten alive than, than, than . . .' Shouting at him seems to be having a funny effect on me. I feel all wobbly. I think even my lip is wobbly, because the words aren't coming out properly. I'm running out of breath, and words, and everything. And I might be about to burst into big, noisy, messy tears.

'Oh shit, Sarah.' He's banged the door shut, and somehow his arms are wrapped round me and his lips are on my eyelids. 'I'm sorry.' He's kissed my nose, then his hard, cold lips are on my mouth.

It's so urgent and passionate, it makes me dizzy. I feel safe. I feel all funny and liquidy inside.

I think I'm clinging on to him, but I'm not sure. He tastes like home and all good things, and the pine smell of his hair, and coldness of his face under my fingers is making me laugh and cry all at once. And I'm all hot and bothered, but it doesn't matter.

He's holding me tight, his fingers in my hair, and I can hardly breathe, but I don't want to. I don't need to, I just want to be kissed like this for ever. Rocked in his arms, pinned against the hard wood and kissed. Did I already say kissed?

Something inside me wells up, a hard lump of pain that is mixed in with lust and fear, but more than anything, want.

I want him. I need him to carry on. I'm going to explode if he does, but it doesn't matter. Nothing matters.

It's how I imagine a last kiss would be, grabbing what you can before you die . . . except I bloody hope this isn't one. I'm too young to die, and I am not, not, not intending to become the waste product of a polar bear.

He pulls away and stares at me. I gulp in air and stare back. Slightly dazed. Shocked. This is touch-me-not Will I'm looking at.

'Wow.' It's the first thing that comes into my empty head. I touch my tingling lips.

The corner of his mouth tips up. Then drops again. It wouldn't do to smile too much, would it?

'Sorry if I scared you, but shit, Sarah, have you no idea how dangerous it is out here at the moment?' He's as breathless as I am, but it's like he's trying to act normal. And that's good. As long as he's not going to pretend that never happened.

'Bears?' It comes out as a croak. Last Supper time.

'Worse. Snow.'

'I wasn't that scared.'

'I was.' He runs his fingers through my hair, pulls me closer again so he can kiss my forehead. This time it's gentle.

'You were worried about me?'

He sinks down onto the floor, taking me with him, his arms still wrapped around me. 'Shit scared. People die out here if they're not careful; nobody in their right mind would come out after a snowfall like that.'

'But you did, you came to get me.' It's a statement, not a question.

'I must be as daft as you.' The corner of his mouth is quirked in a wry smile. 'I was scared shitless, probably more than you were, if that makes you feel better.'

'Nope.'

He laughs. 'I came out in a sweat when I saw the snow-mobile and no sign of you.'

'Oh hell! The snowmobile, I forgot all about that! Oh God, I'm so sorry, is it insured? I'm so selfish, I just never thought, I—'

'Who gives a damn about a lump of metal? I was just glad you made it here and you're okay. You've no idea what was going through my mind. But from where it was, and the tracks . . .'

'I broke it, though.'

'Bollocks.' He's grinning. 'A snowmobile can cope with more than a slip of a thing like you can throw at it. It's run out of fuel.' He shakes his head. 'Another of Ed's little jobs that he forgot to do.' He tips his head back and stares at the ceiling. 'I tried ringing your phone.'

'It's in the shed.'

'I know. I found it, and noticed the snowmobile had gone. That's why I headed this way. Ed often brings the girls out here for a ride.'

He says it with that lift at the end, a question in his voice.

I think I might have turned slightly pink.

'And you're okay? You didn't fall off . . . ?'

'I stopped to look at the scenery, then it wouldn't start again. I reckoned if I came here I could call, then remembered I hadn't got my phone.' There's a funny grumbling sound, and it isn't Rosie. 'I'm starving, why am I starving?'

'Stress can do that.'

'You didn't bring emergency supplies, then?'

'Only that.' He points at the bag he dropped by the door. 'Dog food!'

'Dog food? You've only got *dog* food? You came to rescue me and didn't even bring chocolate, or brandy? You're useless, you'd never make the grade as a Saint Bernard rescue dog.'

'I figured if you were frozen you wouldn't need food,

whereas Rosie, on the other hand, would have to keep her strength up, to drag your body back down the mountain.'

'Ah, good thinking! So you skied with her?'

'I trust her to look after me, I couldn't have done it without her.' His voice is soft, his free hand reaches out to caress her soft fur, and I don't quite know what to say. So I just swallow down the lump in my throat, and stroke the other side of her. She rolls over onto her back.

'Loony.' He gives a soft laugh, and she seems to be grinning as she looks at him, her tongue lolling out of her mouth. I glance up at him, share a smile. Cuddling a dog, a funny dog, makes all this seem a bit more normal. Acceptable. I get now why they say dog owners are less stressed.

'So, the dog food.'

'Mm?'

'Means we're not heading home?' I don't actually mind being stuck with him here, but it is late, and I am starving.

'Well, it's dry and warm in here.'

'I'll go with the dry, but if you call this warm you've been living like an Eskimo for too long.'

'A bit of body warmth goes a long way, you just need to cuddle up.'

I think my eyes have nearly popped out of their sockets. Will is suggesting cuddling up?

'That's a bit forward, I hardly know you!' I say it jokily, but don't really know why I say it at all. To cover the awkwardness, I guess.

'I meant to Rosie.' He's laughing. I've never seen him so chilled. 'But I'm quite happy to throw extra body heat in.'

I can feel it already. Or that could just be me, anticipating. 'I'm not undressing.'

'Thank God for that!' He chuckles, and it makes me feel all wriggly. This must be like that syndrome where you are so grateful to your rescuer you totally fall for them. I'll be fine when I get back to civilisation, and Christmas dinner, and hot chocolate. 'How would I ever explain that you froze after I'd found you.'

'Ah. Good point. Tricky one, and possibly incriminating. I could ruin your good reputation.'

'I don't think I have one, but thanks for the thought.'

'It's nearly Christmas, and it's Friday night. I'm spending Friday night in a tiny hut with a husky.'

'Could be worse. You might not have made it to the tiny hut.'

That sobers me up.

'I don't want to endanger anybody else, so I've just texted Jed and suggested he come first thing with a can of fuel. The snow will have settled better, by then, and it'll be safer.' My stomach rumbles. Loudly. 'And we'll still be back in time for lunch tomorrow. I can make you pancakes if you like?'

'Don't talk about food! It's making it worse.' It's like watching running water when you're dying for a wee. Not a good thing. 'Shall we sing carols to keep our spirits up?'

He groans and puts his head in his hands, but I can tell

he's still smiling. 'I'll call Jed, tell him I'll pay him double time, that it's an emergency!'

'Don't you dare. Don't you know, I'm the karaoke queen?'

'I should have guessed.'

We sit in companionable silence for a bit. Then he spoils it.

'Why did you leave your phone behind?'

'It was an accident. I just forgot to pick it up.'

He raises an eyebrow, just a smidgen.

I sigh. How can I lie to him when he's risked his life to check I was okay, and we're stuck in a wooden box together for the night with a wolf dog for company? 'I know, it was a bit stupid, but I needed to get away.' My mobile is like an extra body part. We are inseparable. I never forget it, I left it because I needed to be on my own.

'Oh, Sarah.' He cups my face in his big, capable hands and takes a deep breath. 'Why on earth? What the hell made you come out here?'

I look at him, and for the first time ever I want to tell somebody. 'I was lonely.'

'But you've got—'

'I was the only person there who didn't have . . . someone. I'm never good enough. Everybody leaves me, eventually.'

'But what about the Callum guy? Ed said . . . I thought . . .'

'We split, it's over. We're just friends. He'd have gone soon, when he realised that it wasn't going to work. I just let Ed think . . .'

258

'Come here, you're in shock, let me warm you up.'

He pulls me into his arms.

'Why don't you think you're good enough?' His voice is soft in my ear. I'd not expected that. I'd expected platitudes, expected him to say I was being daft. All those meaningless words people say.

I shrug. It's complicated. My head hurts, which is why I came here on my own.

'Tell me about what happened here, Sarah. Why you've really come back.'

'I came back to sort this place out.'

'Why?'

'Because you were messing it up, ruining it, and our clients . . .'

'You.' He spreads his long legs out, drapes a heavy comforting arm round my shoulders. I want to cuddle up to him. Curl up. Suck my thumb. Where did that come from? That makes me feel so uncomfortable and stupid. Vulnerable.

I must have stiffened up, because he pulls me more firmly against him.

'Let's talk about you.'

'Oh, you don't want to do that.' My silly shrill laugh echoes in the cabin. Even more embarrassing.

'We've got all night, and I'm sick of hearing about all my cock-ups. Your turn! Why's it important we sort things out here? Or would you rather talk spreadsheets?' He wraps his arms round me tighter and groans in my ear, which sends a shiver down my spine. 'I'm not sure I can stand spreadsheets for two hours. Save me, Sarah.'

He makes me laugh, his tone so desperate, his breath tickling my neck. Aunt Lynn used to hold me like this, tight, whisper in my ear. Well, not quite like this, but I feel safe like I did with her. I want to sit back, rest against him, let the words come out. I'm all cocooned. This is just for here, for now, and when we go back to the resort the words will have disappeared and everything will be back to normal.

'I think it was Aunt Lynn's idea for us to come out here. Her and my mum didn't really stay in touch that much because they had totally different lives. I suppose they were both a bit like hippies when they were younger. Lynn flew all over the world, spent time in Asia, Australia . . . she was totally footloose and fancy free.' I take a deep breath. 'Mum was more Stonehenge. She had an old camper van and loved all the mystical stuff. She used to spend a lot of time in Cornwall.'

'Do you remember much about it?'

'What?'

'The van, Cornwall?'

He's done it again, asked a different question. The 'do you remember your mum' question always has me gnashing my teeth. How am I supposed to answer that? I was young, she'd left nothing tangible, and the haziest of memories. It makes me angry, defensive. The therapist said I should try to be open and express my feelings. Then I got detention when I rolled Molly Parker down the slope because she'd called me 'awful orphan'. Yeah, right, I learned pretty quick that it's just the good feelings you're supposed to express. Apparently, shouting out 'I hate you all, you don't understand' and kicking the teacher is not the correct expression of pain.

But Will hasn't asked 'the question'. I can talk about the camper van. That's fine.

'It had dreamcatchers and cushions, and red and white checked bunting.' I squeeze my eyes tight shut to stop the stupid tears escaping. I loved that camper van, with its pretty, summery bunting and all the little treasures. It was like finding a secret cave full of the most wonderful things a little girl could imagine. Throw in a unicorn and it would have been totally watertight, 100 per cent unbeatable.

'There were little bowls full of crystals, all the colours of the rainbow, and she used to let me pick out the one that looked best and hold it tight.' I'd forgotten the crystals, forgotten Mum telling me I'd be drawn to what I needed most in my life. All I'd remembered, all I'd let myself remember was the day she left. The fact she left nothing behind, but me. 'I had a tiny stool that Dad made for me.' I blink, and I can see it. If I reach out, I'll be able to touch the wood. A lump hardens in my throat. 'He painted a ladybird on the seat, it was the only thing he ever made for me. That ladybird made me laugh.' I'd loved Dad, back then. I'd loved his hugs, his sense of fun, the way he'd make me laugh.

'If I'd have been good enough, they wouldn't have left me.'

'It's not about you being good enough, Sarah. It was about them.' His chin is resting on my head, and his words vibrate through me. 'I guess that's something I've finally started to realise: it's never about you.'

'Parents are supposed to love you.' I guess that's the problem. 'When we're little, the people who look after us are supposed to have all the answers, do all the right things. Love you unconditionally.'

'They are – and how do you know they didn't?'

The anger bubbles up inside me, burning, fighting its way out.

'You don't frigging abandon somebody if you do!' The words are staccato, sharp. My heart is starting to race, my mouth drying, that familiar feeling of panic that I've tried to leave behind is back. I take a deep breath. Think about blowing into paper bags, which has always seemed far too ridiculous to actually do.

'People make mistakes, Sarah, none of us are perfect. People run away for all different reasons, even when they shouldn't.' His grip tightens round me, makes me feel more grounded, his slow, measured words crumbling some of the hate. 'Why don't you find them, ask them? Isn't it time?'

'I can't.' I scrunch my knees up to my chest. He's still holding me, and I haven't shrugged him off. Yet. But I'm closing up, wrapping myself in the cocoon that has always protected me.

He squeezes, just a little. Just enough to tell me he's not going to be pushed away. 'But, you can if—'

'No if. The day after they walked away from me, my mum was killed.'

'Oh God, I'm sorry.' There's a long, long silence. Only broken by the little whiffling noises Rosie makes. I want to put my hands over my ears. To block out what I know is coming. But I don't. 'But your dad? Surely he—'

I can feel the bile rise in my throat and I swallow the bitter taste down and squeeze my eyes shut. The lump in my throat doesn't want to let the words out, but I have to say them. I've never said them. I wouldn't to the therapist. I wouldn't to Auntie Lynn.

'It was his fault. He murdered her.'

I've lived with this inside me, my horrible secret, for most of my life. And I don't know quite what I expect now it's out in the world, but there's no sensation of a huge weight lifting, no fanfare. Just hot tears on my face and the blanket of silence.

They'd called it an accident at first. That first day, when Aunt Lynn had to try and explain that they weren't coming back. But by the New Year, by the time we were home my funny, zany Dad was a murderer. And I was that 'poor child'. And even though I was young, I took in every word and squirrelled them away. Then I slowly built a barrier so that those words would never get out and hurt me again.

But Aunt Lynn was right. It's taken until now, in this

place, with this man who's been damaged in his own way, to realise that I have to admit what happened in the past, what's made me who I am, before I can have my new beginning. My fresh start.

'He's been locked up and I hope they've lost the fucking key.' The shaky words explode from my throat. 'My mum abandoned me, and then my dad made sure she could never come back. If he hadn't, if . . .'

I've had these 'if's' with me all my life. Would everything have been different if she hadn't died? Would she have come back, explained why she left? Or would it all have been the same?

The sound of Will's steady breathing is in my ear. the thump of his heart against my body, and suddenly I need somebody to hold me.

I throw myself round, grab his jacket and scrunch it up in my fists. Bury my head in his jacket and wail. Horrible, snotty messy tears cover my face, and dribble all over the coat of a man I hardly know. He rocks me in his arms. My throat hurts, my chest hurts, my lip hurts from where I'm biting it. My head hurts and my body aches, I want to hit something, but instead I hang on, my nails digging into the palms of my hands.

It stops. Eventually. I have run out of emotion.

The shaking and trembling eases, but not the pain. I'm hot, my face wet and sticky, my hair plastered to my face. A total mess. Clinging to a man, scared of letting go.

Then I feel a new warmth. Rosie is licking the side of

my face. I turn slightly, look into her wise, understanding eyes. It's like she's trying to draw the hurt from me.

One deep breath, two. I unfurl my fingers, open my hands. Let go.

I'm not quite sure how I get out of this one.

'Sorry.' I try and peel myself off him, without being too obvious. Then throw an arm round Rosie, which seems to work as a good escape route.

'No problem. I suppose if I was a real man I'd have a hankie to give you.' I risk a glance. He doesn't look all over-sympathetic, or shocked. Or horrified. He's watching me closely, but it's understanding, not sympathy in his eyes.

'No hankie?' I hiccup and spoil the trying-to-be-cool look.

'No tissues, nothing. Just dog food.'

'Terrible. What kind of a man are you?' I try a smile. He tries one back.

'I guess I'm the kind of man that should try and get this resort back to what it was.'

'Not what it was – as good as it was, but different is fine.' Different can be good. 'But you don't want to be here, do you?' I don't want him to ask about what happened, I don't have the answers to give him. And I need to think about how to get them, if I want them, in my own time. It's easier to ask about him.

'True. But the biggest problem is the cash; Ed has more or less bankrupted us.'

'And I've lost the snowmobile.' How could I be so selfish,

how could I do this to him? He already has enough problems and now I've added to them.

'I told you, forget it, I know where it is. And anyway, we've got insurance.'

'Why were you so angry with me when you got here?' I try and ignore the catch I know is in my voice. He rattled me, which is why all that emotion spewed out in an unstoppable torrent. It was like a panic reaction. I know all about them.

'Was I?'

'You lost it completely!'

He looks embarrassed and his cheeks are pink tinged. So that makes two of us. Nice to be in this together.

'You need to respect the weather here, the snow.' There's a gruff edge to his voice which is definitely sexy. 'You wouldn't go surfing in a gale, would you?'

'Well . . .' I grin, I can't help it. 'I quite like some wild weather, a bit of a storm.' The familiar frizz of excitement wells up in my chest, pushing some of the throbbing pain away.

'You're crazy.' He grins back. 'I quite like it when it's heavy myself. It's like when you ski on virgin snow, you're totally alone out there, just you and the elements.' He's got a dreamy edge to his voice that I'm sure I get, and he's not looking at me, he's lost in his own world.

I get it. For me being out there in that massive ocean, just tiny, insignificant me and the elements is as good as it gets. My heaven on earth.

'So what happened to skiing on virgin snow, then?' I try and keep it conversational, no pressure. 'It must have been some crash to leave you with a limp, so I guess you weren't on the nursery slopes?'

There's the tiniest glimmer of a smile, but it doesn't reach his eyes. 'It was some crash. I was snowboarding, going at a lick.'

'Speed merchant like Ed, then?'

'Oh yeah, I could kick his ass any day of the week, he's a total amateur.'

I study him more closely. Ed had called him the golden boy, the one who was good at everything, the one the women flocked to. We never got to the punchline – some hobbit kid had tried to wipe me out and put paid to that conversation.

'He looked pretty good to me.' While I was hanging on to him.

'That's his problem. It's all about looking good, not *being* good.'

'But for you it's about being the best?'

'Being the best I can. There's a difference.'

'So, you were good?'

'Not bad.'

'And the best you could be now?'

'Is so far off the mark I might as well be dead.' This seems a bit extreme, but I can kind of relate. There have been times when changing my life completely has seemed the only way to cope.

'It was my life, Sarah. I'm not cut out for all this.' He waves an arm expansively, and Rosie ducks, which makes me giggle. That crooked smile's tugging at his mouth as he fondles her ears. 'Limping around running a resort isn't what I thought I'd be doing any time soon. I used to travel, live out of a rucksack. Surf in the summer, snowboard in the winter.'

'Nomad.' It's not a question.

'Yeah, Mr Itchy-feet, that's me.' We share a look, and it's nice. 'I'd travel from competition to competition. Live a proper life instead of this existence. I need to be free.'

'I do get the living out of a rucksack thing, I used to do that. I think itchy feet is the one thing I inherited from Mum.' The normal lump in my throat when I mention her isn't quite as big this time, so I just swallow and crash on. 'It's how I used to be, before a nicked scooter, black eye and stolen passport made Lynn reel me in. I don't blame her, I was only a kid, and . . .' I wasn't stupid, I knew it could have been worse. I was reckless back then, not valuing life. 'She wanted me to learn the value of life, learn to love myself a bit, before I wrecked it.'

'You're lucky to have her.'

'I am.' I nod. I know that. 'You've got Ed.'

His eyebrow shoots up so high it makes me laugh. I think the high altitude is making me giddy. I need to think about work, bring myself back down to earth. Stop staring at the man who's rescued me, stop those little thoughts that we're so alike in some ways, so different in others. 'I don't get it then, why buy Shooting Star?'

'I didn't. It was supposed to be Ed's project, I just put some cash into it. But I don't want to be here, Sarah. It's just a reminder of what I can't do, my old life. I only came back because he was so desperate.' He runs his fingers through his dirty blond curls. 'Stupid twat. What does he think I can do that he can't? I'm not a businessman, I'm a – *was* – an athlete.'

He looks so genuinely upset I want to cry again. I think when I get back I might need a new therapist to help me talk less and build all the barriers up again. Can you get those?

'Well, you seem to be doing something right.'

'Not enough, from what the reviews say. Come on, Sarah, you know it's a disaster! And I guess I'm not an athlete any more. I feel like a caged animal.' There's a hint of a lift at the corner of his mouth, I'm not sure it's humour, though. 'Probably why I spend so much time with the dogs. I went looking for you down there, then heard your phone ringing.'

'Sorry. Sitting with Rosie wasn't enough.' She looks at me, so I give her another hug and whisper in her ear, 'You know I wanted to bring you with me.' She licks my nose; I'm forgiven.

Will shrugs. 'I get that. Today is the first time I've come out on skis since it happened; not sure if that's a good thing or a bad thing.'

'Oh. So, what's "it"? What happened?'

There's a heavy sigh, and a long silence. But I'm pretty sure he's thinking, not blanking me. I know defensive body language when I see it. I am the queen of defensive, and Will isn't doing it right now.

'It was just before Christmas. I was getting ready for a competition, trying out some new moves and I wanted one last go. I thought I could beat the elements, get one up on the weather.' He shrugs. 'Bad weather never stopped me before, unless it was really bad. I was heading for the high ground and reckoned the snow had settled enough. I liked to make the first tracks.'

'But it hadn't settled?'

'I was riding on an edge when there was a fall, an avalanche. It wasn't major, but there was nowhere to go, I couldn't outrun it. So I jumped.'

I can feel my jaw drop. 'Off a mountain?'

He laughs. Genuine humour, and it makes me feel happy inside.

'It's what snowboarders do. I'd busted a three and it was pretty awesome, me and all that pure snow.'

'What the hell are you talking about now? Busted a what?'

'A 360 degree spin. Only trouble was, when I came down it was straight into a crevasse that you couldn't see from the top.'

'And?'

'I fell wrong. End of jumping, end of competing, end of.'

'But you survived. Surely that's good?'

He gives me a bleak smile. 'You survived what happened to you too, didn't you? Did that make everything hunky-dory?'

'Yes, but . . .'

'The scars sometimes run deep, don't they? A shrink told me I had to wait for the right time to move on, I couldn't force it. Just cos my body was patched up, it didn't mean my mind was.'

'And what did you say to that?'

'I told him to sod off. Load of jumped-up crap.'

I laugh. 'Poor therapist.'

'Poor my foot, you should have seen the bills!' He sobers up then. 'I don't want to interfere, but Ed, well, he likes to . . .'

'Play the field?' I can't help but smile. 'Oh, I already worked that one out. He's a fun guy, though.'

'Great fun.' His tone is so dry you could strip paint off with it. 'I just don't want . . .' The look is meaningful. Heavy. It takes a while for the penny to drop, then I get why I'm getting the treatment. It's funny. Gawd, this is like being on a roller-coaster: one minute I'm crying, the next he's making me laugh, then feel all warm and fuzzy and huggy. Which is *so* not me.

'I'm not looking for a guy, Will. I want fun, that's all.'

'Callum?'

'Was fun, then we split just before I came out here.'

'I'm sorry.'

271

'Don't be; it was getting a bit heavy for me. Time to split. Though he was lovely.'

'I'm sure he was.'

'What about you?'

'Me?'

'No girl?' I can't help thinking about what Ed said, about Will grabbing all the girls on the slopes.

'Nope. Not for me. I'm a free spirit.' The laugh, I reckon, is what you call ironic. 'Apart from this boulder called Shooting Star hanging round my neck. And Ed.'

If he says the word 'free' one more time I might have to strangle him. I get it. No ties. Not interested. Despite the mega tonsil-curling snog.

'Do you ever miss the slopes?'

'You just move on with life, don't you? No choice. Anyhow, it was nothing, just a daft sport, just a stupid accident, not like what you've been through.'

But I know it's not 'nothing'. It was his life. He's had it taken away just as badly as I've had things taken away.

'There's no such thing as nothing; if you chose to do it, then it meant something. But yeah, you just move on.' You have to.

We sit then, side by side. Thinking. I'm thinking about him, crashing in the snow, not able to do the one thing he loves most. And I think of Mum, cupping her hands round my own as I hold on to one of her crystals.

'You reach for the things that can help you,' she'd said, 'you'll be drawn to what you need.' And I wonder what it was *she* was reaching for, what it was she needed the day she left me.

And I really wish she was still here to tell me.

And then I think I must have fallen asleep.

Chapter 21

My watch tells me it's just after midnight. My left arm is asleep – I can't say dead because it is all tingly and uncomfortable.

Rosie is gently snoring, and Will is watching me.

'You talk in your sleep.'

'Better than snoring.'

'True. Feel okay?'

He doesn't say better, which I like. I like a lot of things about Will.

'Stiff. I'm not used to camping out, not done it for ages.'

'Me neither.' He stretches, and I guess his bad leg is uncomfortable.

'And I'm bloody starving. These pockets are big enough to pack a picnic in, so why didn't one of us?'

'I can't say picnics were top of my list when I set off.'

'Mine neither.' We share a smile. Nice. 'Oh hell, I've just remembered, I have put something in mine. Wonder if it's edible?' Unlikely but worth checking.

'What?'

'I've got a present.'

'Really? You brought presents out here with you?'

'Just one. Aunt Lynn hid it in my bag, then when she rang yesterday she told me.'

'Ah. She rang.'

'She did; she wanted to check I was okay and let me know she was celebrating Christmas early, so she said Happy Christmas.'

'Early? It's not until Monday!'

'I know.' I frown. 'She said she and Ralph were off on a trip down memory lane in the camper van, but I wonder if he's having to go into hospital over Christmas. You know.'

He nods. He knows. We sit in silence for a second. 'Life can be rubbish, can't it?'

'It can. It can also be good.'

'Very good.' I smile, and fish the package out from one of my massive pockets. 'I wanted to open it out here, on my own, cos we've always done personal presents that really mean something, and you know . . .' He nods. Opening this present in a room full of strangers, or maybe I should call them new friends, would have felt wrong. However lovely they are.

There is a note.

Happy Christmas my darling Sarah. I thought it was time I passed this necklace on to you. Your mother gave me it when I was the same age you are now. Lisa loved her gemstones and crystals and I knew it was a present from the heart. We were sisters and, despite all our differences, we knew each other because we are each other. Which is why I'll never lose her, and I'll never lose you, even if we are sometimes continents apart.

You're the most precious gift I've ever had, I never knew I needed a daughter until you came into my life, and I thank her with all my heart for making sure you were safe.

Remember, she never left you. She never abandoned you. She loved you, and it wasn't her choice to leave you. She'd always planned on coming back after one last adventure. And please remember too, that she loved your dad with all her heart. I've always found that hard to admit, because he was a bit of a tearaway, and it's easier to blame him for everything that went wrong, rather than to admit that Lisa wasn't any more perfect than the rest of us.

Live your life, my darling, live your adventures. None of us know which one will be the last.

Ralph is making the final one – I need to be with him, holding his hand and his heart. I couldn't let him take that trip without me. I made that mistake with your mum. But you, my gorgeous girl are having your first real solo adventure. Treasure every second, the good, the bad, the happy, the sad, the beautiful, the glorious, and the ones that seem boring and mundane. Every single one counts, every single one has a meaning, a place in your life. Every twist, turn and uphill battle is as much a part of the map of you as the swoops downhill and the long happy straights are. And hang this around your neck and know that me and your mum are always with you.

Happy Christmas, darling. Lisa would have been so proud of you – you're as feisty and brave and independent as she was. And I hope you've kicked Mr Scrooge in the baubles and shown him what a proper Christmas looks like – that would have made her laugh!

Love you to the ends of the earth, L xxx

'Okay?'

I don't realise how tightly I'm hanging on to the note, until Will starts to carefully prise the crumpled-up paper from my fist. He gently smooths it out, then carefully folds it and slips it back in my pocket. 'You might want to read that again some time.' He wipes my cheek with his thumb, then touches the little pink tissue-paper wrapped present. 'Now or later?'

'Now. It has to be now.'

I know instantly what the crystal is. Like Mum, I've always been drawn to them, and whether that's something that comes from my heart, or from my upbringing with her, it doesn't matter. 'It's a desert rose.'

'It's amazing.' He traces the edge with his fingertip.

'Mum only had one – she said they're carved by the spirits of American Indians.'

'Oh.'

'I think it's actually a combination of the wind, sand and water that does it.' I hold the stone tight in my hand for a moment.

'Here, let me.' His hands are too big for the tiny clasp,

and my clothes are too thick and clumpy and get in the way.

'Bugger.' He fumbles and the whole lot nearly slithers down my cleavage, but finally he manages to do it up. 'Happy Christmas, Sarah.'

'Happy Christmas, Will.' We smile at each other, in our madness. Who cares if we're early?

I don't know what's got into me, but I can't help myself. I reach out and stroke down the side of his face. He catches my hand.

Then very slowly, very deliberately, pulls it towards his mouth. Kisses it knuckle by knuckle, and I hold my breath. It's like the feeling you get when you've drunk something warm, something strong, the sensation of heat and uncertainty trickling down inside me, and when he moves even closer, my lips part.

I don't want to close my eyes, I want to see him when he kisses me. I want to know how it makes him feel.

This isn't the mad passion of before. This is languid, and sexy, and I want this one moment to last for as long as it can. And it does. In fact, it's bloody annoying. He's stringing me up and I'm getting tighter and tighter like a wound coil. Any second now I'm going to explode, and it might be messy. Every move he makes is measured, and his gaze never leaves me.

'Will!' I shiver and try and pull his head back down to mine, but he resists. Smiles.

'Oh no, you're not getting your own way on this.' The

cool air hits my skin as he peels my clothes off, but it's the trail of butterfly-light kisses down my stomach that make me gasp as the muscles contract, then squirm, trying to get more contact. 'I think I know what I'm doing, and if I don't . . .' He stops, winks, and he looks so bloody gorgeous. 'Then you can show me a different way, next time.'

I don't think I need to show him a different way.

I think, in fact, I'd die quite happy if this was the last thing I knew. Well, no, maybe not. But it would be a damned good way to go if you had no option.

'What are you thinking?'

'Believe me, you don't want to know.'

'You're probably right.'

'I am.'

He pulls me in close against him, tidies my clothes, then kisses the tip of my nose.

We gaze into each other's eyes for a second, or seven, but we don't kiss. Then we stare out of the window, up at the stars and the blacker-than-black sky. I rest my hand over the pendant, and I really don't expect to drop off to sleep again. I just want to sit here quietly, with a man and his dog, and a little bit of the two people who've meant the most to me.

I think I may have finally found my new start. I'm ready to move on.

Chapter 22

'What's that racket?' I can hear a buzzing. It's annoying. How is a girl supposed to get any sleep around here? 'I didn't think you'd get bees here.'

'We don't.' Will sounds amused. 'Not much pollen about this time of year.' He nudges me in the ribs. 'Wakey-wakey, time to get decent. Sounds like the rescue party have arrived.'

'The rescue?' Oh bugger, I'd dreamt we'd waltz out of here hand in hand and walk back to the resort, and nobody would even have noticed we'd gone. Well actually, I'd dreamt I was surfing with a bronzed demi-God who looked remarkably like Will, but we'll skip that, seeing as I'll never see him again once my job here is done.

'Anyway, I am decent, fully clothed and fastened up like an Eskimo.'

'Sarah, about yesterday when . . .'

The normally direct-speaking Will has got all tongue-tied.

'Forget it, it was all just a bit emo, wasn't it? I mean

honestly, forget it. And can you forget all of this as well?'
I wave my arms about. He ducks to avoid a black eye, and
Rosie whines and plasters herself against the door.

'It's just, I can't . . .'

'I get it, Will. Honest. Look, it was just a kiss.'

'It wasn't just a kiss though, was it?' Why did I ever think
his eyes were steely blue? They're searching, not piercing.
Kind, not hard. And right now they're worried.

'You live here, I live in the UK. We've got businesses,
family . . .' My words tail off, and just in time, Jed bursts
through the door. Holding a can of fuel in one hand, and
what looks remarkably like a parcel of bacon sandwiches
in the other.

Well, I say looks; I mean smells. Even Rosie helps when
I leap on him. Which means we go tumbling straight out
of the door and land in a waggy heap in the snow. Well,
Rosie is waggy, I'm more kissy.

Chapter 23

'Oh my God the Teletubbies are here!' I am totally and utterly knackered, my head is also all over the place with thoughts of Will and kisses, and Lynn and Mum, and I hardly know what day it is. And that's my excuse and I'm sticking to it. But as we get closer, I realise that there are too many of them. 'Is Father Christmas about to arrive, or something?' There is a small crowd gathered outside the reception area, a very brightly coloured crowd. 'It's only Christmas Eve, eve.' Even in my current mental state, I know Christmas doesn't come this early for anybody.

If they are expecting the man himself, they're going to be very disappointed. I have no Ho Ho Ho or big sack. And we are on snowmobiles, not a sled.

The crowd is starting to bounce around and wave. Rosie barks.

I spin round, in case I'm about to have my head taken off by low-flying reindeer, or (more likely) he's snuck up on the snow. Being trampled by Rudolf and his gang is so not how I want the day to end.

There is nobody behind us. Apart from Jed.

'I think it might be a welcome party just for you.' Will breathes in my ear.

'Me? It can't be, what have I done?' I hiss back, sideways out of the corner of my mouth.

'Disappeared into the mountains on a Friday night? It's kinda noteworthy.'

The man has a point. Although, as, a) I have no family here to miss me, and b) I tend to do my own thing most of the time anyway, then c) why should anybody care?

'Nooooo.'

'Yep. Come on, let's get it over with.'

'Shouldn't they be inside wrapping presents or something?' This is embarrassing. Very. I was hoping we'd be able to sneak in unnoticed (like you do, with a rescue party tagging on behind). They were supposed to be tucking into a hearty breakfast and doing general Christmas stuff. In fact, if they'd been necking Bucks Fizz like me and Lynn usually are by this time the Saturday before Christmas, they wouldn't have noticed if a tribe of polar bears had joined the party.

Ed must be as disorganised as Will has told me he is. He's probably still in bed with one of his snowboarding groupies.

I'd quite like to be in bed, actually; last night was, well, stressful. I've been wrung out (and a few other things that we won't go into), and now I'm all floppy and need time to regain my form.

'Sarah!' Something metallic blue hurls itself at me, and we both land in a heap at Will's feet. 'Oh, Sarah! Where've you been?' My face is in its clutches, and I'm being kissed. It's like being molested by a giant cartoon dog.

I open an eye. I'd closed them in the name of self-protection.

'Sam?' It can't be. 'Sam!' I look at Sam, who is sitting astride on top of me, then up at Will, who mouths 'I forgot to tell you', which is hard to believe.

'Yeah! It's me!' She claps her hands and grins and sits back slightly too heavily so that all the air is forced out of my lungs.

'I – I . . .'

'You're speechless. I knew you'd be pleased! Surprise!' She bounces, and the remaining air whooshes out of my lungs.

I haven't even got the energy to thrash about. Just squeak. 'I can't breathe!'

'Oh. Sorry.' She giggles, and wriggles back a bit. It's a good job I've not eaten much for hours.

'I *am* pleased. But what are you doing here? How the hell did you get here?'

'Taxi, plane, minibus thing. Isn't it fab? We're going to be together, on Christmas Day. All of us!'

Her voice is full of exclamation marks. She's excited. In fact, she's bouncing about a bit and I think my ribs are about to crack and I'll fold up like one of those camp beds with a hinge in the middle.

'Sam, please stop bouncing.' She stops. 'All of us?' What does that mean?

'Surprise!'

A vision in pink looms over the top of me, blocking out the snow, the sun, the whole world.

'We're here too, darling!' The figure is dressed in a very (and I mean very) bright shade of pink (think neon pink and add a bit), with massive goggles strapped to her head. First impression is very embarrassed minion. 'Oh my goodness me, oh goodness. Oops a daisy!' Her feet are skidding all over the place and she's plopped down and just missed landing on my face. 'Oh my, nobody said it would be this slippery!'

'It's ice, Mum.' Sam rolls her eyes.

'But it's extra slippery ice, dear.' She thrashes about until she's on her knees, then somehow gets to her feet, grabbing on to everybody and everything as she goes, spiky shoes threatening to leave parts of my body perforated like a teabag. If Sam hadn't still got me pinned to the ground I'd be out of here quicker than a pro-snowboarder jumping off a mountain (I'm still struggling with the image of Will doing that). 'Our ice at home isn't at all like this! Do they make it differently here, Samantha?' Sam shakes her head. 'Oh well, no harm done. It's us, Sarah! Us!'

'Ruth!' She's moved back a bit, and cannoned into Will, who manages somehow to remain rock solid on his feet.

It is Sam's mother.

I feel faint. I can't deal with this. Not just Ruth. The whole unexpected visitor thing.

I need a shower, a blanket, a big glass of wine. 'Aren't you supposed to be big-game hunting or something?'

'Oh, aren't you funny? There isn't any big game in Canada, silly sausage! All of us are here! David! David, come here, come here and say hello to Sarah. You remember Sarah, don't you, dear?' She has dragged Sam's dad over to peer down at us. I feel like an exhibit. 'Sarah works with Sam.' Her feet go all slippy-slidey again and I cringe. Will grabs one of her elbows and David the other, and I breathe again.

'I know that, dear. How are you, Sarah? Lovely to see you again; we were rather worried that you were in absentia when we arrived.' Luckily, Sam's dad doesn't talk as much as her mum. Though they are both very nice.

'Shush, darling, don't dominate the conversation. Jake's here as well, Sarah – Jake, come and say hello to Sarah!' I am surrounded by Sam's family, and they are all standing in a circle and peering down at me and Sam as though expecting an encore. Jake gives me the thumbs-up. He is Sam's boyfriend, an up-and-coming actor, and a very dishy one.

I'm not quite sure what to say.

'Now, isn't this lovely, dear?' Ruth smiles expectantly. I am expected to speak.

I nod. Speechless. Then do what I really didn't expect. Burst into tears.

This place is having a very weird effect on me.

Maybe I died in an avalanche. Or am delirious from the cold.

'Oh Sare, don't cry, I thought you'd be pleased.' Sam looks like she's about to cry as well.

'I am. Totally. These are happy tears.'

'Everybody say fish fingers or something before my bollocks turn to ice!' A tall, lanky figure in a leather jacket (*so* not the right thing to wear) has joined the crowd. I don't recognise him and crick my neck trying to get a better look.

'Who the . . . ?'

'Get a grip on those girls, Jake boy! Perfect.'

I am blinded by the light, literally. A flash has gone off and immortalised my puzzled look for ever. At least Ruth wasn't sitting on me, which is good. I think.

'Sod off, Larry. Can't you give me five minutes' peace?' Jake never sounds cross, even when he is cross. But I can tell by the look on Sam's face that he's not happy. She can tell. Luckily.

'Five minutes' peace? When you get five minutes' peace then you know you're old news, mate. See yous all tomorrow.'

'Chill, Jake, we'll hide from him tomorrow.' Sam blows him a kiss, then turns her attention back to me. 'He's a reporter; he followed us from the airport.'

'Ah.'

'Jake's agent says if he's nice to the journos then they'll go away when they've got a couple of shots.'

'Ahh.' I hadn't realised Jake had got *that* famous. Mind

you, those pictures of him stripped to the waist on a Cornish beach had certainly attracted a lot of attention.

'What are you still doing down there, Sarah?' Ruth nudges me with her toe. 'You'll get a chill – it's very cold, you know. David, help the poor girl up or she'll catch her death.'

Sam clambers off me and Will hauls me to my feet before Sam's dad gets a chance.

'Bloody hell, Sarah. We thought you were dead when we got here and there was no sign of you! Oh my God, are you okay? Ed said Will was . . .' Sam tails off and stares. 'Tall . . .'

'Tall? Ed said Will was tall?'

'Sorry, I got distracted. He said Will was a one-man rescue party.'

Her mum stares, then points. 'Oh my God, that's Will! You're Will.' She shakes Sam's arm. 'It's Will, that photo you showed me.'

Oh God, how many people has she shown that photo to?

'He's that terrible man who doesn't believe in Christmas and doesn't have marshmallows.' She manages to inject utter incredulity and disgust all into a few words. Her acting skills are obviously improving. 'But he rescued her, so he can't be a total dead loss, can you, dear?' She pats his arm. 'You rescued her! David, he rescued her.' She looks at me. 'He rescued you! You've never rescued me from an avalanche, David!'

'You've never been in avalanche, darling.'

'It wasn't an avalanche.'

We all talk at once, but Ruth just carries on regardless. 'Now aren't you a lucky girl? I think this calls for a mince pie and mulled wine! You do have mulled wine, don't you, William? And chestnuts? Do they have chestnuts in this part of the world?'

'We're not on Mars, Mum.' Sam rolls her eyes. 'And it's too early to hit the mulled wine, you won't want your dinner.'

'Oh nonsense. Well, now you're back safely I think I'll strip off this outfit and put my après outfit on. Except we've not been skiing yet, have we? What's before in French, Samantha? I need a before-ski outfit. You did GCSE French, come on, darling.'

'I only got a grade C.'

'Oh, but you were better than that, you must know that word! What is it, David? Oh, you won't know what it is.' She waves him away dismissively. 'I bet Edward does, he's clever. I'm off to find Edward, and I'm sure he'll be more than happy to find me a nice little glass of mulled wine to warm me up, then we can unpack the presents!' She pulls the goggles down. 'So bright out here! How about a photograph of me and the hero? Come on, don't be shy. I need to get some pictures of my ski gear. Do you know how much this cost? But I thought, well, you never know who you'll be mixing with, do you? The Royals ski, you know! And really famous people do, like that James Bond chap.

What was his name? Oh, it doesn't matter, it will come back to me. Now, come here young man, yes you.'

'Plenty of time for photos later; come on let's get in. Sarah needs to sit down.' Will summons a charm I didn't know he had, mingled with a firmness I've seen plenty of. And which makes me blush.

'Of course, of course. And you need to tell me all about what you got up to in that little hut in the mountains. I'm not one to gossip, but that brother of yours is naughty. He called it a lurve-cabin, champagne and roses, how romantic.' Ruth giggles coquettishly and fans herself. 'You're just what our little Sarah needs, a nice man. She needs to think about settling down, and that Callum she was seeing, well, the things he did with gladioli . . .'

'How many people have you told about that?' I hiss at Sam as we follow the others inside, and the warmth hits me so hard my nose tingles.

'Well, not her, what do you think I am? I told Jake, and she must have overheard. You know she's a secret ninja.'

I do. Ruth is always saying she's not a gossip and can keep a secret – neither of which is true.

'Come on, let's go and put the presents under the tree. We were waiting for you.'

Bugger. Presents.

I look at Sam. 'I've not got a single present. Nothing.' My hand goes automatically to my chest, to cover my pendant.

'I don't want a present. All I wanted was to see you.' She hugs me, and it brings silly tears to my eyes again. I'm going to have to find a way to deal with this. 'You don't mind, do you? Us all coming?'

'Of course, I don't mind. It's fantastic, the best thing ever.' It *is* great, a wonderful Christmas surprise, and the nicest thing anybody has ever done for me. But I guess I'm in shock after an emotional night with Will, and I'd been expecting some downtime on my own to get my head round stuff. To work out what happens next. What happens with Will. I hug her tighter, no way do I want her to think I'm not totally grateful and thrilled to see her. 'But why? I don't get it.'

'Well, it didn't seem right you being here on your own, no Lynn, and not being at home doing normal stuff. And after I cocked up that booking to Kenya, Mum said she'd seen *Out of Africa* and it was all dusty and she wasn't sure it was right going somewhere like that, and she was pretty sure that Robert Redford wouldn't be there, or might even be dead, or sells sauce or something these days.'

'Isn't that Paul Newman?'

'Anyway, she said what was the point in going? Then I told her about Lynn and you, and here, and she got all excited and rushed out to buy après-ski gear and actual ski gear that will never see snow, and well . . . we booked!' She pauses. 'I didn't cock up, did I? I mean, we've not gate-crashed a thing going on between you two, have we?'

'No "thing", and no, of course I don't mind, it's brilliant! It's lovely – I'm so lucky having you as a friend.'

'Well, you were so brilliant after the shitty Liam thing, I really owe you one.'

'Friends don't owe. They just do stuff.' Liam was Sam's ex, and he *was* shitty. Very shitty. If I'd had my way he'd have had a one-way ticket to somewhere horrible, with spiders and clowns, but as Sam wouldn't let me do that we drank lots of wine together, stuffed our faces with pizza and watched back-to-back romcoms, until she met Jake.

'So, he's okay then, this Will? He looks nice, not at all Scroogey, and we met Ed. He is *SO* cute! You should have seen him with Mum, she was practically simpering, which is a bit disgusting, really, but it's funny as well; it meant Dad could go out and have a cigar in peace. This place it totally amazing!'

I'm glad she moved on quickly from the Will question. 'It is?'

'It is! I knew you could do it! It's fantastic, so warm and cosy and our cabins are fantastic. Oh Sarah.' She hugs me again. 'You've totally transformed the place in a few days. Nobody could ever give this place a bad review now. I love the new website as well, and those videos, and the snow.' She runs out of breath, her cheeks glowing. 'Lynn will love it! She'll promote you even higher.'

I laugh. 'That isn't possible.' But my cheeks are glowing as well. I guess I hadn't really had time to stop and look at what we've actually achieved. But the place *is* looking better – I'd even go so far as to say magical.

'It's fantastic, you're a Making Memories ambassador! You can go out and make all the other places even better than they already are!'

'This wasn't just me, it's been a team effort, and . . .' I don't want her to get carried away. But I have to admit, Aunt Lynn's idea of us going out and exploring new places has sounded better by the day. I've loved getting out of the office, being here. Doing things. My fresh start.

'Will's a bit of all right too, a real outdoorsy type; he suits you.' She hasn't moved on from the Will question it seems.

'Sam!'

'Well, it's true. Are you sure you haven't, you know . . .?'

'He doesn't do relationships, or settling, which is why he's not happy here. It's not his thing.'

'Well, nor do you. so he's perfect for a fling.'

I hadn't thought of it like that. She has a point.

'Oh, my goodness gracious. Now isn't this nice? Isn't this nice, girls?'

Sam's mother is 'projecting' from her seat near the fire – apparently Jake has been giving her lessons. Personally, I think he and Sam have been extracting the Michael a bit, the flamboyant hand gestures make it all a bit too theatrical. Like she's auditioning for a part in *Macbeth* or something, but she's happy, and that's what counts.

'What a nice young man you've found, Sarah. Come and sit here and tell me about him.'

'I haven't . . .'

'I wouldn't even bother.' Sam is shaking her head. 'Deny this and she'll fix you up with somebody else. Wow, though, he *is* a nice young man!'

Will is looking awkward, and balancing a large tray, and Jake is standing behind him looking much more comfortable, and also carrying a tray. He can act any part – waiter is a piece of piss.

'I thought, seeing as I wasn't here to sort your welcome packs out, I'd try and make up my way.' Will puts the massive drink in front of me. 'Hot chocolate.'

'Oh my God, you have got to be kidding me? You call that a hot chocolate? I love you. Well, obviously not actually love you, it, I love it, it's, er fab, well . . .'

Then he stops me.

By putting his lips over mine.

Very effective.

'Drink up.'

'You're not running away, then?'

'Not yet.' He grins and sits down next to me, just as Sam slopes off to share sloppy kisses under the mistletoe with Jake. 'Maybe in January.'

'Wow.'

'The hot chocolate, or . . .'

'Both.' There's cream, chocolate, real chocolate flaky bits, marshmallows . . . I need a picture, to post everywhere. I need Instagram. Or another kiss. 'Did you mean to do that?'

'I did. I'll do it again to prove it if you like.'

'Cool.' It comes out a bit breathy and weird, but doesn't stop him.

'Are you sure nothing happened in that hut?' Sam is leaning between us, looking like the cat that's got the cream.

Literally. I wipe a splodge off her top lip. Then notice the sprig of mistletoe she's got in her hand.

'Cabin. It was a cabin not a hut. Sod off, Sam, go and slurp all over Jake, he's pining already. And where did you get that?'

'There's loads of it, everywhere.'

I look at Will. 'Ed. He's addicted to the stuff – you know, any opportunity.' His voice is all rough and sexy. He is staring into my eyes. He's got very nice eyes.

I want him to kiss me again.

Maybe this is why I couldn't kiss Ed. Maybe this is the answer. It wasn't just guilt about letting Will down. It was Will.

I blink. It's a bit of a scary answer.

I glance down so I can avoid his gaze, just in case he can guess what I'm thinking.

'Oh God! What are you wearing!' I think my laugh is hysterical. But it is funny. As distractions go it's brilliant.

'It's my Christmas jumper. I thought you'd approve – you know, getting in the spirit and all? You said I had to be festive.'

'I didn't quite see *that* coming. It's terrible, but wonderful.' We share a grin and it makes my toes curl. 'As jumpers go, that is zinging.' I do what I always do and fill the gap with words when I get a bit embarrassed.

'Zinging?'

His entire chest is covered by a giant reindeer head, with a very furry bright-red nose and antlers that reach his armpits.

'Squeeze his nose.'

'You just want me to touch you.'

'Well, there is that, but . . .'

I squeeze and his antlers light up. Will's chest is a mass of flashing red and green lights. There's a squeal, then Poppy races over and jumps on his knee. Then starts to pummel him in the chest.

'Oof!' I hope the sound of pain is because she's landed on his stomach, and not a bit lower down. 'Stop it, you little minx.'

'Oh, let her, she's excited.'

'I bet you used to be like this, didn't you? I can just imagine you as a little girl.'

'What do you mean? Used to be?' I affect my hurt look, then join Poppy in a competition to see who can keep Will lit up for longest.

'Stop it, the pair of you.' He manages to wrestle us both to the ground, one under each arm. Poppy carries on attacking, but I stop and look at the man I've just spent the night with.

'Not quite the result I was after.'

But his eyes are bright, and he's grinning. Letting a little girl pummel his chest and squeal as the lights go on and off. As Christmas surprises go, he might even have gone one better than Lynn.

'I like it.' I do. Who can't love a man in a terrible jumper, tickling an over-excited little girl just before Christmas?

'Why didn't you warn me this lot were going to descend?'

As we're on the floor, and Poppy is distracted, I think it's safe to ask. Nobody can overhear.

'It was a last-minute booking, and I was warned that if I breathed a word to you I'd have pine cones stuffed into orifices I didn't know existed.'

'Sam said that?'

'No, her mum did.'

'Would you like to see my ham, Sarah?' As this has come from Ruth, and not Will, it's a tad disappointing. 'I brought one in my suitcase, a massive one, just in case there wasn't any food!'

Will frowns. 'No food?'

'Well, you can't be too careful, can you? I mean, all the shops will be closed on Christmas Day, and after we'd seen that horrid video? Not that I believe it for a moment, it was just attention-seeking, trying to get looks-at or whatever they're called.'

'Views.'

'I brought nuts as well; you have to have nuts to crack at Christmas, don't you, David?'

David doesn't comment.

'And dates. Oh, and we mustn't forget the Stilton! It's the proper stuff, you know. I did try and sneak some bucks fizz and brandy cream in, but that horrible man at the airport confiscated it, along with my lovely cranberry sauce. I bet he'll be having a real slap-up meal.'

'What does she mean, video?'

'*The Worst Christmas Ever* one that I told you about.'

'Ah. Should I watch it?'

'Probably better not to. You know, clean slate and everything. Where on earth is she going now?'

We watch Ruth head out of the lounge at speed. 'I hope she's not gone to find her huge ham.'

***

She hadn't. She is back twenty minutes later.

'Do you like it, Sarah? Isn't it absolutely chic?'

'It's very, er, red.' As I said, we're not talking hams here.

'Cherry. They call it cherry, darling. It's my ski-ing outfit! The lovely lady in the shop said I'd kill them on the slopes.' She pulls her white bobble hat down a bit more firmly on her head. I think she's waiting for us to take photographs. 'You can put me on that Instant Gran site if you want!'

'I think you mean Instagr—'

'I think she was closer first time.' Sam hugs her and kisses her cheek. 'Oh, Mum!'

Sam's mother is wearing a bright-red ski suit with white go-faster stripes down the sides. She looks like a Mini out of the Italian Job.

'Now then, girls, who's going to join me on the slopes? Enough sitting about, let's work off those Slimming World Syns before tea time!'

I wasn't aware I'd committed any sins (recently), or that there would be any tea.

'I've seen them do this on *Ski Sunday*, even children can

do it, you know, so I'm sure it's easy. Come along, come along.' She tosses her skies over her shoulder and the waitress dodges, but gets caught on the rebound.

She's flinging the door open, fuelled by wine, whisky and a bucket of sambuca before anybody can stop her. We watch her stomp past the window.

'What did you put in that hot chocolate?'

Will holds his hands up. 'Nothing to do with me, honest.'

'I think you need to stop her.'

Jake and Will look at each other. 'No rush, she's not going very fast.'

'No, but she might take a window out.'

There's a squeal and everybody rushes to the window to see her sliding down the path on her bottom.

'She's not even got her skies on yet.'

Jake and Sam lure her back in, with the aid of a bottle of port. Ed, who is laughing so much he can barely stand up straight, barricades the door so she can't escape again.

I need my bed. On my own. Now.

I look at Will, but the funny quip I'd prepared in my head dies on my lips. He's staring at me. His gaze intent. 'Is it time to beat a hasty retreat?'

***

We do. We practically jog all the way to my cabin, and I'm panting when we step inside and he closes the door firmly behind us.

'I think we have some unfinished business from last night.' His voice is gruff. 'I need to have you to myself, on a bed, with no dog for company. I need to look at your beautiful body in the candlelight; I need to show you just how perfect Christmas can be.' He's down on his knees, sliding my top up, his lips against my skin. 'Without a single bauble or scrap of tinsel in sight.'

My knees are trembling, a shiver of goose bumps is spreading over my body and I thread my fingers through his hair as sensations I've never felt before wash over my body. I push myself against him, clutch him close and shut my eyes so that I can hold on to every single second. Just me and him.

I feel the change in him, a new urgency, as he sweeps me off my feet and then lays me on the bed. Tantalisingly slowly, he undresses me – and I want to scream with impatience, but I don't. And as I watch him take his own clothes off I know that. being here with Will. is what I've always been waiting for.

He pauses for a moment, the moonlight dancing over his muscles, highlighting his toned body, his strong jaw, then lowers his body over mine. 'Sure?'

There's no need for words, I just let a small smile linger over my lips, then I reach up and draw his head down to mine.

Chapter 24

O h. My. God. I'm famous! It's like in one of those films when the main character answers the door naked apart from a strategically placed miniscule towel, unwashed (the star not the towel), and with his hair a mess, and there are a crowd of strangers staring at him. Taking photographs and shouting loudly.

It is just like that. Except I am not naked; I am fully dressed because the weather is flipping freezing, and I am showered and heading for breakfast.

So not exactly like it, but the shouting and photo-taking is spot on. Why didn't I think to put make-up on? Why did I not put my sexiest après-ski clobber on? Or more to the point, just why? Why are they here?

'You've made a mistake, Jake isn't here!'

There's a brief pause in the noise, then one voice rings out.

'Who's Jake? It's you we want, darlin'. Give us a pout!'

I think I am preening. They want me! I am doing that thing Sam's mum, does touching her hair. I do a little bow.

'Can you jump in the air and shout woohoo?'

There is a mass of clicking of shutters, even more when I slip and land on my bum. That gets a round of applause and thumbs-ups.

'Looks like you've fallen for him, then, love?' I don't know who shouts this, but it makes them all laugh.

'Head over heels, I'd say,' yells another. This gets an even bigger laugh. They're all very friendly and jovial.

I get back to my feet. Being wanted is easy. And fun.

'As long as she's not heading for a fall, eh?'

'Headlong crash?' They all seem to be taking notes.

'On the slippery downhill slope?'

This has taken a turn I'm not quite sure I like. Asking me to leap for joy was obviously a nasty ploy. They knew I'd land on my arse.

'What the . . . ?' Will insisted on escorting me home last night; he said this was to make sure I didn't run off with the snowmobile again. He said and did a lot of other things as well. And he stayed with me, in my bed, to make double sure. He's very thorough.

He is behind the door and drags me in then slams it shut.

'What are you doing? I do actually need to go – I need coffee.' I try to reopen the door, but his foot is wedged behind it. But not even a pack of polar bears can stand between me and the first coffee of the day, let alone a bevy of excited men.

I might have to modify that last bit of the statement at some point.

Will is running his fingers through his hair at such a rate, it's standing up more than mine is. Plus, mine is a paid-for look, his is just cute in a I-need-a-hug way.

'The press are here!'

'I know, but why?' Had they heard about my skills on a snowmobile, and our tryst (I've always wanted to use that word) in the mountain cabin? Am I now a minor celebrity? If so, I need to open the door quickly, before my fifteen minutes of fame expires.

'They're after me, not you.'

'Oh.' Bit of a bummer, but not entirely unexpected. 'Are you sure?'

'Positive.'

'Why? You're not a serial killer, or drug smuggler or something are you?'

'No.' I had hoped that would lighten the atmosphere (though it was a question I needed to ask, seeing as it had been one thought before I came here). There's a glimmer of a smile on his face, but it's mingled with frustration. And frustration is winning the day. 'How the hell did they find me?'

'What do you mean, find you?' We both stare at each other. 'Er, it wasn't when they took pics of Jake, was it? We were all in them and . . .'

His jaw hardens, there is a twitch. 'Shit.'

'This is why you didn't want to be in my livestream, isn't it?'

He nods.

'This is why you didn't want your photo on the website?'

'Yup.' He looks distracted, as though he's planning an escape. Which he probably is.

'But why—'

'I'll explain later, I just need to get rid of them first. Hell, this will be all over the papers, everybody will know.'

'It looks like everybody already does.' I point at the door.

'That, darling, is not everybody.'

He called me darling, and he's not a darling kind of person. Does that mean he is actually going to stop harping on about being free for a bit and make the most of this?

'What do you mean though, "everybody"? What "everybody"? Who? Will, stop. What will they know?' One minute I've spent a rather energetic night with a man, and think I'm getting to know him. The next he's talking in riddles and I haven't a clue.

'Later. I'll explain later, but I need to get out.'

'Can you go out the back?' On my reckoning I've used up at least six minutes of the fifteen and might as well make the most of a once-in-a-lifetime opportunity.

'There isn't a back door.'

The man has a point. 'The window?'

'Look, you go, and I'll stay here until they get bored. They won't follow you. They don't know who you are. With any luck they'll decide I'm not here.'

I am slightly miffed by this. However, he does have a valid point. The tale of me riding off into the night on his snowmobile is obviously not tabloid fodder.

We are both wrong. They do follow me.

'How did you meet him?'

'When's the wedding?'

'How did you hook up?'

'How long have you been together, babe?' The 'babe' bit makes me glare in indignation, and I realise it was a mistake. They all capture the moment forever. If I was going to be famous, that wasn't the look I was aiming for. This is almost as bad as the one of Ruth almost sitting on my face yesterday. I don't think I'm cut out for fame.

Hang on. Hooked up? Wedding? I am not hooked up. What are they talking about?

'We're not—'

They are not listening, they are clicking away and waving microphones willy-nilly.

Now, do I lock the door and risk trapping Will in? Or leave it open and risk a press invasion? I lock it. From the look on his face I reckon he'd rather be trapped than swarmed all over and have cameras stuck up his nostrils.

'What are you planning next? Is he back competing?'

'I am planning coffee. And pancakes.' I aim for the centre of the pack, as that is where the path is.

I would have been better sidling up the side, and tramping through the snowdrift.

The path is packed hard, and frozen. I slip-slide my way along, manage not to fall by grabbing onto a few coats and elbows as I go. It's not graceful, but it works. Like pulling yourself along a rope bridge. Wobbly and inelegant.

Ed is grinning through the window when I get to reception. He does not come out to rescue me (the sod) but he does let me in (I was beginning to think he might not), and pushes the door firmly closed behind me. And locks it.

'What did they mean, competing?' I stamp the snow off my feet, and glare at him.

'What?'

'One of that lot asked if Will was going to compete again.'

'I better let him explain that.'

'Tell!'

'Sorry, Sarah, but he's actually even scarier than you are.' He ruffles my hair. 'He's going to go ballistic. What have you done with him?'

'I think he was going to climb out of the back window.'

'Chop-chop, Sarah! We're all going skiing.'

Today, Sam's mother is a vision. Well, I say vision, I think she's impaired mine. She is dressed head to foot in purple. Shiny purple. She has arrived at breakfast fully prepared for the day ahead. How many bloody ski suits has the woman got?

'I'm not very keen on—'

'Oh nonsense, it will be such fun!'

'And I need coffee.'

'Well, drink up – we don't want to waste the day, do we? That snow won't be there for ever!'

'I think it might be there for quite a while, Mum.' Sam shoves a mug of coffee in my hand and tries to steer her mother back towards the table. Ruth dodges. And waves her poles about.

'I'm not sure you'll want to go out yet. There are all these photographers, out—'

'Really? Photographers!' Her hand goes automatically to her hair. 'Oh, how splendid. Jake, Jake, they're here again. I do love you having a famous boyfriend, Samantha. Much better than living with a boring fart who works in a bank.'

We both raise our eyebrows. Jake and Ed smirk.

'They're not actually here for J—'

'Did you slip something in Mum's coffee?' Sam is grinning.

'Just a swift tot to keep her warm.' Ed waves a flask about then slips it back in his pocket.

'You youngsters these days have no sense of adventure. When I was a girl . . .'

David rolls his eyes, and mutters something that sounds remarkably like 'well, that was a long time ago.'

He is not dressed in ski wear. He has a thick jumper on, and a newspaper in his hand. Which is good. I dread to think what kind of snow outfit Ruth might have bought for him. I doubt conservative or brown, his favourite style and colour.

'You could all go out through the kitchen, avoid the paparazzi?'

Jake nods vigorously at the suggestion from Ed. We all troop through the kitchen, which is probably against all health and safety guidelines, and Ruth's skies are on her feet before she's even cleared the back-door step.

'Come on. Tally-ho!' Ruth seems to think we're about to

go hunting, whereas I feel more like the hunted. 'Isn't this exciting, girls? Come on, Jake, keep up! You can tell them I'm your mother-in-law and the next Dame Judi. Oh, what larks!' Her two feet head in opposite directions, and Ed and Jake herd them back together. It's a bit like watching Bambi standing up for the first time.

'To the ski lift!'

It is surprisingly quiet at the back of the building. Too quiet. Apart from Ruth that is.

'Oh my, look at those slopes!' Ruth breaks free from Ed and Jake, and sets off at a surprising speed.

'I thought she couldn't ski?'

Sam shrugs. 'You know my best mate Jess at school? Well, her mum, Juliet, was the village summer fete dry-ski champion—'

'Summer fete?'

'It was too dangerous in the winter when there was snow. She was champion when we were six years old. So . . .'

'Your mum had to try and beat her?' I've heard all about the competitive streak that has existed between Jess's mum and Ruth, ever since Jess's first, very advanced, demonstration of pencil control on their first day in nursery class. Sam had been too busy inspecting the boy's toilets to notice.

Jess and Sam didn't care about the comparisons. They had become best friends who wouldn't compete.

So their mothers did it for them.

'Yep. She had Dad on his bike, towing her through the

park on her skies every night. It was so embarrassing. Then at the fete, she cannoned out of control into the cake and homemade jam stall and ended up looking like a murder victim.'

'Could have been worse – it could have been the cacti stall.'

Sam giggles. 'It was the buttercream that upset her most; she said the dog wouldn't stop licking her crotch when she got home and it left a nasty damp patch.'

I try not to laugh.

Ruth has got halfway up the nursery slope and is waving madly. We wave back. I'm glad she didn't go on safari, I don't think the wildlife would have been able to resist her.

'Are we going?' Sam holds up her skies.

'Are we buggery. You can, but—'

'There!! There they are!!' There is a hollering like a pack of wildebeest on the run, and a stampede as loads of people pile round the side of the building.

'Oh my God, who do you think they're after now?' They have either hunted Will down and devoured him, or they've got a new target.

'Well, it's not Jake!' Sam points as they steam past Jake nearly sending him into a spin. 'Well, his agent did say if he was nice to them for one day they'd leave him alone.'

'It must be somebody *really* famous. Sorry.' I grin apologetically at Sam. 'I mean, I know Jake is famous, but . . .' I take a deep breath. 'I think they're here because of—'

'It must be somebody who's properly famous. Maybe it's Kit Harrington – he likes snow.'

'I think that's the part he plays, not him.' We both wheel round though, but there is nobody remotely resembling Jon Snow (sadly), or anybody else for that matter. 'Sam, I think they're after Will.'

'Will?'

'They were all outside my cabin this morning, lying in wait.' Gears are whirring in my brain. 'He told me that he used to snowboard, to compete.' I talk slowly as they start to click into place. 'Ed called him a golden boy, I think maybe he was quite good . . .'

'*Very* good?'

'Maybe very good, and then he had a crash and—'

'Where is he? Where's the bugger got to?' The leader of the pack slides to a halt, and I grab Sam to stop myself falling over.

'Who?' I try and look blank. It isn't difficult.

'What's he like to snog?'

I don't think I should answer that, but I don't have time anyway. Maybe a good thing.

'Were you his nurse?'

'No, I—'

'Bed baths bring you together?'

'Now there's a headline, Jason, I like that.'

I might as well not be here. They are quite happy to chat amongst themselves and make up the answers. 'If you aren't going to listen, how can you get the facts right?'

'They're not interested in facts, sweetie, believe me.'

A woman I have never, ever seen before (I'd have remembered), has appeared from nowhere and hooked her arm through mine and is smiling widely. She is looking her best – well a lot better than me.

'Who the hell . . . ?'

Then she sidles over towards Jake and drapes herself over him.

Sam snarls.

'That,' Ed shakes his head slowly, 'is Dominique.'

Dominique not only sounds French, she looks French. In a sleek, well-groomed, look-sexy-and-tousled-in-any-kind-of-gear way.

She is also surrounded by men with cameras. I feel sick.

'And why is she . . . ?' I don't think I should have asked that question. I don't think I want to know the answer. Which is why I have left it hanging.

The photographers who had been following Jake on the slopes yesterday, have multiplied.

'Oh darling, I've come for Billy!' Dominique sounds husky and gorgeous. There is a collective passing of air (as in sighs) from the press and they go into overdrive.

How can she hear when she's that far away? Who is Billy?

'No Billy here!'

Ed whispers in my ear. 'She's talking about Will.'

'Will?'

'Everybody used to know him as Billy when he was snowboarding.'

'What does she mean, she's come for him?' I hiss at Ed, right in his ear, so Dominique can't hear. He flinches.

'Well?' I poke him in the ribs, hard.

'Maybe she wants him ba—'

There is the sound of an engine, and the snowmobile skirts the crowd, dangerously near, showering us all in snow and nearly burying one reporter. For a split second I could swear it's Will; I've some to know the shape of his body, the way he holds himself, his every move, so well. It's the only bloody thing about him I have come to know, though.

Billy? How could I not know he was a Billy? And that he had a Dominique. Who is back.

And then he's gone. There is silence.

I feel queasy.

'Look at me, over here! Over here boys!'

Ruth is hurtling towards us, crouched down like Eddie the Eagle.

'Oh my goodness gracious, make way, make way. David, David, how do I stop? It was never this fast with the bicycle!'

I want to kiss Sam's mother, who is careering towards us, with her pointy sticks aimed forwards as though she intends to kebab most of the crowd. I rather think she'd prefer to be caught, though.

They part. At least they do have some common sense.

Ruth hits a hillock, stops abruptly and face-plants with a screech. Jake and Sam rush over to heave her back upright, and she swoons back to the floor.

'Call a doctor, Jake, call a doctor. Oh my goodness, the stress of having a movie star in the family.'

It does distract the press for a moment, quite a few of them needing to check out who the movie star might be, and who *she* might be.

'Where's Will?'

Ed shakes his head. 'He'll be lying low.'

'Why are they here, I mean . . .'

'Somebody spotted him on the photos they took of Jake yesterday.' Ed holds out his mobile as we walk back in and I look. There are tweets. Many tweets. We have gone viral.

The startled picture of me, underneath a pile of friends. With Will looking on.

Billy is back in business!

On the slopes, or sloping off?

Are the model couple back together – or is it timeout with a tattooed lover?

Ed flicks through the tweets and stops at one. 'Do you really have a giant tattoo of a dragon all over your back?'

'No, I don't! What are you talking about, Ed?'

'This tweet says it clashes with your hair!'

'It's a dragonfly tat, not a dragon. Honestly! And it's small, like tiny. Who told them about that?'

'Can I include that?' A woman reporter has managed to sneak in after us. 'Talk to me, sweetie, I can do a story from your side; you know, how you got him back on his feet and all that crap.'

'What are you talking about?'

315

'We can pay – double if you can get him to talk.'

'What does she mean, get him back on his feet?' Ed is edging off. He doesn't do 'tricky' or 'difficult'.

'Why would he . . . I don't get . . .'

She opens her eyes wide and then suddenly smiles. It's not a particularly nice smile. More crocodile than Father Christmas.

'You don't know much about Billy, do you?'

'Billy? He's . . .' I look at Ed for support, but he's looking shifty and tugging at my arm. But I don't want to go, I want to hear what this woman has to say.

One minute I'm pouring my heart out and drinking hot chocolate with a man who might not be as bad as I originally thought, now I realise I don't know a thing about him.

He's not Will, he's Billy.

He's got a glamorous girlfriend on the prowl.

He is famous.

'You really don't know who you've been shagging? You're shitting me?'

'I shit you not.' What is the woman on about? 'And anyway, how do you know I've been . . .' I'm beginning to suspect he must have been more than 'very good' on his snowboard, and that he's missed out a few of the finer details.

'That photo said it all, love. That was the look of love, and we're printing that bit whether you talk or not. And if you haven't been humping your brains out, babe, then there is something seriously wrong with you. I mean, look at him!'

She's waving a photo about that isn't my Will. It is an old photo. It is vaguely familiar. Then I realise: it was one that popped up (repeatedly) when I was googling Will, trying to find out more about him when I thought he was Ed.

I had dismissed it, because 1, It was a bloke called Billy, and 2, It didn't look anything like the picture on the resort website (which it wouldn't, seeing as that one was Ed). I think my brain is going to explode.

I think the whole of me might explode.

'When I get hold of—'

Ed is making shushing motions.

'Yeah, well, nice pic, but he can be quite grumpy.'

'I wouldn't give a monkey's about his moods, sweetie – when you get to my age it's hot or not. That, my girl, is *the* Billy Armstrong. Shit-hot pro snowboarder, champion, and all-round hottie. And that,' she waves at where Dominique is still pouting and posing, 'was the other half of the supermodel couple. Forget Posh and Becks, this pair were the real deal. She disappeared off the scene after his crash.' She gives me a look that says she feels sorry for me.

'So why is she . . .'

She looks at me shrewdly. 'Well, I guess she's come back for him now he's back in one piece?' She folds her arms. 'Now, do I get that shot of you two cosying up under the mistletoe?'

'No.' As I haven't a clue where he is, the answer to that one is easy.

'Well, I guess it's the heartbroken break-up and make-up ex story then. Any chance of a threesome angle?' I'm going to hit her. 'No? Thought not.'

Chapter 25

Will is in his office. He is shredding paper. It looks like he'd actually like to be shredding much more – so I keep my distance.

'What are you doing?'

'Tidying up before I go.'

'Go where?'

'Who knows? Who bloody cares.'

'I think I might.'

He sits down with a heavy sigh and thumps his feet up on the desk. Will never puts his feet on the desk. This makes me very uneasy.

'Oh Sarah.' That makes me feel even more uneasy. 'Oh God, this is such a mess, I knew I shouldn't . . .' He's gazing straight into my eyes. 'You don't deserve this. I told you I couldn't . . .' He rubs his palm over his face and looks knackered. I want to hug him, but it's not the right time. 'This is why we can't . . .' All his unfinished sentences hang in the air between us. 'I can't stay here with this media circus, that's why I kept my head down after the accident.'

'You hid. Ran away to a different country, a different life?'

'Harsh, but fair.' He rubs at a barely visible mark on his trousers.

'Everybody has shit in their lives, Will. You can't just sit back and let it take over – you have to kick its arse, stamp on it: you can't keep running.'

He shakes his head. 'I can't stamp on this, Sarah. It isn't always that simple.' His voice is quiet, but more determined than ever.

'Yes it is. It is simple if you make it that way.'

'Says who?'

'Stop being so bloody stubborn.'

'Sarah, you know it's not always simple!'

'Come back to the UK with me, start again.' I didn't mean to say it, it just came out. Not only do I now have a five-year plan, it seems I want a boyfriend. A proper boyfriend.

'I can't.'

Well, that put a stop to that, which is probably good. I can't cope with long-term, with commitment. 'Why not?' Oops.

'It will be worse than ever, we'll both be in the news, everything I've ever done, everything you've done, will be spread across the papers, tweeted about, bloody Instagrammed to death. Do you want that?'

'No, but . . .' I think about Callum and his gladioli, Aunt Lynn, my lovely quiet home.

'*All* your secrets.' He stresses the 'all' and gives me his most direct stare. We both know what I'm thinking. Dad.

'They'll forget, move on.'

'Eventually, when they've scavenged every last morsel and regurgitated it so often it's unrecognisable. I need to keep my head down, hide, until it goes quiet. Not stir them up.'

'I could stay here.' My voice is small, and we both know why.

'No, Sarah. You can't.'

I can't. Not really, if I stop and think about this. I've got great friends, fabulous Lynn. My business. My love of travel, my itchy feet, both partly why I loved the idea of working with Aunt Lynn; and when she said me and Sam needed to get out more, that she'd take on a temp I'd not really thought about what it meant. But now I have.

I'm ready to hit the world, go out to more of our resorts, check new ones, encourage the old ones to pull their socks up and be even better.

'I could try, for a bit.' We both know I can't. But I can't let this beat me, there has to be a way, a solution. 'You can't just run away or go back to hiding and being a bloody misery.' I probably shouldn't have said, or rather shouted, the misery bit. But I'm frustrated. He's frustrating.

'Stop trying to run my life – why don't you concentrate on your own.'

'That is so out of order.'

'Sorry.' He slumps down further into the chair. 'Honestly,

I'm sorry, I shouldn't have said that. But if you and your friends—'

'This is all my fault, isn't it?'

He shrugs.

'If Jake hadn't come here, and the reporters hadn't followed him . . .'

'You didn't know, and they're your friends.' He pauses. 'Good friends.'

'But if I hadn't come over here, interfering.'

He does a big heartfelt sigh. 'If Ed hadn't made such a balls-up with this place, and if I'd done the sensible thing and told him to sell up, then you wouldn't have had to come here.'

'True. I wouldn't.'

He stares at me, those steely blue eyes making my heart beat faster. Then he clears his throat. 'I'm glad you did, though.' His voice is low, but I hear every word.

'So am I.'

'I guess you're right, though, I can't hide for ever.' He picks at a sticker on the printer, slowly peeling it off. His tone is flat. I don't like flat. It makes my insides churn.

'Who are you hiding from, Will? Dominique?'

The smile on his face isn't humour. It's got a twist, which means it hurts. She hurts. Now I hurt.

'Ha ha now that's a funny one.' He laughs. But obviously doesn't find it funny. 'No hiding from Dom. She couldn't get away fast enough; playing nurse was not her style.'

'I can see that.'

He carries on shredding paper and not looking me in the eye. Bad news.

'You were the golden couple.'

He shrugs. 'We were good press fodder, and it didn't do her career any harm.'

'Which was?'

'Wannabe star. I met her when I did some promo.'

'Promo?'

'Snowboarding gear, clothes, you know.'

'Modelling?'

His eyes fleetingly lock on to mine, there's a barely percept-ible nod.

'You were a model?' Something tells me I shouldn't pursue this one. He looks even more unhappy. 'She's French.' Who knows why I said that. It was just the first thing that came into my head.

'How do you know about her?'

'She's here. One of the reporters mentioned—'

'Ah, explains the frenzy on the slope then.'

'Why hide? What are you frightened of Will? They can't hurt you, can they?'

'Failure?' He gives a harsh, short laugh that makes my insides curl up. 'They only want to crow. In fact, I'm not really hiding from anybody – *they* all dumped me. Dom, the press, the advertising companies, the modelling agency, the team . . . I'm a crippled has-been, and nobody likes a failure, do they? I've just been trying to outrun my own bloody uselessness. I don't need to see it reflected back at me by some trash tabloids.'

'But you're not useless. You're just different now.'

'Sarah.' He stares at me. 'I don't *want* to be different. I liked who I was.'

'Sarah, Sarah? Oh, thank God for that; we wondered where you were.' Sam is smiling at us round the door. 'Fancy a drink?'

'Look, go back to your friends, they've come a long way to see you.'

'But you—'

'I've got stuff to do, go. I'll see you later.'

So I do go, but I've got this horrible, hollow feeling in the base of my stomach as I walk away, trying to joke with Sam. I shouldn't leave him, I really shouldn't. We need to talk, work something out. But I don't think he's giving me any choice.

***

I can't help myself. After a drink with Sam I come up with an excuse to nip back to my cabin. I push the door shut. Stand on a chair (I have discovered that an almost passable download speed is available two metres above floor level, just at the side of the front window, if you hold your mouth in a certain way and pray) and google Will, Billy.

Now I realise that I don't know him at all.

I poured out my heart, and he gave me titbits.

I stretch up to enlarge the photo of two gorgeous people in love.

Then a movement outside catches my eye.

It's them.

I shuffle round on the chair so that I can see better, and my mobile phone drops down to my side. His hands are on her shoulders, her hands on his chest. Moving slowly up, until her fingers tangle in his hair and she's leaning in for a ki—

'Shit!' I forgot I was on a chair. Now I'm on the floor. My elbow hurts. My knee hurts. But most of all something inside me hurts, but I still need to know what they're doing. Just how bad this is.

I scramble along the floor like a crab, pop my head up to windowsill height. All I can see is the snow. They've gone. Completely disappeared.

I try and peer round the corner, banging my head on the cold glass. I even open the door and shove my head out.

They've probably gone somewhere more private.

I hate her. I want to hit him.

It's Christmas Eve I should be happy and having fun. And I feel crap.

Why didn't he tell me that as well as a broken body he had a broken heart?

Why is he snogging (or maybe even right now shagging) the wonderful Dominique?

I have been totally stupid. I should never have kissed

him, let alone anything else. I can't say he didn't warn me. But when he said free, I didn't realise he meant free to be with somebody else. And I shouldn't have poured out my heart to him like an overflowing drain. I need to go home.

Except it is Christmas Day tomorrow and I won't get a flight. And I'll let Sam and all her family down after they've come all this way so that I wouldn't be on my own. Going home is not an option.

I need to talk to him. Have this out. I can't not. And as I'm still half out of the cabin, I might as well just get on with it.

Slippers in snow aren't a good idea – my toes are going to drop off. Along with my boobs, or more precisely, my nipples, which are as rock hard as the ice cubes they're about to resemble.

***

One deep breath and I rush into the office before I change my mind.

'Hey, gorgeous!' Ed is sitting on the wheelie chair, with Bianca practically on his knee. Christmas spirit does this to people. Well, normally it's just that whole feel-good happy kind of spirit; this year I think it's the mulled wine and hot toddies that Ruth keeps demanding and Ed keeps making.

'Where is he?'

'Who?'

'You know damned well who! Tell me! Or don't if he's in bed with her, and—'

Ed has a raised eyebrow and big grin. 'Her who?'

'Dominique. I don't want to know if they're thrashing about, no.' Eurghh, that's a horrible image. 'No, stop. I don't mean that. Just get him, tell him I need to see him, when he's finished—'

'Finished?'

'You're enjoying this, aren't you?'

'Well, you *are* being funny. Slow down, who's he thrashing?' He winks at Bianca, who positively purrs in his ear.

'Mmm I like the sound of that.'

'Stop. Stop.' I put my hands over my ears. I now know why Will had a ban on all things festive, and no trace of mistletoe.

'Her.'

'If you mean Domi.' Yuk, Domi. I hate it when people shorten names. It makes them more human and loved, and not horrible people I want to hate.

'Yes, her.' I'm not going to say Domi. No. Way.

'She's gone.'

'But she was – they were – her and Will – snogging out there.' I point outside. 'In the snow.'

'I don't know about snogging, maybe a goodbye peck on the cheek? Though to be honest, I don't think he'd even do that. She totally shafted him. She's gone, Sarah. Home. Left.'

'Home? She's not with Will?' He said he was packing; has he gone with her?

'Nope. He asked Jed to give her a lift back to the airport. Well, told rather than asked. I've not seen him like this for ages.'

'So, where is he?'

'I'm not his keeper, babe. As you well know. He's around somewhere, I reckon.'

'"Somewhere" is quite big round here.'

'Have you tried the kennels?'

I think he's trying to get rid of me. 'Right, fine, kennels.' It makes sense.

'Or the log store? He was muttering about burning the place down, so it figures.' Ed is grinning.

'It's not funny!'

Maybe I'm being unfair, and advocaat girl is doing something under the desk to him that I can't see. Ticking his fancy, Aunt Lynn would call it. 'Oh, come on, Sarah. You know Will wouldn't do it – far too much of a goody two-shoes, plus he'd be worried about the health-and-safety implications. Do you want to borrow some boots and a jacket?'

I look at my feet. I am standing in a wet patch that Will would not approve of.

'Borrow mine, hun.' Bianca stands up.

'Er, thanks.' I am not sure this is a good look, but it probably doesn't matter. She is about two feet taller than me, and she has boobs. At a guess, they're surgically enhanced, because I am absolutely positive that gravity would have a firm handle on anything that big. If it can cope with an apple, these wouldn't stand a chance.

She misreads my doubtful expression. 'It's a good one, babe; my Joey got it me, but he won't mind you lending it.'

I want to correct her to 'borrowing' but that would be mean, she's being nice.

'Joey?'

'He's my fiancé, babe. He's loaded, only buys me the best.'

'Right.'

Ed doesn't look shocked, so I guess he's heard about Joey before.

My arms are slowly swallowed up by the sleeves, then the rest of me is consumed.

I am the child on the first day of school who is wearing castoffs from her (much) older, (much) bigger sister.

'Thanks. That's really kind of you!'

She leans over the desk and buttons me up. Then pats me on the head. 'No probs. I've got Eddie to keep me warm and cosy.'

Eddie looks more than up to the task. He hardly notices as I waddle off like a pregnant penguin, in search of his brother.

Chapter 26

Will is not with Domi. That is good. Will had his heart broken. That is bad. Will snogged her. Bad. Will is not with the dogs. Bad. Will has disappeared. Even more bad.

There seems to be a lot of bad stacking up. I need to find some more good.

Rosie whines and wags her tail. She is staring up the path behind the kennels.

There is no smoke, suggesting he has not started an arson campaign yet. This is good. Though I'm not convinced arson is the brightest idea around here at this time of year. You'd be pretty dense to try it, and he's not dense.

There are tracks from the log store leading up towards the shed where they keep the equipment; this is good! And in this part of the world it doesn't take Sherlock to track him down. I reckon that's why crime is so low round here: how can you kill somebody, hide the body and get away without leaving tracks? Unless there was a blizzard. You'd have to be a meteorologist as well as a deranged murderer.

It adds a whole new level of complication, and practically rules out a spontaneous crime of passion. Premeditation and planning is key.

'All gone then, have they? Come to tell me the coast is clear?'

I gather he means the press. 'Why didn't you tell me about Dominique?'

'It's history.'

'Then why were you kissing her face off just then?' I'm sorry, I can't help it. See it, say it, think afterwards. My nipples are also burning from the cold, now that they've been reheated inside my super-size thermally insulated coat, and it's moved me one degree closer to exploding point.

'I wasn't.'

'You were! I saw you!'

'You saw what she wanted you to see. I was trying to politely stop her jumping on me, that's why I was holding her.'

'She put her—'

'Can we stop this?'

I can't stop this. I'm bubbling up inside (and it isn't the coat). It's never been more important to know what came next, after I'd fallen off the chair. 'She was flashing a diamond engagement ring at the press!'

'Was she?'

'How could you not notice? It was massive! I've seen smaller icebergs.'

'Is that counting the bit you can't see?'

'What?'

'The underwater bit.'

'Maybe I should have said ice cube.' That raises a glimmer of a smile, and I suddenly wonder what I'm trying to achieve here. I am so insecure that I can't just accept that Domi has gone. That whatever she used to mean to him, it's long since over. He's sent her packing. Ed said he'd sent her home.

'We were never engaged, or close to engaged.'

'I'm sorry, I just thought I saw . . . and . . .'

'She came because she saw the reports, because some newspaper rang to ask what she thought. She came because,' he takes a deep breath, and his eyes are all set and steely, 'because she didn't want to be landed with a cripple, but a rich property owner is another matter. Okay?'

'You lied to me! How am I supposed to believe you now?' Even as the words come out of my mouth I know what I'm doing. I'm hitting out, forcing him away the same as I've always done, because it will be easier that way.

'I have never lied to you.'

'You said you wanted to be free; was that all just bollocks to brush me off? Have some fun, walk away cos it's all fine, you told me the score so that's hunky-dory.' I need to shut up. I'm way out of line. But I can't seem to.

He stares. Gazes straight into my eyes, and I haven't a clue what he's thinking. 'You haven't got a clue, have you?'

Got it in one. 'Well, give me one.'

'You know what? You're right. I do need to be free; I

need to get as far away from this place as I can. And to be honest, it doesn't matter what you think, whether you believe me or not, does it?'

And with that he brushes past me. Or stomps would be more the word.

As departures go, it's pretty dramatic. I'm so glad I asked.

No. I'm not. Asking was the worst thing I've ever done in my life. Why do I do this? Whatever happened to the new me, the fresh start?

Whoever said that breaking up was hard to do? Will and I have it down to a T.

Chapter 27

'Is he all right?' Sam is hovering at the door of my cabin, chewing the side of her thumb.

'He's fine.' Why do we always say that? 'Well, he's not fine, actually. He hates me, he hates this place, he says he hates Dominique, even though I was sure I saw them kissing.'

Sam plonks herself down on the rug next to me and stares at me glumly. 'Oh bugger, this is all my fault.'

'Don't say that!'

'But if we hadn't come here . . .'

'You coming here was the nicest thing anybody has ever done for me.' I hug her. 'It's not your fault that he's completely screwed up and was hiding. I mean, how were we supposed to know he was a fugitive?'

'I suppose it explains why there was just that pic of Ed on the website, and you couldn't find anything out about him.'

'True.' That thought had occurred to me and made me realise that most of this was my fault. I should have accepted things as they were, and not tried to dig. Then I might not have been taking snaps of him while he wasn't looking, and warned him that Jake is a bit of a photo-magnet. Except I didn't know Jake was coming here.

'All kinds of stuff comes up when you google Billy Armstrong instead of Will.' She waves her phone in front of me.

'I know.' I feel miserable. I don't know why I feel this miserable. He's a holiday fling, this place is an assignment that I've actually done quite a good job with. I should be proud of a job well done and go home. 'Shouldn't you be with your mum? Is she okay after that head-plant thing?'

'Ed offered her a cup of tea and she told him it was bad for her head, and a hot toddy would be better. She's now planning an afternoon of charades so that she can show off her acting skills. Are you going to come back over?'

'Maybe in a bit.' I need to go. They've come all this way to see me.

'Look!' She waves her mobile under my nose.

'I shouldn't. Last time I nearly broke my neck.'

'What?'

'I was standing on that chair trying to get decent reception, and I fell off.'

'Well, I've downloaded this stuff.'

'Cor, you've been busy.'

'You did it for me, when I first met Jake. You found out all about him and made me go for it.'

'I hope you're not trying to matchmake here? I told you that you were getting like your mum.'

'Rubbish. Just being helpful.' She says it in a far-too-practiced casual way.

'Hmm. But this is different to you and Jake.'

'But you do like him. Will.'

'I do.'

'And you did do stuff in that shed up the mountain?'

'My base layer has indeed been viewed.'

'Well then.'

We look at the 'Billy' pictures. He has twinkling eyes and a dimple. He looks much more like Ed. He also has medals draped around his neck. And, in some of the pictures, Dominique draped around the rest of him. She is like a cashmere wrap, all clingy but sophisticated.

'I wish he'd told me.'

'About her?'

'No, about the snowboarding. God, how embarrassing have I been? I thought he was scared of the snow and ice like me!'

'But he is.'

'Only because of the accident, and he isn't actually scared.' We stare at the reports of Will in hospital. He's strapped up, bandaged up, and hooked up to all kinds of stuff, his bronzed face a stark contrast to the white sheets.

He looks small, and I want to hug him.

'Wow, he was a world champion! Look at this.'

But I'm not really interested in Billy the medal winner;

all I can think of is Will the man I met in the Halfway Cabin. Will, the man who held me, who listened to me, the man I trusted. Will, the man I didn't try hard enough to understand. Will, the man who let me come here and talk him into turning his ski resort into a winter wonderland. Who came back to the place he didn't really want to, to help his fun-loving, slightly (quite a lot) irresponsible brother out.

'Would you think I was a really crap, selfish friend if I went off to find him instead of playing charades?'

'I wouldn't think anybody was crap trying to get out of a game of charades with Mum.' She grins, then hugs me. 'You're not selfish, Sarah.'

'Am I being ridiculous here?' I've never run after a man in my life. Not that I'm running after him in *that* way. I just want to straighten things out. 'He just stormed off when I found him in the shed.'

'Why?'

I shrug.

'Well, he must have said something!'

'I think I might have said something about him lying to me, and he said he hadn't.'

'About what?'

'Kissing Dominique and stuff.'

'Maybe he didn't actually lie to you.'

'But he didn't say stuff he should have, and that's just as bad.' I'm struggling here to justify myself, I know I am.

'He might have had his reasons.'

'We've had two snogs, one shag, and at least three arguments. Not normal, is it?'

'But you're not normal, Sarah. You don't want normal.'

'I feel like a puppy, chasing after him, and he doesn't want to be chased by anybody. He wants to be free.'

'Oh Sarah. Maybe he's ashamed, feels guilty or something.'

In my heart, I know there's something. Not that guilt or shame had occurred to me. But I know that I want to talk to him, *need* to talk to him. Not just because I've realised I fancy the pants off him, but because I don't want him to be like me.

I don't want him to feel rejected or abandoned. I don't want him to feel he's failed or let anybody down. I don't want him to keep running.

Being here has made me realise that I've been doing all of that. And it's time to stop.

I'm all grown up and I can make the decisions myself on how I want my life to be. On how much I let other people, and what they've done, influence what I do and who I am.

Which is all a bit mind-blowing and ultra-serious.

'Go on, find him. Then come and find me after you've talked. I need all the goss.'

Chapter 28

It is frigging freezing standing outside the kennels. In the films, if you rush out semi-naked, you catch the hero, he warms up your cockles, and other extremities, and it's all happy ever after. Why is real life so rubbish in comparison?

This was the exact spot where it all went wrong before. Where I was abandoned. I never got to beg them to stay, to understand why they wanted to go. But I'm not a little girl now. This time I can fight to keep somebody. To at least *understand* why he needs to leave.

Bugger, what if he's actually gone for good? What if I'm too late?

My heart's already pounding harder, unwanted adrenalin seeping into my body. I can't lose him the same way I lost them, I just can't.

'Oh Rosie.' But it's not Rosie's hot breath against my fingertips. It's a different dog.

And now I know. He's not gone for good. He's not left. If Rosie isn't in the kennels, then it means she's with him.

And I know exactly where he is.

I rush back to the kitchens. Stuff my massive pockets with the food I'm pretty sure they were designed for, and run into Sam.

'You're back, you've seen him! What did he say?' Then she notices the bulging pockets. 'Where are you going now? You never said you were packing a picnic! It's Christmas Eve!' She barricades my way with a fire poker. 'You can't go out on Christmas Eve, it's nearly Christmas Day! Have you talked to Will? What did he say? We've got Poppy doing charades, and Mum found a karaoke machine and . . .' She runs out of steam. 'Sarah, what's up?'

'I've not spoken to him yet. He's gone.' I resist the urge to shove her out of the way.

'Gone?'

'But I know where he is.' I'm jiggling from one foot to the other, trying to stand still and not make a run for it.

'You're going out?' Her jaw drops. 'On Christmas Eve? I'll come.'

'No.' I grab her arm, to stop her dashing off to get changed. 'I'll be fine. Honest. I know where he is. I won't be long. But if I am, don't worry.'

'Oh, come here you daft moo, how can I not worry?'

It's good to be hugged by Sam. Even if she has got a painted-on moustache that we are managing to smudge and turn into a black slug. Nearly as good as being hugged by Lynn. Just a bit different.

'I'll be okay. What's with the, er . . . ?'

'I'm,' she lowers her voice, 'Hercule Poirot!'

'Doing karaoke?'

'No, you daft bat, we're doing charades.'

'Oh yeah. And the fire poker?'

'He carries a walking stick doesn't he? Or did I get that wrong? Is that somebody else?'

'I'm not an expert on Poirot. You should have asked your mum.'

'I can't, she's joining in. You should have seen her acting out *Wuthering Heights*! She made Jake kneel down and be her horse.'

If anybody else said that, it would sound indecent. But this is Ruth.

'I'm quite glad I was out when you started this!'

'You won't be long, will you? Ed has made mulled wine, and Bianca is actually really funny and sweet, and she's ace at keeping Mum quiet and the kids happy, and there are hot sausage rolls and stuff, and even some M & S mince pies that Mum smuggled in.'

'I won't be long, don't worry. Save me a mince pie.'

'You are taking your phone this time?'

'I am. I'll let you know when I find him.'

'Promise you won't be too late?'

I shrug. 'Hope not. Thanks for coming, Sam, Honest, it's brilliant you all being here, but I really . . .'

'But you need to find him?'

'Last time I was here I never even got to say goodbye properly to Mum and Dad. I'm going to at least do that this time. I can't stop him going if he's decided that's what he needs to do, but . . .'

'You can make sure he has something to remember you by?' Her eyes are twinkling, and we're jiggling about in each other's arms, hugging and kissing and being so silly it brings a lump to my throat.

'You're the best, Sam.'

She is. And as I pull back and stare at her, it hits me. Even if I'd been silly enough to think there was something more than a five-minute fling with Will, I couldn't move here to be with him. And now it doesn't look like there would be a hope in hell that he'd come home with me.

It's a fantastic place, but I have my own fantastic. Lynn, Sam, a job. My family and friends are the best thing in my life.

I thought Will was fantastic, too. But now I don't know. There is just so much I don't seem to know about him, it makes me wonder if I've even seen the *real* him.

The Will I know wouldn't run without saying goodbye, unless he had a really good reason. And I'm about to find out what that is.

Chapter 29

Ed is not dishing out mulled wine. Ed is standing next to the snowmobile, all wrapped up warmly, as though he's going somewhere. 'I'm coming with you.'

Maybe it was a bit harsh calling him irresponsible.

'It's okay, I'll find him.' Sam wanting to come is one thing, but Ed? Ed is Mr me-me-me.

'I need to check he's there, Sarah. He's my brother, and he's a total twat at times, but he's still my brother. And,' he pauses, 'I quite like you too. He'd never forgive me if I let you head out on your own. You know what happened last time!'

I think I may be turning crimson. I do know exactly what happened last time. But I think we might be talking at cross-purposes here.

'Come on. We'll take both snowmobiles.'

'But . . .'

He's already pulling a helmet on and is sitting astride before I can say another word. 'I promise that if he's there and he's okay then I'll do a disappearing act. He'll never know I've been there.'

345

That is hard to believe. Especially when he's wearing a jacket with 'Piste again' emblazoned on the back and is currently spinning the snowmobile in small circles in a very show-offy way.

I don't seem to have a choice, though. God, these brothers are annoying at times.

Ed insists on leading the way. He also insists on going incredibly slowly, like proper old-man slowly. We'd be over-taken by octogenarians in cloth caps on mobility scooters if such things were common out here.

I'm not sure if this is, in fact, because he has been sampling the mulled wine, or is just taking super-duper care of me so he won't get into trouble.

Normally this would give me a chance to appreciate the glorious scenery, to wallow in the splendour of a winter wonderland, but today I want to run my snowmobile up his backend. If you'll pardon the imagery.

'Stop a second.'

We stop, which isn't difficult at all, given the speed we're going at. 'What now?'

'Fuel.' He checks the fuel, and twiddles about looking at and one hundred other things that I've never seen him do before. 'Okay, that's fine.'

I reckon he's worried. There is no other explanation.

We potter on, along a route I know quite well now.

'Thank God for that.' At last I spot the Halfway Cabin. The snow looks to be flattened by the doorway, which is a good sign. Ed stops a short distance away.

'Maybe you should go on your own from here. I'll watch, make sure you don't come straight out.'

This also is unlike Ed. He must have hidden depths that he doesn't like anybody to see. It would appear that he and Will have more in common than they realise.

'Thanks, Ed.' I hug him. 'You go, no point in you hanging—'

'I'll wait a minute. Check you'll be okay, that he's there.'

I know he's there. I don't know if I'll be all right, but sometimes you have to take a chance, don't you?

This time, if Will leaves me, it won't break me.

***

I'd love to be able to say I leap in shouting 'surprise' and he's pleased to see me. But, as I'm a bit worried about the second bit, I knock tentatively, and sidle in.

Rosie thumps her tail and looks at me slightly apologetically. As though she'd love to say hello but isn't sure if it's acceptable behaviour.

'Is nowhere safe from you?'

'I know that's code for "I'm pleased to see you". I've brought food! Not just dog food, either.' It raises a smile. And a shake of the head. I give Ed a 'bugger off' kind of wave and shut the door.

I empty out my pockets slowly. He's not told me to bugger off yet, so that's a positive. And he's not done a disappearing act yet, double positive 'I didn't know you could eat mince pies with cranberry sauce – is this a British thing?'

I didn't say I'd carefully selected food items, did I? This was more a supermarket sweep. 'It's the best. A new trend – have you not heard of fusion food?'

'You're crazy.'

'You ain't seen nothing yet, mate.' I make a move to rip open the front of my jacket. He looks slightly horrified. 'Don't worry, I'm not naked underneath; I'd have to have a complete disregard for my nipples to even attempt that in these temperatures.'

'Believe me, I'm not worried about you being naked.' There's a lazy grin on his face and his arms aren't folded now.

'Selfish.'

'True.'

'This is better, St Bernard to the rescue!'

I do not have a barrel of brandy, but I do have a flask of whisky, with a picture of a St Bernard dog on the front, which Ed gave me.

'I'm not saying it's better, but it's definitely one of your more inspired ideas.'

'Along with these!' I spread out the rest of the contents of my many pockets. There is what I thought was a block of cheese, but it turns out it's a pack of butter (not a good start), a couple of boiled eggs (I thought these would go with the cheese, but as it isn't cheese I'm not sure what they go with). The pack of ham I grabbed turns out to be a smoked salmon roulade (result!), and there are some mini Christmas puddings that smell like rum truffles. Alongside the mince pies and cranberry jelly, there is something I can't identify.

'What is this? I thought it was one of those, what do you call them, power balls things.'

'Power ball things?'

'For energy. That's it, I mean *energy* ball! You know nuts, fruit, coconut,' I sniff it again. 'Peanut butter, energy.' My voice tails off. It's a bit greasy and unappetising now I've had a chance to look at it more closely.

'It's a suet ball.' Will is laughing at me, and it makes me feel good. 'For the birds. We freeze a whole lot.'

'Oh. So not very nice?'

'Definitely a last resort if we get stuck here. A very last resort. I'm not even sure Rosie would be keen.'

Rosie groans and flops onto the floor, proving the point.

'It's Christmas Eve, Sarah.' His voice is soft. 'Shouldn't you be with the others, not stuck up a mountain with – what did with Ruth call me? That terrible man who doesn't believe in Christmas!'

'And doesn't have marshmallows.'

We look at each other. I've done the food distraction, so now I need to get down to the nitty-gritty, say what I came to say.

'I wanted to be with *you*. I'm sorry I was such a cow; I shouldn't have said that stuff.' My voice is tiny and pathetic, but it needed saying.

He reaches out, and his warm fingers are intertwined with mine in a way that makes me know I made the right decision. Baubles, tinsel and hot chocolate will still be here next year. Will might not be. This isn't five-year plan stuff, this is here and now. 'I can't just let you disappear on me, slip through my fingers, like my parents did, without at least saying goodbye.'

'Oh Sarah, I'm sorry.' The sigh is heavy, but it isn't scary. Something about it makes me sure that this time if I reach out, he won't disappear into thin air. 'I shouldn't have shot off, but I needed some space.' He looks at me earnestly, and the final shreds of trepidation drift away. 'I was going to come back. I wouldn't have gone anywhere without saying goodbye. You do know that?'

I nod. My heart knew it, I just didn't trust the truth that was sitting deep inside of me. There were too many layers of life and hurt muddling up the past and present.

So I squeeze his fingers and pass him a rum truffle.

He grins.

'Is it Christmas you don't like, or just snow?'

He laughs. 'Both. I made festive headlines when Dominique dumped me via text on Christmas Eve, I guess there wasn't much news that day.'

'She dumped you on Christmas Eve?' This goes a long way to explaining the Mr Scrooge image. You'd have to be a pretty die-hard fan (like me) to survive that and still feel the goodwill to all men vibe. 'But you were in hospital, weren't you?'

'I was indeed. The full works, foot in the air, tubes up places they had no right to be. A neck brace.'

'Bugger, what a cow.'

'I couldn't even sit up to throw the mobile across the room properly, only had enough strength to crack the screen.'

'Oh Will.'

'I went from hero to zero overnight. Daft thing is, I hated all the attention, all the posing, the modelling. But when you get that type of rejection, from everybody, it hits kind of hard. Nobody actually liked *me*, they liked my success, they fed off it. Even breaking up Domi-style was done for maximum affect – she told me and the rest of the world all at once with a tweet and lots of emojis.'

'And she thought she could just walk straight back into your life?' This is one ballsy woman. Not that I can admire this particular type of ball-breaking behaviour.

'It was all about attention, and she only came because her career's taken a bit of a downturn. She's doesn't know what grow old gracefully means and she can't compete with the new kids. She's desperate for headlines – modelling is as brutal a job as sport.'

'All the press have turned up now, though, they still love you.'

'They're only here because I was off the radar for years, and now they've heard I'm back on the slopes. And Domi told them she'd be here. They must have been expecting us to be reunited and me miraculously recovered and back on the board. A great Christmas story, eh?'

'Oh.'

He drapes an arm over my shoulder and pulls me closer. Rests his chin on my head. 'I let everybody down, Sarah. It wasn't about losing the limelight, or even just about not being able to compete, though it did hurt. I realised Domi never loved me and I know sponsorship disappears when you're not top of the game. All that is fine, kind of. But I let people down. It was all my stupid fault. If I hadn't been so confident . . .'

'But you have to be confident in a sport like that, don't you? Isn't it all about mind over matter.'

'Sort of. You have to be mentally tough. But I was stupid. My parents weren't rich and they gave up everything in the UK to move out here.'

'You were born in England?'

'I was, but I hardly remember it. We moved out here when I was young, when I first fell in love with snow sports. They sacrificed everything to give me the best chance, poured every spare penny and every hour they'd got into my training. It was their lives as well as mine. Then pow! it was all gone. Overnight. And now I can't do anything else. Snowboarding was my life.'

'Parents do that.' I swallow. 'They do what they can for their kids.' Most of the time. And maybe mine did, in their own way, except it all backfired.

'I need to get a grip, though, don't I?' I nod. 'I need to stop running and talk to my parents properly. I think I've known all along, really, I just wouldn't admit it to myself.

That's why I came to give Ed a hand when he screamed for help.' He gives a heavy sigh. 'I don't think I want to face any more press, though. Not yet, not for a while.'

'I think they've gone – rumour is that certain members of the royal family have fallen out with the Queen and headed onto the slopes.'

'Really?'

'I think it might just be a rumour, maybe started by Jake's agent. But they have buggered off.'

'Thank God for that.'

'Can we stay here tonight?' The thought has crept up on me while we've been talking, and it won't go away.

'You'll miss out on all the fun. What about the carols and mulled wine, and all that stuff you keep telling me about? And your livestreaming?'

He grins and nudges me in the ribs, and he's got crinkly lines at the sides of his eyes, and a dimple at the side of his gorgeous mouth. And the warm feeling inside me spreads. 'I think I'd rather be here with you, a big sky full of stars, and a snoring dog. Tinsel can't top that.'

'I think you could be right.'

'Oh, and a weird and wonderful squashed picnic. Can we pretend we got snowed in? Tell everybody we couldn't get back?'

'Again?'

'Maybe not.'

'Even Sam's mum would probably notice it hasn't snowed today.'

'They won't mind. Sam will cover for me. Please?'

I've never spent Christmas Eve in a wooden hut, on a snowy mountainside with nothing remotely commercial, and a gorgeous man.

I think I probably should have done though. Will was right. Why come here if you're not going to appreciate the scenery?

***

The food is surprisingly good, though we pass on the suet ball. Time trickles by and we chat, share Christmas stories, talk about surf and snow, and dreams and loss, about forgiving, forgetting and moving on, and before we know it, it is midnight.

'It's Christmas Day.' I think I have some kind of inner alarm that goes off at midnight so that I won't miss a minute.

'Happy Christmas, Sarah.' Will leans closer and drops the lightest of kisses on my lips.

'Me and Aunt Lynn always say Happy Christmas as early as we can, and have a hug. It's a rule.'

'Well, I'm honoured to have replaced her this year.'

'Me too.' I give him what feels like a shy smile. Not awkward, just quietly pleased and trying not to show it too much as he leans in and gives me the best hug ever. I love Aunt Lynn hugs, but this is so big, and warm, and, well, manly. And the kiss isn't like an Aunt Lynn one at all. Which is quite a relief: that would just be weird.

'We'll make it a good one, shall we?' He passes me the whisky flask, and the unspoken words, that it has to be a good one, because it will be the only one, make me sad.

I blink away the sudden fire in my eyes.

He strokes his finger down my cheek, rests it on my lips. 'We will meet again – we'll make sure we do. You can come out surfing, I can come and look at your Houses of Parliament.'

'Nobody has ever called them that before.'

I look down at my chest, and so does he, and he laughs. 'We'll work it out. Okay?'

'Sure.' Who knows, though? It's a big world. He's got his life, I've got my job, my family, my friends. 'But let's not talk about it now, eh?'

'No.'

The whisky burns a path down my throat. Gives me an excuse for talking with a raspy voice. 'Last mince pie?'

'Sure. But no cranberry jelly, that is just too weird. Are you going to show me your dragon then, my tattooed lover?'

'It's a dragonfly, I told you. Expect a dragon and you're going to be very disappointed.'

'I'll never be disappointed by you, Sarah.'

'I've got to do one thing I need to do first.' Apart from hide my face, because that has to be one of the nicest things anybody has ever said to me. I text Aunt Lynn and wish her a Happy Christmas, even though I suspect she'll be sitting in a hospital, holding Ralph's hand, and won't see her phone until much later. Then I text Sam and tell her we're safe (though I'm sure Ed has done that!). Then I turn my mobile phone off, but not before I get a text back. The funny dancing elves make us giggle, the two reindeer doing things that Rudolph really shouldn't, make me laugh.

Then I glance his way, and my laughter fades as my gaze meets his. He reaches out, strokes one warm finger down my cheek with infinite care, and I close my eyes as the heat of his breath caresses my skin. My lips tingle with anticipation for the Christmas kiss I know is about to happen.

Chapter 30

'You're back!' Sam races across the room and wraps me in a big hug. 'Happy Christmas! And Will's with you!'

We took Rosie to the kennels, then snuck into my cabin to get changed, before heading over to the main building.

I wanted to check the dining room out first, just to be sure that Ed had actually remembered it was Christmas Day, and had laid the table properly.

'How could I miss Christmas Day? Sarah would never forgive me.' Will squeezes my hand. I think he's forgiven himself for a lot of things, and although I'm not entirely sure I can forgive my parents, I know I've come to terms with some of the stuff. I know they didn't leave because I wasn't good enough and didn't deserve to be loved.

Will told me. He also told me that he's never wrong, and I want to believe him.

'No one is allowed to miss Christmas Day!' A familiar smell prickles at my nostrils and I look around, taking the room in properly for the first time. 'Wow, this looks totally amazeballs!'

Sam grins. 'We all helped out, though Ed and Bianca have been so fab. Bianca can even fold napkins into animal shapes, how cool is that? Good, eh?' It is indeed good. It is more than good. It is the perfect place to eat Christmas dinner.

The place is festooned with fairy lights, the tables covered with white tablecloths and gold and red runners that sparkle in the candlelight. Everywhere I look there are holly, berries, pine cones and the most gorgeous garlands, and the Christmas smells of cinnamon, cloves and fir trees hangs in the air.

'This is amazing, but posh at the same time!' It's got that thrown-together look that never actually looks good when I try it myself.

'Come on, come and see the lounge, we're all having pre-dinner drinks!' Sam grabs my hand and we don't have much choice but to follow, even though I'm feeling a bit dazed.

There is a cheer when we walk in. Slightly embarrassing.

The fire is blazing, but it's the warmth of the whole scene that brings a lump to my throat.

I glance up at Will. 'It's perfect.'

'Of course it bloody is, what did you expect? Here you go.' Ed shoves glasses of bubbly into our hands and looks very pleased with himself.

'You did all this?' I can't help the incredulous edge that creeps into my voice.

'Of course. Well, with a little help maybe.'

Bianca has glided over (I've never met anybody who can

move so gracefully in six-inch heels before; I think she's been to a special high-heel finishing school) and slipped her hand through his arm. They look very comfortable together. Will raises an eyebrow but doesn't say anything.

'Perfect timing for the turkey.' Bianca smiles.

'You might, er, need this?' I fish out the jar of cranberry sauce that really didn't go with any part of our picnic.

'Brilliant! Right, time to carve, darling!' And she's ushering Ed over towards the kitchen at a speed that surprises both of us.

'I reckon Ed's met his match at last, somebody who knows how to make him work!'

***

I don't want to say it's the best Christmas ever, because Lynn isn't here. But it's shaping up to be pretty damned good. Everybody is crammed into the dining room, Jack is chortling, Poppy is skipping round showing everybody her special fairy dress, and even Tina is finally looking chilled.

'Ta dah!'

God knows where they found a plate big enough, but Jed and Ed are staggering under the weight of the massive turkey, before they plonk it on the sideboard, and everybody applauds. Partly out of relief that it's made it safely all the way, I think, and partly because it looks so brilliant.

'That is some mahoosive turkey, Ed!'

'There's another one in the kitchen if we need it. Right,' he rubs his hands together, 'let's get carving, bro.'

'Well, I didn't know that you could get a turkey that size, are you sure it isn't an emu?' Ruth is out of her seat, taking a closer look.

'I don't think they get emu's here, Ruth.'

'Oh silly me, I'm getting confused with our Kenya trip.'

'Emu's live in Australia, love.' David very subtly pushes Ruth's wine glass to one side, and she, less subtly sweeps it up and takes a swig.

'Well, I must say, it is all so lovely, much better than I expected. I mean, we've all seen that video from last year, haven't we? So rude of them to record your terrible dinner, Will. I'm sure it wasn't your fault.'

'It wasn't, I wasn't here.'

She ignores him. 'And you've done much better this time. I was going to pack a turkey in my suitcase, just in case, but it would have meant paying for excess baggage, and I never like excess anything, do I, David? And look at the size of these sprouts!'

'They're alligator eggs, a Christmas delicacy.' Ed manages to keep a straight face, and keep eating, despite Bianca nudging him hard in the ribs.

'Really? Well, isn't this special! David, David, take a photo for that insta granny thing. I can't wait to tell Juliet – I'm sure she'd have mentioned it if she'd had alligator eggs before, and who would have thought they looked just like sprouts? It must be for camouflage purposes!'

360

'You really must try the polar bear before you go, Ruth.'

'Oh no, oh I absolutely couldn't, they're so cuddly,' she takes another swig of wine, 'and probably a bit tough I'd imagine.'

'Probably.'

David doesn't take a photo. But I do, and I take a short video. If I saw this on the internet, I'd book a room straight away. Or that could just be me, and the warm feeling that seems to have crept into every part of me, but particularly my knee – where Will's hand is currently resting.

'Oh my, is that one of those drinks you set fire to?'

'No, Mum, that's the ladle of brandy for the pudding.'

It's weird not having Aunt Lynn at my side, but nice. I never really appreciated that I had a massive extended family who'd be there for me whenever I needed them. I've never been alone, I've just sometimes felt a little lonely. Today I've realised that sometimes you really do have to live in the moment. I can't change the past, and I can't predict what will happen in the future. But I can enjoy today and add it to my list of wonderful memories.

'Okay?' Will's voice is soft in my ear.

'Perfect.'

PART 3
COMING HOME

Chapter 31

'There's someone at my house that I think you should talk to.'

'Ouch.' This is what happens when you're knackered and have your head in the fridge searching for some kind of edible leftovers and your aunt creeps in on you.

'The back door was open, love.'

I have only just got back from the airport. My clothes look like they've been slept in (they have), and I'm bloody starving. I am also missing Will like crazy, and I thought food might help. I need carbs.

Me and Will made the most of my last few days in Canada, but we both knew I'd have to come home to my friends, my family and the job I love. We promised each other that we'd meet up. He's planning on chasing the surf in the spring, and I'm sure Aunt Lynn will agree that it's time to research some surfing holidays. Then maybe we can decide if this thing is real, or a Christmas holiday fling. Maybe things will be clearer and we'll work out some kind of complicated diary of where we can meet and when.

It needs a lot of planning, but right now I miss him, and spring is ages away.

At times like this I wish I was one of those organised people who stock up on food (with long sell-by dates) before they go away, then I'd be sitting on the settee, nodding off, with a pizza in the oven, a film on the TV and a glass of wine in my hand – not thinking about a snowboarder who seems to have jumped his way straight to the centre of my heart.

'I brought you some mince pies, love; they were reduced, and it says on the box that they're okay until the end of January. Isn't that a stroke of luck?' Lynn is nudging me back to the present. 'Are you okay, dear?'

'Fine, fine. Brilliant.' Some people might worry that a mince pie that lasts over a month must be full of additives. I don't care. My body is no temple. Right now it is an empty shell that needs a bit of scaffolding. And anyway, it probably is just an indicator that there is plenty of brandy in them.

Lynn puts the kettle on, plonks the packet of mince pies on the table, and waits. She's looking very serious. We haven't even discussed Ralph, Will or the fact I haven't unpacked my dirty knickers yet, and I've got a distinct feeling I'm in trouble.

'Has, er, Ralph come back with you?'

'No, love. It's not Ralph.'

'Did you meet somebody?'

She shakes her head.

'Don't tell me the press have . . .'

'It's your father, Sarah.'

I stare. And my stomach is all hollow, but I'm not at all hungry now.

'Your dad,' she says it slowly, looking at me all the time, 'has been to see me.'

'But he . . .'

'I think you need to see him, to hear what he's got to say.'

'Dad?'

'I can't make you, it's your choice, love. But how would you feel if you never took this chance to speak to him? He's told me some things that I didn't realise, but you need to hear them from him. I think you need to see him, meet him face to face. Just once, for me. I feel . . .' Aunt Lynn never pauses, she always knows exactly what she's going to say, so this is unnerving. It makes me feel even more queasy than I already am. 'I feel like maybe we never got to hear the full truth, that we've got it wrong. Oh Sarah, I am so sorry,' she's wringing her hands, 'you've got to see him, love. I've always blamed him, everybody did, but I really do think . . .' Her voice tails off. 'Please say you'll see him, hear him out?'

It's odd, but I think I did my wailing and shouting out in Canada, to Will. It must have affected me in some way, because I don't feel the anger I'm sure I would have done if this had happened a couple of months ago. Before I met Will.

I just feel calm. Accepting.

I'm not saying I'll forgive and forget, that would be stupid and totally untrue. But I *am* prepared to see him. The man who stopped being my lovely Dad, and became the man who killed my mother, that Christmas many years ago.

'I'll meet him somewhere else.' Somewhere public, not on my own personal ground. Somewhere I'm less likely to yell at him, or cry, or make a scene. Just in case I'm not as over it as I think I am.

'Come on, love. Drink your tea, I've got the car. Come and chat to him at my house. These meetings in public aren't the way to do things, if you ask me.'

***

He's standing by the window when I walk in with the two mugs of coffee on a tray. My dad. Looking out at the garden. Older than the image I had in my head, but I guess that's because I last saw him when he was not that much older than I am now.

I'd recognise him in a crowd, though. Anywhere. Even though we've both grown older, both changed. When he turns to look at me, I don't recognise the hesitation, the fear in his eyes. That was never there before.

'Hi.' I'm glad Aunt Lynn insisted on making us a drink. It gives me something to do with my hands. Putting them down. Pulling out a chair. Pushing the biscuits into the centre of the table.

He relaxes the tiniest bit and I realise he's scared of what I'll say, do. It's taken guts to see me face to face. And I do want to know what he's got to say.

'This is hard.' He's studying his hands, then glances up and his gaze meets mine. A familiar gaze, a gaze that brings a lump to my throat. My dad. 'Lynn told me you didn't want to see me, and I get that, and I get that when I wrote and asked, you didn't reply.'

'I haven't read the letters.'

'Oh.' There's a long pause.

'I got them, but I didn't read them.'

'I didn't know.'

'I threw them out.'

'I guess I'd have done the same. Well . . . I . . . well, you've got kind of famous.' He holds a hand up to stop words I wasn't going to say, 'I'm not here to cash in or anything. It's great, I'm pleased for you, proud.'

'I'm not famous.'

'But you're mixing with that film-star guy, and now the snowboarder, and well, that's what made me come.'

'Will? Billy?'

He rubs his hands over his face in a familiar way, and I wonder where I've seen it before. Then I realise. In the mirror. We share mannerisms, ways of glancing down, apologising for being there, grinning to ease the tension. 'Yeah, you in the newspapers, all over the internet. I'll get to that in a bit.' He stares into the cup. 'Right. I need to spit this all out, but first I want you to know that your mum was the loveliest person that ever lived. She was beautiful and kind and loved you to bits, okay?'

I nod. Swallow hard.

'She wasn't leaving you – neither of us were. We just wanted to have a few wild weeks and had stuff to sort out before we moved into a flat and tried out this adulting lark properly.'

He makes me smile, the way he talks. 'A flat?'

'Yeah, new year, new us.' He grimaces. 'We'd sold the camper van, left it with a mate when we all headed out to Canada, and he'd got a good offer within days. We were going to use the money as a deposit to rent a place so you'd have a proper school and friends. All this travelling around wasn't fair on a kid, you.'

'You were coming back for me?'

'Of course we were coming back!' He looks so genuinely surprised that I know, with total certainty, that they never abandoned me. That everything that came after was not my fault, nothing to do with me not being good enough. 'What makes you think we weren't?'

Hot tears make my eyes smart.

'Shit. You thought we were leaving you with Lynn? Forever?'

I nod. Bite my lip.

'No wonder you didn't read the letters.'

'But Mum made Aunt Lynn promise to look after me. She told her to look after me, why would she do that?'

'We hadn't made wills or anything so that was just her

being careful cos, in case . . .' His voice tails off. 'Anything happened.' He closes his eyes. 'I'm only telling you this because if I don't, somebody else will. I get it if you still hate me after.' He stirs his tea, ladles more sugar in. 'It's this guy. This guy, Adam, he got in touch; he recognised a photo of you in the paper. He said if I didn't talk to you, he would.'

'About what?' Those reporters have a lot to answer for.

'Your mum and the accident.'

'But I already know—'

'What really happened.' He sounds tired, reluctant, as though it's an effort to squeeze each word out.

'What's it got to do with this Adam?'

He stares at me. Direct. And there is such a sadness in his eyes I want to cry. But I don't know why. 'He was the last person we saw. We were chatting in this bar. He saw us drive off.' He swallows hard, his gaze flickers. 'This doesn't change anything Sarah. Believe me, your mum was the best.'

I wait. The longest wait ever.

'He knew Lisa was driving, not me. He said he was going to the police and this was my last chance to explain before you found out from somebody else.'

We sit in silence. It takes a long time for the words to sink in. Make sense.

'Mum was driving? But you were, she, you . . .'

'The first thing I said when somebody turned up to help us was that it was my fault. Because it was. Then they

Zara Stoneley

assumed I meant I'd been driving, and it seemed the best way out. She'd get better, she'd come back to you, the kid we hit would get better. Then after . . . It didn't matter. I'd lost her, and I knew you'd be better off without me. I knew Lynn would look after you.'

'You weren't driving? You didn't crash?'

He shakes his head.

'You didn't kill her.'

'As good as.' His voice has a harsh edge. It hurts. 'We'd hired this motorbike, and I shouldn't have let her drive, it was too big, too powerful, but she loved her motorbikes. I'd had a drink, just one or two, and was tired. I should have insisted we stay on overnight – we'd driven far enough. I should have.' He closes his eyes, and I can't help myself. I put my hand over his. 'She was upset about leaving you and she wanted to get a move on, not waste time. She wanted to get it over with, get back to you, start our new life. But the roads were slippery, we were both so knackered, and then this guy came out of nowhere, running into the road. We swerved, braked, and we lost control.'

'*She* lost control.' My words are small, lost in his pain.

'We were thrown clear. I thought Lisa would be all right, I thought the kid would. Christ, I shouldn't have let her get on that bike.'

'It was her choice, Dad.' The word Dad comes out naturally, hangs in the air between us. A word I never thought I'd get to say again. I know my voice is soft, but I know he hears.

372

'It was my fault. I said it was my fault.'

'And they thought you meant the crash.'

'I did.'

'But you weren't driving.'

'I should have known better. I was the man, for God's sake, I was supposed to take care of her. I was supposed to take care of both of you. We should have stayed at that place overnight.' He's close to tears, and I don't know what to do. 'I didn't want you to think bad of her, Sarah. She was talking to me, lying in the road, saying it hurt, and I said it would be okay. I thought it was okay. There was no blood and I thought it would be okay. I didn't know . . .'

He's not looking at me now, he's staring out of the window and I've moved closer to him before I realise, wrapped my arms around a man I barely know.

'I was wrong. I was wrong about everything. And that poor kid. She didn't hit him, love, it wasn't her. The bike did. It spun out of control and we went one way, it went the other.'

For a long time we just sit. Think. Then he starts to talk again.

'His mates said he'd told them he was going to top himself, but the family said it was crap, he'd had a few drinks, was a maudlin teen, hadn't been looking where he was going. He jumped right in front of us, though. Ran at us.'

'And Adam?'

Zara Stoneley

'The kid was in a coma for a while, then a wheelchair, then he died a few weeks ago. He told his mum he had tried to kill himself, and this last time when he told her again, a nurse was there. She knew Adam, it was a small town, they got chatting.' He shrugs. 'They both saw the photo of you, and Adam tracked me down. He said it was time to wipe the slate clean, time everybody knew. When I told him I hadn't seen you since I came out of prison he said I was an arsehole. And when I told him about the letters he said he never did trust writing stuff down, said I had to find you. Tell you to your face, or the police would do it for me, and what kind of a coward did that make me?'

'You're not a coward, Dad.'

'Maybe not a coward, but I'm a fool, a silly twat who's ruined a whole lot of lives.'

I let that lie. 'Where were you and Mum going?'

He sighs. 'We'd been involved in this conservation project and we needed to tie the loose ends up, explain we weren't going back.'

I looked at him. Properly. My free-spirit Dad. The guy with a camper van, a woman he loved, a kid, and a whole big world he liked to explore.

'Prison must have been horrible.'

He shrugs. 'Not the best, but it's in the past. I don't expect you to forgive me, Sarah. I should have been there for you.'

'I wish I'd known, about everything.'

'I want you to remember your mum as she was, the

374

perfect mother, not all this. This is crap, Sarah, this isn't about her. I thought it would be a fine, I'd get a driving ban, something like that, and I'd be able to come and collect you. But some witnesses who saw us head out of town said we were going too fast, that we'd argued before we'd set off. We hadn't, love, we were just trying to work out what to do and, like I said, she was upset. It was an accident.'

I think about the bike, spinning out of control, crashing. I think about Will taking off, racing the snow, spinning out of control. I think about hate, disappointment, fear and anger, but the tears only start to well up when I think about love.

Isn't that what it's all about? Loving so hard that you think you've let people down. Not loving yourself enough to realise you haven't. Loving enough to walk away if you think it's the best thing to do. Loving enough to walk back and admit you've made a mistake.

He squeezes my hand. Rubs the tear away with his thumb.

'I'm sorry.'

'So am I. I thought you'd left me, that you didn't want me.'

'I could never leave you. I never left your mum, either; she's here, in my heart.'

'I'm sorry I didn't read the letters.'

'I guess it doesn't make a difference.'

'But I hated you for so long.'

'I deserved it.'

'You didn't, Dad.'

We stare at each other, both blinking away the mist in our eyes. He swallows, recovers first, though his voice still cracks at the edges. 'So where's your snowboarder guy, then?'

'Will? In Canada, it was just a holiday . . .'

'Holiday?'

'I was there working, really, now I'm back again.' I shrug.

'Bollocks. You can't fool me, even if you can fool yourself. In those photos you were looking at him in the same way your mum used to look at me. Listen to me, love, I might have been a total crap dad, but I do know what it's like to lose out. Twice. Your mum, you.'

I stand up. I need time to get my head together.

'Don't let him get away, if you love him.'

'I won't. And Dad,' I pause as I reach the door, 'you only lost once. We can chat again, yes?'

'I can make you another ladybird stool? Full-size, this time.' He grins then, and I know it's going to be all right. 'I can send you some photos of us all – if you like, that is?'

I nod. 'I'd like that. Thank you.'

***

I go upstairs, hear him saying goodbye to Lynn. Listen as the door quietly shuts, then there's the sound of her footsteps coming up the stairs.

She lies down on the bed next to me, like she did when I was a little girl.

'Are you all right, love?'

'You know what happened?'

'He told me yesterday, when he came looking for you. He was quite cut up that you weren't here – I think he'd got it all stored up, what he wanted to say.'

'Why didn't I know?'

She sighs. 'It was easy to just go along with what he said, what they said in court, because it hurt so much. He'd always had a bit of the bad boy about him, which was what your mum loved so much. The easiest thing was to believe the bad, and when the prosecution said all those things . . .'

'They loved each other, didn't they?'

'Oh, they were head over heels. I always knew she was, but was never quite so sure about him, until now. He'd have done anything for her, but you do, don't you if you love somebody? Here,' she places a large envelope on the bed between us, pats it. 'I kept these for you.'

I know instantly. They're the letters that I threw out.

And I know instantly where and who I want to read them with.

'I have to see Will, don't I? Before the spring.'

'I think you do, love.'

'But you need me here, and there's work to do, and I could go and see him when I'm looking at new resorts for the business, but we're busy this time of the year.'

'Not that busy, love, and you need some time off. We can talk about business trips and new resorts later. Look,' she takes my hand in hers, 'I'd never hold you back if you wanted to do something different, be somewhere else, you do know that?'

'I do, but I want to be with you.'

'I wish I'd spent more time with Ralph, darling. You can fit more than one person in your world, you know, and wherever you are, you'll still be with me. I'll always be here for you to come back to if you need me. You could spend a year exploring with Will, checking out new places if that's what you need to do.'

'I don't know what I need to do.' I'm tired, I want to bury my head in the pillow. 'I do want to see Dad again, though, and there's Will, and you.'

'I know, Sarah. I know. That necklace I gave you, do you know what the crystal is?'

'It's a Desert Rose. Mum's favourite.'

'And do you know what it symbolises, darling? It means all things are possible, helps you throw off all your restraints and things that hold you back and go with what your heart tells you. It helps you find your purpose in life, love. That,' she brushes the hair back from my face, 'is why it was the right time for you to have it. Your mum would have wanted you to be brave, to go after your dreams, and I'd have failed in my promise to her if I didn't make sure you did.'

'She went after her dreams.'

'She certainly did, and now it's your turn. Have a nap

first, though; it'll keep until tomorrow, won't it?' Then she gets up, pulls the covers over me and shuts the curtains. I smell her familiar perfume as she kisses my forehead, and I'm that little girl again, safe in my bedroom.

Chapter 32

It feels a bit déjà vu-ish, writing to him. And I don't know quite what to write. I want to keep things light, but if it's too jokey he might miss the point. And if it's too serious then he might think I'm asking for a commitment neither of us really know we want yet. And it's hard. I mean, how do you say 'can I come and see you, because I miss you, and my dad came, and he told me stuff that's changed everything, and Lynn says I can have time out, but I don't know what I really want' in a ha ha way?

But I've been stuck on 'Dear Will' for quite a while now, so at this rate it'll be spring before I actually manage to get anything sensible together.

There's a brief knock on the front door, then a louder one. 'Oh, bloody hell, go away.' Then it's thrown open. Oh Christ, burglars, that's all I need, unless they're literary and witty. It might be worth asking if they can help me with my letter before they cosh me, or gag me, and put me in a cupboard.

The door slams shut. I don't think burglars normally do

that. It's more hit and run. Oh bugger – Sam! I'd completely forgotten I'd asked Sam to come over. We were going to sort through our photographs and videos and decide which ones to put on the website. I wish I could ask her to help me write this email, but it's personal. Too personal. 'I won't be a minute, put the kettle on!'

'Where is it?'

That's not Sam's voice. Maybe it *is* a burglar. I freeze, then slam the laptop lid down, leap off the bed and slide down the bannisters. It's the type of trick you never forget.

He's stood at the bottom of the stairs, and neatly catches me, whirls me round so that he ends up staggering. He's laughing.

'What the hell?'

'I hear you've got decent surf in this little place called Cornwall?'

'We're nowhere near Cornwall, Will.'

'Oh, come on, an island this size? You're near everywhere!'

'But what . . . ? When . . . ? How did you get here?'

'Lynn picked me up at the airport, she's just dropped me off.' His eyes are all twinkly, lovely little lines fanning out from the corner. I want to hug him. I need to hug him. So I do.

'Lynn picked you up?' My voice is a bit muffled, as it's buried in his coat, so I move back, and he kisses me. Which is rather nice.

He stops. 'I emailed her.'

'Why?'

'I missed you. I can't wait for some meet-up in spring; I needed to see you now. I need to try and make this work, Sarah. Did I do wrong?' He's holding me at arm's length, and I want to be back at kissing distance.

'No.' It's a whisper. 'I was just trying to write to you, ask if we could get together, if I could maybe come over or something.'

'Or something?'

'Well, I thought you were busy with the resort, and—'

'You know what? They don't need me; my job there is done. Bianca has got it all in hand.'

'Bianca?'

'She came clean after you'd all left. I thought there was something fishy about her – she was too bloody smart and organised to just be a holidaymaker, and if she'd got some rich boyfriend, why wasn't he there?'

'Joey?'

'Yeah, Joey. Joey doesn't exist, he was part of the cover story, and a way of keeping Ed at arm's length, which didn't work.'

'Cover story?'

'She works, well, worked, for this big chain. They thought we were ripe for a takeover and she was checking us out, seeing how desperate we were. How low we'd go. She's a clever cookie, that one.'

'Worked?'

'She handed in her notice; seems Ed is as irresistible as he keeps telling us.' He's grinning, the smile is even in his voice.

'But he's . . .'

'As smitten as she is. She's the first woman he's been happy to take orders from and he's like a puppy dog running after her. My little brother has finally met his match, somebody who plays hard and works even harder. I've no idea if it'll work out, but good luck to them. And they certainly don't need me hanging about, so, here I am!'

'Oh Will, I am so happy to see you.' We get a bit tangled up then, but when we finally untangle a bit I know it's the time. I need to do something. 'Will you come somewhere with me?'

'Anywhere.'

'It's a long way, and you must be tired and—'

'I said anywhere, and I meant it.'

'I'll pack a picnic.'

'No cranberry sauce with mince pies.'

'You just have no taste at all, Will Armstrong.'

***

It is later, much later, when we pull off the road and park. Then I lead him by the hand down a narrow footpath that I remember from long-ago summers with Aunt Lynn. Canada had been our first bittersweet Christmas together, but here had been our first summer. Our new start. It seems appropriate to bring Will here. We've shared the sad, now it's time to share the happy. The place of new beginnings.

The wind whips at our clothes, picking up sand that smarts our faces, but it isn't far and we soon find a sheltered spot and Will lays out his coat for us to sit on.

I pull out the bundle of paper from the bottom of my oversize tote bag, and we hunker down in a sheltered spot on that windblown beach, and I finally read my letters. Letters from a father to his daughter.

As I read each one I let it go, watch it soar and flutter until it lands in the sea and is tossed around by the waves before disappearing for ever.

And I finally know I'm free of the past.

'I'm ready to move on now.'

'Good.' He takes my face in his large hands and kisses me, oh so gently, my lips, my nose, my eyelids, and he takes such care as he slowly undresses me and finally looks down at my body. 'That makes two of us.'

He traces my tiny dragonfly with one finger. 'Why?'

'It's a family thing. Lynn has one, Mum had one. A dragonfly is delicate and beautiful, its symbolizes purity,' we both smile, 'and strength. It lives life to its fullest, makes every moment count.'

'Perfect.' His lips find the spot, then they're travelling all over my body, hot and demanding, and it's so right that it's in this wild spot with only the waves and the wind for company.

A note from the author

Thank you so much for picking up a copy of this book. I hope it makes you smile, laugh, maybe shed a tear, and ultimately feel that warm and fuzzy festive feeling.

Like Sarah, in the story, I love everything about Christmas, but the best part of all is being able to share the season with my family and friends. There's always that slightly sad moment when I think about the people who are no longer here to share it with – but I know I'm very lucky to be surrounded by so many special people.

I hope you have a wonderful Christmas, wherever you are and whoever you share it with.

Zara x

Acknowledgements

Many kind, inspirational and wonderful people have been involved in the writing of this book.

My amazing agent, Amanda Preston, who is funny, clever and wise, and always there when I need encouragement and support.

The fantastic team at HarperImpulse/HarperCollins, with special thanks to the legend Charlotte Ledger who has vision and a spot-on commercial instinct as well as being a brilliant editor and all round lovely person, Emily Ruston who is editor extraordinaire and knows exactly what I'm trying to convey and helps me put it into words, and Kim Young who never fails to inspire and motivate. Thanks also to Eloisa Clegg and Claire Fenby, and the fabulous cover designers for creating the perfect image for the story.

My fabulous author buddies Mandy and Jane who keep me going on the days when the words won't flow and share the joy when they do.

Sarah, Nicky, Wendy – you're truly the best for sharing

laughs, life, cocktails and good times with, and a wonderful support when things aren't going quite so well. Quite simply, you make life so much better.

Alex, who puts up with the ups and downs, supplies the right word when all I can remember is the initial letter and 'kind of what it means', and need it right now but can't remember, and who is also a brilliant storyteller who helps me see life in a different way. And who supplies brilliant graphics when I need them *right now*.

Paul, who makes sure that I do leave my desk from time to time and takes me to wonderful inspirational places, and shows me that there's plenty of magic and romance all around.

My parents, who have always loved, listened and supported me.

And last, but definitely not least, a massive thanks to you for reading my books and sending such fabulous messages. Without your support this book would never have been written ☺

HELP US SHARE THE LOVE!

If you love this wonderful book as much as we do then please share your reviews online.

Leaving reviews makes a huge difference and helps our books reach even more readers.

So get reviewing and sharing, we want to hear what you think!

Love, HarperImpulse x

Please leave your reviews online!

amazon.co.uk   kobo   goodreads   L♥vereading   iBooks

And on social!

f/HarperImpulse   **🐦**@harperimpulse
📷@HarperImpulse

LOVE BOOKS?

So do we! And we love nothing more than chatting about our books with you lovely readers.

If you'd like to find out about our latest titles, as well as exclusive competitions, author interviews, offers and lots more, join us on our Facebook page! Why not leave a note on our wall to tell us what you thought of this book or what you'd like to see us publish more of?

/HarperImpulse

You can also tweet us ✔@harperimpulse and see exclusively behind the scenes on our Instagram page www.instagram.com/harperimpulse

To be the first to know about upcoming books and events, sign up to our newsletter at: http://www.harperimpulseromance.com/